DATE DUE

11/14/0?		
01/15/02		
02/20/08		

Demco, Inc. 38-293

THE ARK BUILDER

CONTENTS

Hence, loathed melancholy,
Of Cerberus, and blackest Midnight born,
In Stygian cave forlorn,
'Mongst horrid shapes, and shrieks, and sights unholy.

—John Milton, *L'Allegro*

Aye on the shores of darkness there is light,
And precipices show untrodden green,
There is budding morrow in midnight,
There is a triple sight in blindness keen.

—John Keats, *To Homer*

To the Family

Adena
Rena
Naama
Akiva
Bill

Copyright © 2001 by Chaim Potok

All rights reserved under International and Pan-American Copyright Conventions. Published in the United States by Alfred A. Knopf, a division of Random House, Inc., New York, and simultaneously in Canada by Random House of Canada Limited, Toronto. Distributed by Random House, Inc., New York.

www.aaknopf.com

Knopf, Borzoi Books, and the colophon are registered trademarks of Random House, Inc.

The Trope Teacher first appeared, in slightly different form, in *TriQuarterly*, a publication of Northwestern University.

Library of Congress Cataloging-in-Publication Data

Potok, Chaim.
Old men at midnight / Chaim Potok.—1st ed.
p. cm.
Contents: The ark builder — The war doctor — The trope teacher.
ISBN 0-375-41071-6 (alk. paper)
1. Storytelling—Fiction. 2. Aged men—Fiction. 3. Jews—Fiction.
I. Title.
PS3566.O69 O44 2001
813'.54—dc21   2001033861

Manufactured in the United States of America
Published October 30, 2001
Second Printing, Before Publication

OLD MEN
AT MIDNIGHT

Chaim Potok

Alfred A. Knopf

NEW YORK

2001

OLD MEN
AT MIDNIGHT

I

NOAH WAS BROUGHT TO OUR BROOKLYN
neighborhood by his aunt and uncle, and into my life
by an announcement on the bulletin board of our synagogue: SIXTEEN-YEAR-OLD BOY FROM EUROPE NEEDS
ENGLISH TUTOR.

This was early in the summer of 1947, two years after
the end of the Second World War. No name, just a telephone number.

I called that night. A woman answered.

"Hello, who is it?" She sounded fretful, harried. "Who
is calling, please?"

I said in Yiddish, "A good week."

There was a slight pause. "Ah, a good week," she said.
Her tone softened.

I said in English, "My name is Davita Dinn. I'm calling
about your request for an English tutor."

In the background I heard children crying. Turning
away from the phone, she shouted something in Yiddish,
which I did not understand. Into the phone she said, "You
have done this before, teach English?"

"Yes. But not to a European survivor."

"How old are you?"

"Nearly eighteen."

"Where do you live?"

I told her.

"We will come to you. Is it all right tomorrow at three?"

I was alone when they arrived. Answering the front door bell, I saw a stocky, plain-looking woman in her thirties, garbed in a dark-gray dress that reached to below her knees. The dress had a frilly high neck and long sleeves. Standing a little behind and to her right was a thin boy in his teens, wearing a white long-sleeved shirt, dark trousers, and a dark skullcap.

I said, "Hello."

The woman said, "I am Sarah Polit."

"Come in."

We went into the living room. The afternoon sun fell on the pale-blue carpeting and the brick fireplace and the large painting of flowers on the wall.

The woman and the boy sat on the sofa. I took the easy chair across from them. The woman turned to the boy and spoke to him in Yiddish.

The boy had been staring at the fireplace. Now he looked at me, cleared his throat, and said something in Yiddish in a shaky voice.

I said, "I'm sorry, I don't understand Yiddish."

Sarah Polit said with surprise, "You speak no Yiddish?"

"My parents raised me in English."

"Your parents are in America a long time?"

"My mother came in early 1920. My father's family has been here since the seventeenth century."

4

"The seventeenth century?"

"Yes."

"What does your father do?"

"My father is dead."

"Ah, I am sorry."

The boy sat looking at the two of us. He had oval features: pallid skin across his cheekbones, a straight nose, a pointed chin. His hair was cut short and black, and his wide dark eyes darted from me to his aunt. I did not know how much of the conversation he understood.

Sarah Polit asked, "What did you say your name is?"

"Ilana Davita Dinn."

"Dinn is your father's name?"

"No, my stepfather's."

"What does your stepfather do?"

"He's an immigration lawyer."

She looked at my blond hair and blue eyes. "You observe the commandments?"

Her questions did not surprise me; she wanted to be sure about the kind of home to which she was entrusting the boy.

I told her that I observed the commandments.

"And you have taught English to people who have come from Europe?"

"Yes."

She was quiet.

I turned to the boy. "What's your name?"

The boy looked at his aunt.

"Tell her, Noah."

"I am call Noah Stremin."

"Where did you hear English?"

"American soldati after war."

Sarah Polit was looking closely at my blond hair and blue eyes. She asked, "What was your father? What did he do?"

"He was a journalist."

"What was his name?"

"Michael Chandal."

"You took your stepfather's name?"

"He gave me his name when he adopted me."

Sarah Polit sat back. I had the notion she had decided to ask no more questions. We were a religious family, and she was fortunate to have found us. Most teachers didn't want to work during the summer months; many took their families to bungalows in the country to get them away from the streets.

I asked, "Where in Europe are you from, Mrs. Polit?"

"I came in the twenties from a town called Kralov, not far from Cracow."

"I know about Cracow. About sixty thousand Jews."

"Well, Kralov had four thousand Jews, a Jewish market, small synagogues and schools, and a wooden synagogue. Both our families were from Kralov."

He was sitting next to her, looking at the carpet. His face without expression. It was not possible to tell if he understood what she was saying.

"There was a pogrom in Kralov in the late twenties, and my father sent me here to America. He, my mother, and my two brothers, they stayed. May their memories be for a blessing."

The boy raised his hands, turned them over, and looked at them. A grimace crossed his face. Putting his hands back on his knees, he sat staring at the fireplace.

Pronouncing the words with care, I asked him, "Noah, is there anything special you like to do?"

He raised his head and looked at me blankly.

"I thought we might start with words for something you enjoy doing."

Sarah Polit said, "He was three years in a slave labor camp and two years in a displaced persons camp. He just now arrived in America. He does not yet know what he likes."

"Can he come twice a week?"

"Twice a week. Yes."

"Sundays and Wednesdays."

"What do you charge?"

"Five dollars a lesson. We can start this Wednesday at three."

"What should he bring?"

"A notebook and a pencil."

"That's all?"

"For the time being."

"I thank you."

She spoke to the boy in Yiddish. He got off the sofa, and I saw him go through the entrance hallway to the front door. As he opened the door he gave me an over-the-shoulder look, and I felt his dark eyes on my face. He closed the door behind him.

Sarah Polit remained seated on the sofa, looking at the door. Then she turned to me.

"Noah is the only one who survived."

"The only one in his family? I am sorry."

"The only Jew in the town."

I felt cold to the bone.

"Four thousand Jews, and he is the only survivor. My husband and I, we say to ourselves God saved him for a reason."

I sat very still.

She rose from the sofa. "He knows, of course. He has terrible dreams." She looked around the room. "Tell me, is three o'clock the only time you have?"

"It's best for me."

She smoothed her dress. "He will be here on Wednesday, God willing. I thank you very much for your time."

She went out the door.

From the window of the living room I watched them walk along the street together in the hot shade of the early summer maple trees.

HE ARRIVED WITH HIS AUNT AT THREE O'CLOCK ON Wednesday, carrying a yellow pencil and a blue notebook of the kind issued by yeshivas. The notebook had ruled pages, a drawing of Moses ben Maimon, the medieval Jewish philosopher and rabbi, on the front cover, and the Western Wall on the back. He wore dark trousers and a white long-sleeved shirt, and she had on a light-colored long-sleeved dress. She explained that Noah had not wanted to walk alone. She would wait in the living room while he had his lesson.

"You are alone in the house?" she asked.

I told her that my parents were at work and my little sister was at a day camp.

"I will sit here," Mrs. Polit said. "The heat is terrible outside."

She took one of the easy chairs.

I motioned to Noah. He followed me slowly through the living room and dining room to the kitchen. He was about an inch shorter than I and walked with a gait slightly favoring his right leg.

"When did you come to the United States?"

"Two week," he said.

"Two weeks ago."

He nodded.

"Noah, repeat after me. Two weeks ago."

"Two weeks ago."

Inside the kitchen, he stopped and looked around. We had moved into this President Street house a year after my sister, Rachel, was born, and the kitchen had been renovated. He stood looking at the bright tile walls, at the new table and chairs, at the two sinks, at the stove and refrigerator. I asked him if he wanted a glass of milk and a cookie.

"No, I eat already."

"I *ate*."

"Yes, I ate."

"Our home is kosher."

"I no worry."

"I'm *not* worried."

"I am not—worried."

He followed me through the kitchen into the den.

There were cushioned chairs and a couch, a rug, and a large floor radio. The far wall was mostly two bay windows and a door in between that gave out onto a wooden porch with a round table and chairs and, a few feet away, lounge chairs. Down the stairs beyond the porch a paved path defined a lawn. Inside it a rock border circled a birdbath and peony bushes. Across the path to the right of the lawn, pink roses rambled along a fence while yellow and white honeysuckle climbed the fence opposite. In this heat the aroma of honeysuckle was particularly strong. Against a wall formed by the rear of backyard neighbors' garages hung a basketball hoop, a few feet from a swing-and-slide set. The screened bay windows were closed. Fan-cooled air blew from the inside, not a wisp of the air from the outside.

We sat down in chairs, facing each other. He had long thin fingers and a long thin face. His neck was scrawny and fronted with a prominent Adam's apple, and his face was damp with perspiration.

I said, "Is it okay to call you Noah?"

He said, "My name Noah." He pronounced it "Noyach."

"My name *is* Noah."

"My name is Noah."

"You can call me Davita."

"Like David. Davita."

"Are your aunt and uncle very religious?"

"What means 'religious'?" The words came out as "vat mins 're-lee-gi-us'?"

I said, "Are they shomrei mitzvos?" The Hebrew term means "keepers of the commandments."

"Oh, yes."

"What synagogue do they go to?"

"It called Bris Achim."

"It *is* called."

"It is called."

"I don't know that synagogue."

"It is small."

Suddenly he was very still. He sat with his eyes wide and staring. A shimmer of sweat lay across his forehead. He stirred and closed his eyes. Then he blinked a few times. The perspiration lay now dripping on his forehead, and he wiped at it with his open palms.

I said, "Let's start the lesson."

"Lesson, yes. Came for lesson."

The script for the Hebrew alphabet was printed on the first page of his notebook. I turned it over and wrote the letters of the English alphabet on the back page. Then I wrote the verbs *build, speak, write, sleep, wake, dress, eat, walk*—in first, second, and third person singular and plural. I gave a list of words for things he would find around the house and on the street. I explained verb and noun, and tried him on a reader I had used with a previous student. He could hardly make out the words. I told him we would start on an easier book. He sat there, perspiring. I looked up and there was Mrs. Polit, standing inside the entrance to the den. I had no idea how long she had been there.

She said, "You give a long lesson."

"I lost track of the time."

We got up off the chairs and started through the kitchen. I asked, "Noah, would you like a cookie?"

"Cookies are not good for him," Mrs. Polit said.

We entered the living room.

"Wait outside for me a moment," she said to Noah.

When we were alone she said to me, "It's not possible for you to have the lesson later?"

"Would four be better?"

"When your parents are home."

"I have a five-year-old sister. The house becomes noisy."

"Isn't there a quiet place you can go?"

"There's my room on the third floor. We can study with the door open."

"With the door open all the time?"

"Yes."

"I worry and my husband worries. You understand."

"He can come next Sunday at seven-thirty."

Noah stood on the front stone step. Mrs. Polit came out the double wrought-iron door, and he followed her down the steps to the lower landing, past the hydrangea bushes and the small lawn and the fence. Looking through a living room window, I saw them hurrying beneath the trees.

MINUTES LATER I CAME OUT THE SAME DOUBLE wrought-iron door past the hydrangea bushes and the small lawn and fence and turned left and walked along President Street. I passed Kingston, Brooklyn, and New York and turned up Nostrand Avenue, crossing the trolley tracks and going past Union Street and the Loew's Kings movie on Eastern Parkway. On the corner of Eastern Parkway near the movie was Mr. Wolf in his newsstand, and I waved to him and he waved his good arm back at me. The streets shimmered with afternoon heat and were filling with rush-hour traffic. On the wide pedestrian islands of the parkway few kids roller-skated, and fewer old people sat on benches in the shade. It was too hot. A tricycle ice cream cart rode by. The two orange day-camp buses were pulling up in front of the synagogue to unload the children. Rachel came down off her bus and we started home.

She was full of a five-year-old girl's chatter about her day. The camp was located in Prospect Park, and that day they had gone to the zoo near the park. The elephants and the sea lions and the tigers. And the apes and monkeys. They were so funny, the monkeys. Jumping around. Rachel walked at a rapid pace, loudly imitating the monkeys, screwing up her lovely face and making monkey noises. People looked at her and moved out of her way. Then a block from the house she suddenly needed to go to the bathroom, and we hurried the rest of the way home.

During supper I asked my mother and stepfather if I could teach Noah at seven-thirty instead of at three.

"Why seven-thirty?" my mother asked. She was in her forties, long raven hair flecked here and there with a touch of gray, and smooth-skinned and trim, with petite lips, pointed chin, and high cheekbones. The visible sadness of our missed life with my father seemed to have left her, though there were times when we were alone together or I came upon her suddenly in a room when I thought I could see the early years in her eyes.

"She wants you or Dad to be home."

My stepfather was a quiet, courtly man, thin and tall, with hair turning gray though he was in his early fifties. I liked him, I respected him, I carried his name, Ilana Davita Dinn.

"They're very religious," I said.

My mother asked, "Where will you teach him?"

"I thought in my room with the door open."

My stepfather said, "Who are these people? What's their name?"

"The boy is Noah Stremin, their nephew. The family is called Polit."

"Polit. I don't know that name."

"I have no objection," said my mother.

"Neither do I," my stepfather said.

"Is Noah from Europe?" Rachel suddenly asked.

"Yes."

"If he tells you stories, will you tell them to me?"

"Maybe."

"Rachel, finish eating," said my mother.

Her father said he would play her a game of checkers if she finished her food. They busied themselves with her. When I was done eating, I went upstairs.

The door harp that hung on the back of my door went *ting tang tong tung ting tang.* Soft waning daylight came into the room. I left the windows closed and turned on the fan. My room faced the rear of the house and I looked out at the peony bushes and cyclamens and mock orange blossoms and the maple tree. We had been without rain for two weeks; an intolerable heat lay mornings and evenings over the neighborhood. Rachel was in the den, playing checkers with her father, and I could hear her high and happy voice.

I BROUGHT NOAH UPSTAIRS THE NEXT SUNDAY, AND the sounds of the harp startled him as I opened the door to my room. He stopped at the door and looked at the harp, listening to the *ting tang tong tung ting tang* of the balls.

He asked, "What it is?"

"What *is* it?"

"Yes, what is it?"

I explained that the guitar-shaped door harp was made from a piece of butternut wood, nearly one inch thick and twelve inches long. Four maple-wood balls were attached to four varying lengths of fish line from a thin strip of wood near the top and lay against four taut horizontal wires. When you moved the door the balls struck the wires and made the sounds. I told him the harp had hung over the front door of every place we had lived. When my mother and Mr. Dinn were married, they gave the harp to me.

Noah listened and when I was done he asked, "Harp is where from?"

I said the harp had come from Europe. My father's older brother was in the American army in France during the First World War. He bought the harp in France. Then he was wounded at Belleau Wood and sent back home, and before he died he gave the harp to his younger brother.

Noah stood inside the doorway gazing into my room. The rear wall and its three windows faced the back yard and the gardens. Across the room to my left was my maple desk and to the right were my bookcases and, on the wall, my photographs of my father and Jakob Daw. I saw Noah looking at my paisley-pattern rose bedspread, at my small oriental rug, at the books on my shelves and the pictures on the walls. Then a corner easy chair, a dresser, a closet. The bookcases stood across the room opposite my bed. There were not many nights when I went to sleep without my father or Jakob Daw, whose presence was real to me and not to be talked of here. I heard my mother call to Rachel. At the same moment the telephone rang in the living room. It rang twice more before it was picked up.

Pointing to the bookcases, Noah said, "Books from your gymnasium, your school?"

"These books are mine."

He said something in Yiddish.

"I don't understand."

He pointed to my eyeglasses. "Always wear?"

"Yes."

"Brother Yoel always glasses."

"Your brother Yoel?"

His eyes glazed. He brushed over them with his hands. "Yes."

"What happened to your brother Yoel?"

"Always glasses," he said. He looked at the wall of photographs. "What are horses?"

"That picture belonged to my father."

"Horses running?"

"On an island near Canada."

The name seemed to startle him. "Ca-na-da?"

"The country north of the United States. Prince Edward Island."

I heard my mother call again to Rachel.

He said, looking at the wall, "This your father?"

I nodded.

"And this?"

"He was a writer. A very close friend of my family. Jakob Daw. He died in France during the war."

There was a silence. Looking at the photographs of my father and Jakob Daw, Noah said quietly, "You have pictures. I have nothing."

I did not know what to say.

"No remember, Papa's and Mama's faces. No remember. Yoel, I remember. Reb Binyomin, I remember. With animals and birds and flowers. Not Papa and Mama. Not all uncles and aunts and cousins."

I had brought a chair to the desk, and he sat opposite me, squinting his eyes at the blue notebook. His eyes focused on the notebook and on the right hand that lay across it. Finally he said, "Begin lesson?"

We reviewed the words I had given him Wednesday and then I assigned him additional vocabulary. He read haltingly from a second-grade primer. We worked hard on pronunciation.

When we were done I went down with him. At the door, he said dismally, "So much to learn."

My heart went out to him. New language. New culture. "You'll learn enough this summer."

"You can do?"

"Yes."

He went out into the heated evening. I started back upstairs. The door to Rachel's room was open. My mother sat on Rachel's bed, reading her a story. I went to my room.

THE NEXT DAY I RAN INTO HIM WHILE CROSSING the trolley tracks on Nostrand Avenue, walking toward Union Street and the Loew's Kings movie. He had turned onto Eastern Parkway, carrying a heavy paper shopping bag. I went on Nostrand Avenue toward the corner with the newsstand. Mr. Wolf waved his good arm at me. He had been with the American army just south of Soissons and his right arm and shoulder had been smashed by a high-explosive shell. He was a short, thin-built man with a high voice, craggy features, and thin, graying hair. He wore jeans and a T-shirt. I went over to read the headlines, keeping an eye out for the camp buses.

"Ilana, ninety-seven hot enough for you?"

I said, "Hot enough."

"Tomorrow they say'll be ninety-nine."

I looked along Nostrand Avenue and saw Noah going into a greengrocer.

"Buses coming," Mr. Wolf said.

I thanked him and turned right onto Eastern Parkway and waited at the synagogue for the buses. Rachel was wearing her two-piece blue sunsuit and wide-brimmed yellow sun hat and came off the bus amid a tumult of campers and parents. She looked bronzed in the sun, vividly dark-eyed, lustrous. Her dark hair was done in two braids, and wisps of it lay helter-skelter on her neck and face, while her fingers and arms went into an account of what had happened that day.

She walked beside me, prattling on about how the boys in her group kept chasing her. The camp had again been taken to the zoo. The tigers and elephants and leopards and seals. The new lion, prowling in his cage. The monkeys screeching and jumping.

We started along Nostrand Avenue. Sunlight fell in great cascades broken sharply by the shadows of buildings. And there was Noah, emerging from a candy store, with an empty shopping bag in his hand. He did not see us. He wore a long-sleeved shirt and dark trousers, and he moved slowly in and out of the afternoon sun that bathed him alternately in light and shadow.

I called out, "Noah, hello."

He was standing in the sunlight and he raised his left hand to his forehead, shading his eyes. For a moment he was lost among the people who passed between us. Then he saw me.

"Davita."

"What are you doing here?"

He briefly raised the shopping bag. "Delivering?"

"Yes, delivering."

"This is my sister, Rachel."

Still shading his eyes with his left hand, he looked at Rachel.

"Noah is one of my students who is learning English."

I could see Rachel looking closely at Noah. The sun was hot on my face and arms. We were a small island in the middle of the street, and people kept eddying around us.

Rachel suddenly asked, "You like baseball?"

"Bezbol?"

"You like to play?"

"American soldat play bezbol."

"They play in Prospect Park."

"Who play?"

"Boys like you."

"She means Hasidic boys," I explained. "Hasidic boys play running bases."

"I not Hasid."

"They play near the lake."

"I not Hasid," he said again.

"I *am* not a Hasid."

"I am not a Hasid."

Rachel reached up and tugged at my hand. "Ilana."

"What?"

"I need to make pee-pee."

"Then let's go home. Noah, I'll see you on Wednesday."

But I saw him again the next day on Nostrand Avenue, a block from where I had seen him the day before, in front of a jewelry store. He carried the shopping bag and entered the store. I waited in the shade of an awning and he emerged and stood for a while in the sunlight, staring at the glittering watches and rings in the window. I walked past the newsstand and glanced at the headlines. Mr. Wolf nodded and waved his arm. I went up Eastern Parkway to pick up Rachel, and when we were again on Nostrand Avenue, I looked along the street and did not see Noah.

HE CAME TO THE HOUSE THE FOLLOWING EVENING, and when I opened the front door to let him in I felt the heat thrust against me. All day the air had been sweltering and now had become an implacable brownish mist. The windows were closed in the house and the fans were on. He brought inside an odor of hot, stagnant air. Beads of perspiration ran down the sides of his face and chin.

I closed the door. He stood breathing with difficulty.

"Are you all right?"

He said something in Yiddish.

"I don't understand."

"Never Poland hot like this."

"I'll get you a glass of water."

I hurried into the kitchen. My parents were in the den, listening to the radio. I did not see Rachel. Fans whispered in rhythmic undercurrents to the voice of a radio announcer. As I put ice cubes from the refrigerator into a glass, I heard news about British forces in Palestine moving to intercept surviving European Jews and interning them on the island of Cyprus. I glanced into the den and saw my mother and stepfather looking at the radio. I filled the glass with water from the faucet and went into the living room.

Noah was standing in front of the fireplace, peering inside. It was two feet deep, lined with red brick and fronted with a wire-mesh screen. I handed him the water and he recited the blessing and drank with his head tipped back, his Adam's apple bobbing, liquid sounds issuing from his throat. I heard the tinkling of the ice cubes and, at the same time, someone hurrying down the stairs. Rachel, wearing a one-piece yellow sunsuit and carrying drawing pencils and a coloring book, halted at the foot of the staircase and stood watching Noah drink.

She said, in her high voice, "I had a class in swimming today."

Noah finished the water. I turned to Rachel. "What did they teach you?"

"I learned the backstroke."

Noah handed me the glass.

Rachel looked up at him. "Do you swim?"

"Swim? I no swim. No."

"You should learn to swim."

I said, "Let me take this back to the kitchen," and left them there. In the den my parents were still listening to the radio. Demonstrations were taking place in Tel Aviv. When I returned to the living room—I could not have been gone more than two minutes—Rachel was saying, "All right, draw something."

Noah said, in a barely audible voice, "No, cannot."

Rachel said, "You just told me you can."

"No do now."

Rachel stood with her head firm, her lips set. Dark eyes suspicious. "Why not now?"

Pale color had risen to his neck and face. His right hand moved up as if to ward off her anger. His left hand held tightly to his notebook and pencil.

He turned to me. "Lesson now upstairs."

Rachel insisted. "Draw the house you lived in."

A look of dread came upon his face. "The house?"

"Yes, yes."

"In Kralov?"

"Yes, yes, in Kralov. Draw the front of your house."

"No."

"The front, just the front."

"No, no."

She stamped her sandal-shod right foot.

He said in a low, tight-lipped tone, "Can no draw now."

She announced suddenly, "You don't play baseball, you don't swim, and you don't draw. Don't you have fun?"

"Fun?" Noah asked.

"I don't think fun is important to Noah," I said.

She gave him a puzzled look and marched off toward the kitchen.

Noah stood very still in the ensuing silence, his eyes soberly following Rachel.

"What happened when I was in the kitchen?"

"Ask if she use pencils for coloring or for drawing, and she say coloring, and she ask if I draw."

"Can you draw?"

"Once I drawed."

"Once I *drew*."

"Once I drew."

"Can you draw now?"

A vague tremor shuddered across his face. "I no draw. No want to draw."

From the den came Rachel's voice raised to a cry.

"Hurt Rachel?" Noah said, sounding distressed.

"It probably has nothing to do with you," I said.

He followed me up the stairs. We could no longer hear Rachel crying. A while into the lesson he asked if he could have a glass of water, and I went across the hall to the bathroom. There was no ice, but it was good Brooklyn water. I filled a glass and brought it to him.

The walk through the hall to the bathroom, letting the water run to cool down, filling the glass, bringing it to him in my room—it all couldn't have taken two minutes. I found him at my desk drawing with his left hand on one of the pages of his notebook. The fluorescent light from my desk lamp illuminated his moist face and pale fingers. His hands were shaking. He sat with his face close to the pencil and the paper. A drop of sweat gathered at the tip of his nose, hung there quivering, and then tumbled onto the lower right corner of the paper. I stood there watching him draw. He seemed unsure of himself; there were marks of hesitation; it all took a long time. Straightening, finally, he put the pencil on the desk and took a tremulous breath.

"We live inside," he said, pointing to the drawing. "Reb Binyomin live floor on left side." He folded the page along the inside edge and tore it from the notebook. "Please give to Rachel."

I took the drawing.

"No want make Rachel cry."

I told him I didn't think he had made Rachel cry.

He wasn't listening. "First hear many people cry. Then years no hear anyone cry. No little child, no anyone."

I stared at him.

"I go home now."

I glanced at my wristwatch. "Now?"

"Very tired."

"I'll see you on Sunday."

"Yes."

"Would you rather go to the park on Sunday?"

"The park?"

"Come here at about two-thirty and we'll take the subway."

"Have lesson in the park?"

"Yes. We'll sit under a tree or on a bench."

"I ask Aunt Sarah."

"If you want me to, I'll call her."

"Yes, call."

I gave him exercises for homework. We started down the stairs. The door to Rachel's room was closed; she was preparing for bed. We passed through the living room. I felt the fiery evening on my face as I let him out of the house.

My mother was coming down the stairs. I asked her what had upset Rachel.

"Camp."

"I thought she loved camp."

"She was tired out from the camp. She's having too much fun. She needed to go to sleep. How is your Noah?"

"I think we'll have our lesson in the park next Sunday afternoon."

"Yes? Well, take him to the zoo. Rachel says they have a new lion."

Inside my room, I sat at my desk and studied Noah's drawing. It was a facade of a three-story stucco apartment house, clumsily rendered, with tall windows and wrought-iron balconies on the second and third floors. Wooden shutters hung open from the windows. An arched entranceway led to an inner courtyard and disappeared into dissolving shadows. The left corner of the drawing was still moist from the drop of sweat that had fallen onto it.

Noah's home in Kralov, Poland.

From a drawer in my desk I took a pale-blue eight-and-a-half-by-eleven lined spiral notebook, of the kind commonly used in high school. Seated at my desk, I opened the notebook to the front page. There I wrote in pencil the name "Noah."

The next day I called Noah's aunt and told her that I wanted to take Noah to Prospect Park that Sunday afternoon. About a ten-minute subway ride.

She said, "Take care how you cross the streets with Noah."

"Mrs. Polit, can I ask you, does Noah ever draw?"

"Draw? What do you mean, draw?"

"Does he ever make pictures?"

"He works in the store or he watches the children or he studies. When would he have time for pictures? Has he been making pictures?"

"He drew a small picture for my little sister."

"How old is your sister?"

"Almost six."

"That's very nice. How is he getting along, my Noah?"

"Very well."

"He is a good student?"

"Yes."

"You are satisfied with his progress?"

"Oh, yes."

"So he draws a picture for your sister. Can there be harm in it?"

I came into Rachel's room that evening and handed her Noah's drawing. She was playing on the floor with her dolls. "From Noah," I said. "His house in Kralov." She glanced at the drawing, seemed momentarily to study it. Then she put it on her bed, and went on playing.

My mother asked me later, "What did he draw?"

I said, "His house in Kralov."

That Sunday afternoon Noah showed up at my home with his notebook and pencil, and we took the subway to the park and the zoo.

2

THE SUBWAY TRAIN SWEPT INTO THE STATION. Noah backed away from it. We entered the car and found seats. I asked him if this was his first time on a subway. He stared out the open windows at the rushing darkness and nodded.

The train was not crowded. It entered the next station and halted with a grinding of brakes. He looked at me.

"Two more stops," I said.

The doors slid shut. He stared out the windows. The air hovered on the edge of combustion. He held tight to his notebook and pencil. I could not imagine what he was seeing.

The train pulled into our station. The ride had lasted about ten minutes. We climbed the stairs to the street.

I was wearing a print skirt with a white blouse, and he had on dark trousers and a white long-sleeved shirt. We emerged on the edge of Grand Army Plaza. There was not much traffic on the vast sweep of street around the Civil War statuary. The air was liquid with heat. We walked past the main branch of the Brooklyn Public Library, crossed Flatbush Avenue, and went down the hill to the park. Families sat under trees and children raced about and there was a baseball game in one of the fields. Beyond the field was the lake, with people in rowboats. Not far from the baseball game, on this side of the field, three youngsters about Noah's age were playing running bases. They wore white shirts and dark trousers, with skullcaps and fringes, all playing sweatily in the heat.

We stopped to watch them play. The two playing the bases were heavyset, and the one racing against the ball was short and thin, with his right hand holding his skullcap tightly to his head. The base-players were yelling in Yiddish from their bases, and the thin one stood still, and then they got off their bases and quickly moved toward him, throwing the ball to cut down the space between them, and he suddenly swept past the one on the right and reached the base and raised his hand in triumph. One of the heavyset ones wiped sweat from his face with the sleeve of his shirt, and then he spotted Noah and came over. The others noticed and joined in. A brief conversation in Yiddish followed, nothing of which I understood. We walked on.

Noah said, "They from Hungary."

"When did they come to America?"

"Not ask."

I looked back. They had begun another game.

We found a bench under a tall oak and sat down. I had brought along a new reader, and he proceeded to read from it aloud. He had gained some confidence in the past weeks, and he read now with a steady voice. His dark eyes were fixed on the page, his long, pale fingers pointing to each syllable as he mouthed the words.

In the field before us, the three boys had stopped playing and now came to the road, disheveled and sweaty, and nodded to Noah. The thin one, glancing at me, spoke to Noah and a conversation began that went on for a while.

From time to time they glanced at me. Then finally they headed out of the park.

I watched them go.

"What did they want?"

"They want to know name and where I from. They ask if you my sister."

"What did you say?"

"I say not my sister, you teaching me English to get me into school. They say they don't need much English for their school."

"Let's finish reading the story."

He turned back to the book. Just then something occurred to me. I asked him how many languages he knew.

"How many? Fier."

"Four?"

"Yiddish, Hebrew, Polish, and German. I learn German to-to"—he was searching for a word—"to not be killed, to—"

"Survive?"

"Yes. Survive."

"Where did they send you from Kralov?"

"To Auschwitz."

"You studied German in Auschwitz?"

"When Germans came to Kralov, Papa got me teacher for German. Papa said my life—how you say—my life—"

"Depended on it."

"Yes. Depended."

"What did you do in Auschwitz?"

"I made drawings."

"Drawings? What sorts of drawings?"

A shiver turned his face away. "Please, we continue lesson. Please."

He continued reading aloud from the book until he was done, and then we reviewed the vocabulary I had given him the previous Wednesday. Looking for an empty page in the notebook, I glimpsed a new drawing. I did not say anything.

I asked him if he wanted to go past the zoo. He said he had never been to a zoo before. We walked past the baseball game and the families lying on blankets under the trees and the expanse of lake and then beyond into the natural habitat where about half a dozen elephants stood in the baking heat. One elephant, immense and dusty, ears flapping indolently, huge trunk moist and curling, eyes small, was searching for peanuts along the moat surrounding the compound.

Noah said to me, "First time I see." He could not stop looking at the elephants.

We passed tigers and leopards and cheetahs. Before the aviary we stopped, and I watched him looking for a long time at the flying multicolored birds, doves, lorikeets, macaws, kingfishers, and even a kookaburra alighting in an old gum tree and laughing. They flew before his eyes, and on his face was a slowly growing rapture and I heard, as if subtly beneath the crowd, "Reb Binyomin? Reb Binyomin?"

Just then my eye was caught by a form in the nearby cage: a lion rising lazily and stretching. He stood there for a moment gazing out of yellow slitted eyes at the crowd of about a dozen people in front of his cage. Flies buzzed around his tawny form. Then I saw him amble to the front of the cage and he began to move his huge jaws and maned head back and forth, and he suddenly roared in a deep-chested moaning that seemed to unsettle the air. Noah, startled, looked at the lion, who roared a second time, shivering the air of the cage. People leaned against the railing, laughing and applauding. The lion raised his head and roared again and a kind of quiet spread itself slowly upon the crowd. A child let out a wail and was hushed by a father. The crowd waited hesitantly. There was a brief low-throated roar. Then the lion turned and ambled away, settling indolently among the other lions in the rear of the cage.

A dimness came over Noah's eyes. He looked around furtively. He seemed to be waiting for someone.

The primate house stood just inside a large rotunda. We entered the house and found ourselves in a huge, echoing area. Along both sides of the house were floor-to-ceiling cages with chimpanzees, orangutans, monkeys. It was very crowded. At the far end of the house in the gorilla cage a female was tossing feces at a male to force him away from her. A raging din of noise came from the exasperated male.

Noah stood inside the entrance to the primate house. I saw his eyes widen. From the far end of the house the female was cheered by the crowd as she chased the male around the cage. Noah suddenly put both hands to his nose with such force that the pencil scraped against his cheek. He turned and stumbled out. I followed quickly.

We found a bench and sat down. His hands trembled. I put out my hand to steady him. His skin was hot.

"There's a fountain," I suggested.

I walked with him, then watched as he drank. His mouth was dripping water and the front of his shirt was wet. He wiped his lips with the palms of his hands.

I asked, "Are you okay?"

"I think yes."

"What happened?"

He looked away. "We go home now."

We walked along the street to the subway.

The train was not crowded. He opened his notebook and carefully tore the new drawing out of it.

"Give Rachel. First drawing not good."

The train entered the station and we climbed the stairs to the street. Mr. Wolf nodded to me from his newsstand as we went by, looking curiously at Noah. Noah accompanied me to the house. "I will see you Wednesday." He turned and went along under the trees, the only one now walking in the heat on President Street.

I looked at the drawing.

It was the same house he had drawn earlier, but the lines of the entranceway and the windows were clearer, laid out now by a ruler. One could see cobblestones on the street and a small park across from the homes set nearby, the road going off into a stone bridge across a river, and in the distance a courtyard with an odd-shaped synagogue, and beyond that the tall spires of a church.

I let myself into the house. A low voice came from

the radio in the den. Something about boats diverted to Cyprus. I went upstairs and knocked on Rachel's door. There was no one inside, so I left the drawing on her bed. Then I went to my room and closed the door and turned on the fan.

I sat at my desk, looking down at my notebook. Noah. I felt myself alone and scorched by the heat. On the wall, partially hidden by shadows, were the photographs of my father and Jakob Daw. After a while I took off my clothes and stayed at my desk in my underwear. How unbearably hot it was! I started to write. Minutes went by. I closed my notebook and put it in the desk drawer.

Showering, I thought of Noah's drawing. I didn't know very much about drawing, but it seemed to me marvelously well done: the proportions of the house, the cobblestone road, the bridge across the river, the road leading through a courtyard to the synagogue, the strange-looking synagogue itself—more a barn than a synagogue—and then the spires of the church beyond. How had he learned to draw that well?

I dressed and went down to supper.

Rachel ate quietly and busied herself with her drawing. Her long dark hair was pulled back from her face and pinned with a barrette, and her tongue worked furiously.

My mother said to me, "How is your Noah coming along?"

"We went to the park and the zoo. Everything was fine until we got to the primate house."

"What happened at the primate house?" my stepfather

said. He wore a white short-sleeved shirt and light-gray summer trousers.

"He ran out."

"What do you mean, he ran out?"

"He put his hands to his nose and stumbled out."

"Ah," my stepfather said. "Of course, of course. He remembered the latrine smells of his concentration camp."

That was unnerving to me. I had not linked the two together, primate house and concentration camp.

"His next hurdle will be Tisha B'Av," my stepfather said. "I wonder if Noah will be strong enough to observe a day-long fast. Especially one that commemorates a national destruction."

"I hadn't thought of that. But we can have the lesson here in the afternoon. Are you going to be home?"

"No."

"His aunt won't like him studying alone with me. Maybe we'll go back to the park."

"I wonder where he was last Tisha B'Av," my stepfather said. "And the one before that."

Rachel suddenly interrupted, "Ilana, would you give this to Noah when you see him?" She had made a drawing of herself standing between her parents, holding their hands. They were stick figures, drawn in black, all on a barren plain. But from one edge of the page to the other the sky was passionate with brilliant colors.

"It's a rainbow," Rachel said.

"That's very nice," said my mother.

"For his drawing."

"What drawing is that?" asked my stepfather.

"The drawing that he made for me."

"Oh?" said my mother.

"I'll bring it down," said Rachel. She slid off her chair and went out of the kitchen.

"Last Wednesday," I said. "When he came in. She went by with some colored pencils, and he asked if she could draw, and one thing led to another. He drew her the house he lived in in Kralov, and today he gave me a better version of it to give to her."

We sat there eating. I looked at Rachel's drawing. The stick figures were cutely drawn, my stepfather with a bow tie and dark hair and a mustache, my mother with short dark hair and a yellow skirt, Rachel with long dark hair and sunglasses. I was not in the drawing.

She came back into the kitchen with Noah's drawing in her hand and showed it to my mother, who first glanced at it, then gazed at it with interest. She then handed it to my stepfather, who studied it thoughtfully.

"How old is he?"

"Going on seventeen," I said.

"Where did he learn to do this?"

"I don't know."

It is a measure of that night that I can remember going to a concert with friends, but I can't recall anything about it. What I do remember is falling into a half-sleep and waking into the darkness of my room from a dream. My father and I were trying to rescue Noah and Jakob Daw from screeching apes.

WHEN HE ARRIVED AT SEVEN-THIRTY I WAS IN MY room, and Rachel let him into the house. I was reading and didn't know he was there. It was nearly ten minutes later when I glanced at my watch and hurried out of the room.

As I came down the stairs, I heard Rachel say, "Was it a big park?" and Noah's response, "No, not like yours, but big for us." Rachel said, "You didn't have a zoo?" Noah said, "No zoo." Rachel said, "Then how did you know about animals?" Noah said, "From pictures in books and synagogue." Rachel said, "Synagogue?" Noah said, "On walls in synagogue, pictures of birds and animals. Me and my brother, we help Reb Binyomin paint."

"You had a brother?"

"Yes."

"Was he older?"

"We—how you say—born same time. Twins."

"What happened to him?"

Noah turned away. "He not here anymore."

I came into the living room. They were sitting on the couch, Rachel in a pink-and-red dress and Noah in his white long-sleeved shirt and dark trousers. On his knees was his drawing of his Kralov neighborhood. Under it was another sheet of paper, which I assumed was Rachel's drawing.

Noah said, "I drew church and gave to Janos."

Rachel said, "Who is Janos?"

"He Polish friend."

They were so at ease together on the couch, she leaning

into him and pointing at the drawing, elbows on his thighs, her head poking through the opening made by his hands over the paper.

She said, "And the stone bridge. I like that."

Noah closed his eyes for a moment.

I said, "Noah has a lesson now, Rachel."

Noah rose from the couch. Rachel grimaced. They exchanged drawings. We went upstairs.

It was hot in the room. The floor fan quietly whirred. From the wall the pictures of my father and Jakob Daw looked across the room, and over my headboard the three stallions galloped across the empty beach at Prince Edward Island against a tranquil sea. I saw my open notebook on the desk and reached over and closed it and put it inside its drawer.

We sat at the desk and worked on the lesson. I gave him an additional fifteen minutes to make up for the time he had spent with Rachel. I told him to go on reading and I stood up and went to the window.

Rachel was on the lawn soaring on the swing. Long black hair, brown-eyed, quite beautiful. Her mouth a pastel contouring of the gentlest of Cupid's bows. And the bronzed skin of her face rounding into the soft smoothness of her chin.

Noah went on with his reading. I returned to the desk. He struggled over a pronunciation and I helped him get the word out. We were both perspiring. Tiny beads of sweat lay on his forehead. His moist cheeks, I noticed, were filling out, his face losing its angular quality, though his dark eyes still held that doleful gaze.

Later, as we were going down the stairs, he said, "Why does family call you Ilana?"

"My name is Ilana Davita. My friends call me Davita."

"Davita, this Sunday night Tisha B'Av. We cannot have lesson."

"Would you want to go to the park in the afternoon?"

"I talk to my aunt."

He called the next day. "My aunt say okay."

"Good."

"I see you Sunday."

"I *will* see you Sunday."

"I will see you Sunday."

WE TOOK THE TRAIN TO THE PARK. IT WAS A GRAY-ish day, the air hot and stagnant. Leaves hung listlessly from the oak under which we sat. I listened to him read, correcting him from time to time, and after a while I closed my eyes and heard only his voice. Soft, nasal. He read on. I opened my eyes and looked around the park. Families sat about, a ball game was being played on the field, dozens of boats were on the lake.

Later we left the park on one of the paths that went through the zoo. In front of the lions' cage he opened his notebook and with care drew the head of the lion that had roared the week before and now lay still. He drew the mane and the mouth and the whiskers and the leather nose and the eyes nearly closed to yellow slits.

He said, "That Reb Binyomin lion."

"You mean Reb Binyomin made lions like that?"

"For ark."

"He made the lions for the ark."

"Ark in wooden shul. We make leopards, deer, eagles, lions. Bright purples and greens and golds. I give this to Rachel," he said, indicating the drawing.

We headed for the subway. When we got off at our stop after the ten-minute ride, it was raining heavily. We waited in the entrance of the station for it to let up, and then, in a drizzle, started across the parkway. We were on the other side when it began to rain again, and we stopped for shelter at Mr. Wolf's newsstand.

"Wet enough?" Mr. Wolfe said in his high voice from behind the stacks of newspapers. He was on a stool. His right arm cradled in the palm of his left.

I said, "I'm okay, Mr. Wolf."

He looked at Noah. "And how are you, fella?"

The rain turned torrential. I said, "He's okay too."

An occasional car came along the street, splashing rain. The stores were closed and there were no pedestrians. Rain struck the puddles on the sidewalk and the rivulets near the curbs, forming small lakes and streams. I saw Noah gazing at the rain and rivulets. What was he seeing?

I asked, "Mr. Wolf, do you carry notebooks without lines?"

He reached into a shelf behind the stacks of newspapers and brought out an eight-and-a-half-by-eleven-inch unlined notebook.

"This is what you want?"

40

"Thank you."

Noah had continued to stare out at the rain.

"You just come to America?" Mr. Wolf asked him.

Noah, aware that he was being addressed, turned to me.

"I'm his English tutor," I said.

Mr. Wolf looked at Noah. The rain had begun to let up.

"Well, lots of luck," Mr. Wolf said to Noah.

We went up the street and crossed the trolley tracks at President Street and walked to my house. Only an occasional car made its way through the puddles. This was the first day of rain in weeks. It added to the steaminess.

"Noah, come inside for a minute."

We went up the front steps. The hydrangea bushes were wet. Inside he gave me the drawing of the lion to give to Rachel, and I gave him the new notebook.

"Draw in this," I said. "Don't draw in your notebook."

"I buy new notebook."

"My present to you," I said.

He looked at me and then after a moment nodded. He held the notebook, closed and opened and closed his fingers over it. The Hebrew notebook he folded under his left arm. The pencil was in a pocket somewhere. I let him out the door and watched him walk away under the dripping maples.

There was no one home. I turned on the living-room fan and took Noah's drawing upstairs and left it on Rachel's bed. You looked at the drawing and saw only the head, but you envisioned the lion's restlessness, his immense power, his colossal shape.

I went to my bathroom, and then to my room and turned on the fan. I got out of my clothes and, wearing only my underwear, crossed to my desk. I took out my notebook and must have sat there a long time. I remembered my father and Jakob Daw in the room whispering and then the harp woke me and I slipped into my housecoat and Rachel was at my door.

She held the drawing. "Is this Noah's?"

I nodded.

"I like it."

"It's a lion."

"I know what it is, Ilana."

"Rachel, go find something to do, please."

"I'll make another drawing for Noah."

I could hear her singing along the hallway and down the stairs.

She brought the drawings to supper.

"That's Noah's," she said.

My mother said admiringly, "That's a lovely drawing."

"He's very good," my stepfather said.

"Look what I'm giving him," Rachel said.

She displayed a drawing of three figures in a flower-studded field. The picture had been made with crayons, the figures drawn in bold colors, a green dress for my mother, a bow tie and a dark suit for my stepfather, a pink dress for Rachel. Over the figures was a blue sky with a yellow sun.

"That's very nice, Rachel," my mother said.

MY STEPFATHER, MY MOTHER, AND I ATTENDED synagogue on Tisha B'Av. The day was inexhaustibly hot; the synagogue was packed. We read Lamentations and chanted about the fall of the Temples.

Noah's aunt called me Tuesday evening.

"Noah is sick and won't be able to come tomorrow."

"Oh, no."

"The doctor says he will be okay by Sunday."

"Is he running a fever?"

"It is not a fever. The doctor says he needs rest."

I told Rachel when I picked her up from summer camp. She said, "Then I'll give him the drawing on Sunday."

His aunt called me Friday morning. Noah was better and would be here on Sunday. I was very relieved. But then she called me Sunday morning and told me he could not be there after all.

"He has had a relapse."

"You said he didn't have a fever."

"Not fever. He is trying to remember." A wail of pain wafted over the telephone line. "Another of my children is sick. With fever."

I told my mother.

"Well, see if she'll let you go to him."

I telephoned his aunt.

"It is not a good idea," she said immediately.

"Please ask him."

"I will call you back."

When she called again, she said, "Come at three o'clock."

I told Rachel. She said, "Ilana, you give him my drawing as a get-well present."

On Sunday afternoon I left the house. I wore a short-sleeved white cotton blouse and a blue skirt. My shoulder-length blond hair lay parted on the right side, caught in a tortoiseshell barrette. Blistering heat waves stretched across the neighborhood. I could feel them ripple against my legs. The street seemed ancient, primordial. I walked in the burning shadows of the green maples.

3

I TURNED ONTO EASTERN PARKWAY. THE SUN WAS bright and hot. No one was on the street. I looked at the numbers on the buildings. The Polits lived in a four-story brownstone, with an off-white entrance hall and a reddish floor linoleum. I walked up to the fourth floor and rang the bell of the apartment nearest the stairs. The door was opened by a bearded man in his early forties wearing a round skullcap, a short-sleeved white shirt, and brown trousers.

"Hello. I'm Davita Dinn."

He looked at me carefully. He was some inches taller than I, with dark eyes and dark hair, the hairline beginning to recede. "Come in," he said, and closed the door. "Would you like some tea? A glass of water?"

"Water, please."

He brought me into the kitchen, filled a glass from a

bottle in the refrigerator, and gave it to me. I drank it quickly.

He put the glass in the drain and led me through the hallway to the right of the kitchen and then into the space that was a living room and dining room, with sofa and easy chairs near one wall and a mahogany table set with six dining room chairs against the other. A rug and two end tables were near the sofa, and two rotating floor fans.

"Please sit down. My wife will be in soon. One of the children is sick."

I took one of the easy chairs. He took the other. He looked embarrassed.

"You're very young to be teaching English."

"I'm a graduate of Tilden High School."

"But still—"

"And I'm going to Barnard College in the fall."

"Where is that?"

"In Manhattan. It's the women's college of Columbia University."

"That's impressive."

"Noah was doing very well."

"He did his lessons every night after working for me during the day. We have him going to a yeshiva in Lakewood, New Jersey, this coming September."

Noah's aunt entered the living room. She looked exhausted.

"Hello, Davita," she said. "I have a child who is sick and asleep, and the others are out of the house. Noah has been having nightmares again."

I looked at the two of them.

"I came just to give him a lesson," I said.

"You have a good relationship with him," his aunt said.

"Anything you do, anything, we'll be grateful for," his uncle said.

I accompanied her to the bedroom at the end of the hallway. She knocked on the closed door, then waited. She knocked again. I felt the apprehension stirring within her. She knocked a third time. Still there was no answer. She opened the door.

The room was baking hot. It faced the back of the house, its two windows giving out on clotheslines and fire escapes.

"Noah," she said.

He lay in the bed and looked out the windows.

"It's Davita," she said.

"Davita," he murmured. He turned his head slightly and looked at me.

She pushed me gently into the room and closed the door.

The room was furnished with a bed, a dresser, and a desk and chair to the left of the bed. To the right were two windows.

"I'll open the windows," I said.

I raised the shade and opened the window on the right side of the room. Afternoon sunlight fell upon him. He looked ashen. Heat moved into the room and I closed the window. I had put Rachel's drawing on the desk.

"Rachel gave me something for you."

He took the drawing and let it lie face up on the bed for

a moment. He seemed reluctant to look at it. Then he did, taking in its splash of colors.

"Tell Rachel thanks you," he said.

He reached under his sheet and brought out the notebook I had gotten him. But he could not open it. He lay with head against the pillow and with the notebook on his chest, and he said, "Thanks for you came."

"Thanks for coming. Where's your Hebrew notebook?"

"It here somewhere."

"We'll need it to write in."

He turned his face to the ceiling. "Tisha B'Av bring memories. From Tisha B'Av to first day Rosh Hashana, memories."

He lifted his head and looked at me. "I wanting to tell you about Reb Binyomin."

He put his head back on the pillow and spoke again to the ceiling. Nothing came out. He tried to push up on his elbows, and raising his sleeves to adjust the sheet, he exposed his left arm, the arm that bore the concentration camp number. He sat up, covered by the sheet. I took the chair near the desk and brought it to the bed and sat down on it. He was talking again, in a rush of language. Now I hear him again over the years, talking slowly about it, thinking what he and his brother had done.

"It began with my brother," he said. "We were ten years old. I told you my father was a bookseller. We had our store on the market square and one day I found a book of drawings. I copied some of the drawings in the book and then I drew my apartment house and the courtyard. I gave the drawings to my brother."

He stopped and took a deep breath. Then he continued.

"My father said to me during supper, holding up my drawings, You did these? And I nodded, wondering where he had gotten them and thinking a good scolding was in store for me. He was religious, though not one of the fanatics; tall and trim, he wore a skullcap inside the house and a hat outside, wore modern clothes, and had a short dark beard, a pince-nez, and a refined manner. He spoke Yiddish, Polish, Russian, and German. He said to my mother, What do you think of this? She said, looking at the drawings, He's only ten. My little sister, six years old, asked if she could see the drawings, and my father showed them to her, twelve sheets of paper, and my sister went oooh! Then my father asked me if he could show the pictures to Reb Binyomin.

"Reb Binyomin was the caretaker of our synagogue. A man in his late sixties. Stocky, white-bearded, dark, burning eyes, skin furrowed deep on his forehead, his face frozen with remorse. A non-Jew, about my father's age, and his boy, about my age, swept and cleaned, prepared wood for the stove. Reb Binyomin cared for the books and the coverlets for the stands on the bimah in the middle of the synagogue and for the parochet on the ark, the wine-colored curtains with the lions on them.

"I went to the synagogue on Sabbaths and holidays and sat with my father and my brother and our friends, and saw Reb Binyomin moving about on the bimah or reading from the Torah scroll or sometimes opening the ark doors to replace the Torah scrolls and closing them and standing a moment or two longer than anyone else facing the ark after the final swaying of the curtains and lions.

"He lived across the courtyard from us; we had to pass his apartment before we left our house. Later that week my father gave him the drawings. The next day Reb Binyomin asked to see me in his apartment.

"My father went with me after we had eaten supper. It was a freezing winter evening. We walked on the sidewalk skirting the courtyard and rang Reb Binyomin's bell, and he answered and brought us inside.

"It was a dark apartment. Two rooms and a kitchen. We sat at the kitchen table and his wife served us tea and cinnamon sugar cookies. I copied one of the drawings.

"Reb Binyomin cleared his throat, and wanted to know how long I had been drawing. I said the first drawing just appeared when I saw the book in my father's bookshop. Reb Binyomin asked if I had heard of Bezalel, builder of the tabernacle during the wilderness wandering? Of course I had heard of Bezalel. Then, asking my father to be so kind as to stay behind, he sent me home.

"My father arrived about a half hour later. He said that Reb Binyomin liked the drawings. Why it took half an hour for Reb Binyomin to say that, I never found out.

"And that was where it ended."

Noah lay back. I could actually see movements of flesh and bone chase themselves across the contours of his face. In a near-empty voice he asked for a glass of water, and I went to the bathroom across the hall. The cabinet was full of over-the-counter drugs. I filled a glass and brought it to him and he drank the water slowly and I put the empty glass on the desk. He gazed out the window, then looked at me. He moved his spindly legs under the sheet.

"I very tired," he said. "But I glad you came."

"I am glad you came."

"Better you should give me a lesson now so Aunt Sarah will not think you do not earn money."

"Your Aunt Sarah thought I would have to listen much more than I would have to talk."

"Maybe you should give me very short lesson."

I smiled at that.

We worked on his grammar. When we were done I asked him for a drawing for Rachel. He opened and closed his left arm and drew two deer asleep in front of a bed of some primitive flowers.

"Thanks you," he said.

"Thank you," I said. Then, "Wednesday?"

"Wednesday, yes," he said.

I left the door open and went down the hallway to the kitchen. His aunt and uncle were seated at the table.

"I gave him his lesson," I said. "He's coming to me on Wednesday."

His aunt said, "There was nothing else?"

"He gave me a drawing for my sister."

"What did he say to you?" his uncle asked.

"He told me about his family, about Reb Binyomin, and his drawings."

"My sister wrote us about that," his aunt said. "But he doesn't talk about . . . anything."

"You should know how he carried on," the uncle said. "From Tisha B'Av and on. He cries."

"Please," I said. "If he wants to tell you anything at all, he will."

Noah's aunt accompanied me to the door.

"Something happened to him on Tisha B'Av."

I did not say anything.

There was a hopelessness about her. "Well, good-bye."

I went down the stairs and to the street.

The sky was bright with searing heat. Pigeons scratched in fallen leaves. A few old people sprawled on the parkway benches. I went along past Schenectady Avenue and then Troy and Albany and Kingston. I realized that I had long gone past the street I would normally have turned up to go home, and was brought up short by Mr. Wolf and his newsstand. He saw me and waved his good arm. I waved back.

My parents and Rachel were not home. I left the drawing on Rachel's bed and went to my room, where I switched on the electric fan and stood for a moment, letting the blades blow air over me. Then I undressed and went to the bathroom for a shower. I was in the shower a long time. Back in my room, I put on my light bathrobe and sat at my desk.

There was a pull on the doorknob. I looked at my watch. I'd been writing for over an hour. I started for the door, turned the key and opened the door. The harp sounded. It was Rachel. She was carrying Noah's new drawing.

"This drawing is for me? Two deer."

"From Noah."

She looked at the drawing. "It's very pretty."

"Enjoy it."

She went out of the room. I locked the door.

My mother said to me at supper, "How was your time with Noah?"

"We talked about Reb Binyomin, the caretaker of his synagogue. And we did the lesson."

"What did his aunt say?"

"He's having nightmares."

My stepfather touched his moustache and shook his head.

Rachel said, "Mama, look at the deer."

My mother said, "That's really lovely."

"It's good," my stepfather said. "It's very good."

My mother said, "This is a talented person."

NOAH CAME OVER THE NEXT WEDNESDAY. THE DAY had dawned gray and stayed that way. We were about halfway up the inside staircase when Rachel opened her door. She came up to him and said, "This is for you."

It was a drawing of a field of gaily colored flowers over which a resplendent sun smiled brightly. The sun covered about half the sky. From its periphery radiated spokes of brilliant light.

"It very good," he said delightedly.

"The sun and all the flowers," she said. "I drew it in the park."

"It's really beautiful," I said.

"And you know what? They're teaching us how to swim underwater. Isn't that fun?"

"Yes, it is," I said.

She gamboled past us to the family room.

We went upstairs. I left the door open. We worked a long time making up for time lost. When he was done he asked for a glass of water and when I brought it he thanked me and drank it. Then he put the glass down on my desk and asked me if I had a few minutes and I said yes. He looked at the open door and I got up and closed it. The *tung ting tang ting tang tung* of the harp broke quietly upon the room. Then it faded and the room was left in utter silence. From the shadows of the room came the visible presences of my father and Jakob Daw.

HE TOLD ME THAT HIS BROTHER YOEL AND HE would go to the synagogue courtyard to meet with their friend Janos, who was about their age, stocky and blond-haired, with cornflower-blue eyes and a ruddy face. "In the back of the courtyard near the fence that separated us from the dense woods was a small area where we could build whatever suited us. Scraps of wood, the lower panel of a door, a discarded sheet or a tarpaulin—made to separate us from the world."

He stared at the closed door, then back at me, and went on: "We would sit inside our dwelling and play our games: soldiers and Mongols, Poles and Swedes, cowboys and Indians. Sometimes we would see Reb Binyomin inside, staring up at the walls and ceilings. When he needed Janos's help to move something he would call him, and sometimes my brother and I, we would help as well. Yoel said to me once, Did you notice how Reb Binyomin moves, how his shoes flip-flop over the trail he leaves, how he's afraid to advance, he's an unhappy person. That was Yoel, always in touch with another person's soul.

"We used to hold Shabbos and Festival services in the synagogue, and in the small chapel during the rest of the week. Over the months I got to know the interior of the synagogue, the rooms, closets, ladders, labyrinths. The synagogue's ark and lions and eagles and deer, its ornaments and murals and signs of the zodiac—they were all in very bad shape.

"And then Yoel one day had this bright idea. Ideas came to Yoel from everywhere. He and I were in the shack, waiting for Janos, when his eyes suddenly took fire behind their thick lenses. His face, which was usually deadly pale, was alive. Noah, he said, why can't the two of us help Reb Binyomin by working for nothing? I looked at him and then I looked past him at the wooden synagogue. What? I asked. He said, I don't know what the cost of the materials would be, the paints and glues and oils and varnish. But he did know what the cost of labor would be. Nothing.

"Over supper that night he told our father, who waved the idea away. Yoel insisted. I sat there listening. Inside me was a feeling that things would not ever be the same. We were both ten years old, but this idea had nothing to do with chronological age. Our father scratched his beard, shook his head. He asked, Why disturb an old man with dreams that you can't fulfill? You'll get bored, you'll give up, you'll bring him closer to his grave. My mother said that it was only fair to give Reb Binyomin a say in this. My father shook his head and sighed.

"A few days later my father went over to Reb Binyomin's apartment. Then Reb Binyomin came to our apartment. It was a rainy spring day. We sat in our living room and my mother served tea and cookies. My little sister was in her room. Reb Binyomin cleared his throat and sipped tea and asked if we really wanted to do this? Yoel immediately said yes, if Reb Binyomin could show us what to do. Reb Binyomin said he wanted to think about it. He got slowly to his feet. Soberly, he shook hands with my father, thanked my mother for her tea and cookies, and left.

"Immediately, I wondered what I had gotten myself into. Summer was coming. Yoel did not like swimming in the river, did not like going with other boys into the woods, hunting berries, did not like doing children's things. Yoel longed for fields and meadows, for air smelling of flowers and hay. Yoel loved a Poland free of anti-Semitism, loved it when he could get the three of us to think of university together. He was about ten years ahead of us. Yoel was a dreamer."

Noah paused. The heat in the room was hardly bearable but we couldn't open the window to the even more stultifying heat of the street. In the room below, Mama was putting Rachel to sleep. He passed his hand over his damp face and said he needed to go to the bathroom. I opened my door and he went out and I heard him walking along the hallway.

I shut my eyes. I must have dozed on my feet. He stood in front of me. He was nearly as tall as I. His eyes and chin had almost lost their triangular look. Black hair beneath a dark skullcap; a white long-sleeved shirt; dark trousers. He said, "You are a very pretty woman, Davita." He leaned toward me and gently kissed me on my right cheek, and I was deeply flushed and could smell the sweat of his melancholy smile, and it was sad and good. He backed away, not hastily, a kind of rapture on his face.

"I am going home now," he said.

I accompanied him through the hallway and the double wrought-iron doors to the outside.

After a while I went upstairs and closed my door. The balls of the harp played against the wires. I turned off the overhead lights and moved into the low light cast by the lamp on my desk. I lowered my window shade. I took off my clothes and sat before my notebook in my bathrobe. Purple shadows crossed the room from its disappearing corners.

4

MR. WOLF WAVED AT US WITH HIS GOOD ARM, and I waved back. "Hot enough for you, Davita?" Noah and I entered the subway and emerged some minutes later and moved along the shaded street into the park. We sat under an oak and did the lesson.

There were many people moving languidly about. I gazed across the vast green field. When we were done I asked him if he wanted to go out on the lake. An eager look. A nod of agreement. We walked through the grass of the green field to the lake.

Beached on the edge of the lake were about a dozen rowboats. To the left was a shed against which oars were stacked. A thin man in his early twenties, wearing a T-shirt and jeans and smoking a cigarette, came out of the shed and asked us if we wanted to rent a boat. I said yes and I paid him and climbed into the rower's seat. Noah, balancing himself carefully, sat down opposite me, his knees wobbly.

With a shove the man pushed us from the shore and then stood there watching us row away.

We rowed toward the center of the lake. It was crowded with young couples. The sun was harsh on the surface of the water; people shimmered before my eyes in the feverish air. I saw Noah turn his face uncertainly toward the sky. His eyes blinked in the brutal light and he forced his head toward the fiery sun before he looked down toward the surface of the water. There were largemouth bass and carp and sunfish in the lake, and people were laughing and catching and releasing them. There were sparrows fluttering in the air. There were doves and terns too, and I seemed to remember gulls coming from Sea Gate and Coney Island and Brighton Beach, swooping in and settling on the ground, and there were my father and Jakob Daw and Noah and myself, and we were moving toward one of the coves where we were enclosed by shrubbery and tall wild grasses and streamlets with the movement of water against the shoreline. There I rowed into the cove and pulled the oar blades out of the water and rested the handles against the inner sides of the boat.

My father and Jakob Daw sat visible only to me.

"DAVITA, I SEE NO OTHER FACE BUT REB BINYOMIN. I know my father, my mother, my brother Yoel, my sister. But I do not see them. Reb Binyomin I see. He leaps toward fire and clouds."

Pausing for a moment, he fixed his eyes behind me as if that were where Reb Binyomin was. Then he lowered his eyes and looked at me.

"He had no money for the repair of the synagogue. In the bitter winter of 1934, when the stove went out, he went from one door to the next taking up a collection. A proud man, a lonely man, going from one door to the next with his hand out. That hurt him. From then on whenever he had a panel to fix he kept it to himself. He watched the synagogue fall into slow ruin.

"The truth was he wanted to depend on us, but didn't know if he could. We were children! Two children! Well, he had a panel to repair on the wall near the end of the hall, a deer and some flowers. On the first day of the week, he assigned the deer to me and the flowers to my brother. Yoel whispered to me that he didn't know anything about how to make flowers. I said I would try to help him. Reb Binyomin brought from somewhere little pots of oils, varnish, and glue, and told us what to do.

"He stood there watching us.

"That was a terrible moment. From a pencil being used to make a measurement to a color being used to fashion a hue! From despair to darkness. I could feel myself sweating. What a moment!

"I finished the panel clumsily, resolutely, and then I helped Yoel. My fingers were a mess of color. I wondered how our mother might greet the new synagogue.

"Reb Binyomin stood watching. Finally a deep vibration came from his heart. It was as if he had waited decades for this breath. He straightened, he closed his eyes, he thanked God, he murmured that something respectable might come of all this. Then he turned away and was gone into the shadows of the synagogue.

"Those first few weeks, I do not know how we did it. We trudged home from school, ate our food, and then headed for the synagogue. We changed into rags, picked up colors and varnish and glue, and did what Reb Binyomin told us to do. How he worked us! As if we were ten people! First, a line of flora along the edges, then birds and animals. Slowly, he got to talking about himself—not as a caretaker of an old synagogue but as a new person, someone hidden in the midst of all this messy and tangled construction."

A boat heaved into view rowed by a teenager, with a girl sitting in the seat opposite him. They spotted us. They came to an angled stop against the shoreline, and slowly and reluctantly rode the stream out.

"How he got to talking about himself and the synagogues he built before the First World War! He began at fifteen as an apprentice. Bony, hungry-looking. Going from synagogue to synagogue, seeking worthwhile work. He told Yoel and me that the oldest-known wooden building was at Chodorov near Lvov. It was built in 1651. Other wooden synagogues were known from a later time. The more isolated we Jews were from our environment, the more we created a world of our own in the midst of Polish society. And central to that world was the bimah, the sacred raised area in front of the ark, as well as the holy ark itself."

Noah halted, peering off into the liquid shadows of the invisible ark. We were bathed in our own narrow band of light.

"Ah, the ark, the ark.

Reb Binyomin continued. " 'There were many such wooden synagogues at the end of the nineteenth century, and many arks. Those synagogues were built to resemble a house or a barn on the outside so as not to attract attention, but on the inside they were stunning. Lions stood at the side of the ark opening; they recalled the lion ornaments of Solomon's palace. To the lions were joined deer, a leopard, an eagle. Flower ornaments, birds and animals inhabited the vines and leaves. Fruit, urns, birds, palmettos; a table of showbread appeared on a north wall and the seven-branched lampstand on a south. And the ark, the magnificent ark, in its sumptuous carved frame, stood behind ornamental metal gates, and its lamps, reflectors, and candles increased the majesty of the synagogue. Ah, you don't know what I mean by that? You will. You will.

" 'I acquired three things: a wife, three daughters, and

an uncommon skill with the tools of my trade. At thirty-two, I was given the ark of the wooden synagogue of Kolvel, a new construction to be built from the ground up. Nine years of labor I put into it, all ornamented with legends. Talking fish from the days of the Flood; an elephant with a tower on its back representing strength—'

"Behind me a door opened and quickly closed. It was Janos. He had come to put wood into the stove. In spite of the spring it was cold outside. 'It's raining,' he said. He looked quickly around and was upset at the fence of silence he encountered. He walked out.

"Reb Binyomin waited, breathing deeply. Behind us the shadows took on depths of their own. He waited before he began again.

" 'Eleven years later I was given another ark. Can you imagine what an honor that was? Two in a single lifetime! A wooden synagogue is an expression of the carpentry used by the local population in the habit of constructing many of its buildings in timber. But the ark of that synagogue—that is something very special. It is its soul. Eleven years. I oversaw the wall paintings and the ark itself. Eleven years. For this labor I outdid the one in Kolvel. Two arks . . . If I was ever to have a third . . .

" 'Then I was brought to Kralov.

" 'The community had one of the oldest arks in eastern Europe, worn from revolution and pogroms. I had been chosen to rebuild it. I settled in the town.

" 'Then the First World War began. I waited. The town languished, deteriorated.

" 'Nearly twenty years later, two twin boys talked me

into something foolish and fantastic. Yoel, his eyes alive with ideas. And you, Noah, you could have lived without this. You could continue playing in the woods and the river. But you have the talent. You are Bezalel, you are the first to build an ark out of the wilderness. What marvelous things God puts in our path to overcome. May it be His will!'

"And Reb Binyomin picked up a brush and added wondrous things to a peacock.

"We continued with a vine, a bird, an animal. The days grew warm. Then Janos walked in one day, gazed around, and asked if a non-Jew could help. Yoel, splattered with paint, did not wait for Reb Binyomin to respond. He handed Janos a rag and told him what to do.

"Some of the yeshiva students came over, the ones who are never off from study. They walked in late one night and worked. How they worked! The Labor Zionists arrived one evening, about ten strong. Then the Revisionists and those brazen members of the left, the Bundists, came to lend a hand. They called it 'Our Wooden Synagogue.' Even some Hasidim poked their heads inside to see what was going on, and they stayed and worked.

"What was going on was a synagogue in sudden motion. The last of the Festival holidays came and went. We put up the scaffolding. And from the line of the flora near the ground floor to the signs of the golden zodiac near the cupola, Reb Binyomin played over the synagogue with great authority, a transformed man. The zodiacal plants flowered in the cupola, and it was all lushly painted from floor to ceiling with the colors of flowers and vines, with urns, birds, beasts. From outside, the place was like a courtyard, a plain wooden building of fir and pine with dovetail joints at the corners and interior plank lining. From the interior it was a magnificent wooden synagogue. The measurement was about fifteen square meters. The women's hall was an annex. There was a special additional winter room, a shelter for very cold weather, plastered to facilitate heating. And there was a woodshop near that winter room.

"We took the ark out after Succos. Solemnly, we brought it downstairs. He did his work on it in the woodshop. This went on through the winter and spring and through Tisha B'Av and into the month of Elul. Once I went down with Yoel and we watched him as he applied his workmanship to the making of the ark. It was a hot afternoon. His eyes were ablaze but his fingers were cramped. Yoel asked him if there was any way we could contribute to the making of the ark and he had us raise and lower and adjust it and I watched his hands trembling, his fingers gripping the tools, his white-bearded face a tenacious mass.

"Others came from the villages nearby, to look, some to help.

"Reb Binyomin, two porters, me, and Yoel set the ark in its proper place three days before Rosh Hashana. We watched as Reb Binyomin raised the Sifrei Torah into their niches, settled lamps, reflectors, candles, fixed the curtains with their new lions against the sumptuous frame near the carved gates.

"Three days of strange thudding reverberating noises from west of the town.

"We gathered in the synagogue. The ark poured its beauty upon us. We prayed. We prayed in a new dimension of color, space, and time. The holiness of the place; the sense of the first notes from the shofar; the first harsh call."

My father and Jakob Daw were silent.

"The mysterious stream of strident sound rolled from Reb Binyomin as he gave forth the calling of the notes from the shofar, for he had been given that singular, shattering honor. He put the shofar to his trembling lips. He blew: Tekiah. Shevarim. Teruah.

"On the second day of Rosh Hashana, in the middle of the morning service, the German army arrived."

"WHAT HAPPENED TO YOEL?"

"They took him to forest."

"What happened to your parents and sister?"

"They took them all to forest."

"And you they took to Auschwitz?"

"They took about one hundred to Auschwitz. I had a talent they could use. I drawed."

"I drew."

"I drew."

"WHAT HAPPENED TO REB BINYOMIN?"

"I there with others."

"What happened?"

"They collect Jews and we all watch Germans burn the wooden synagogue."

WE BROUGHT THE BOAT ONTO THE SHORE AND crossed to the zoo. Elephants, tigers, leopards, polar bears. The aviary fluttering with multicolored birds. Heat suffocating. In the distance the deep-chested grunting of a lion. We rode the subway home.

I MET WITH HIM FOR OUR LAST LESSON. HE GAVE ME a pencil drawing of myself, titling it "Davita Dinn." And then he told me what had happened to Reb Binyomin. "He went half-insane with the coming of the Germans, and suddenly there he was, on top of the burning building. We do not know how he got there. The Germans did not see him, because their faces are to us, behind their guns. Then they see him, but an order fills the silence: *"Nicht schiessen!"* He gives a single long loud scream—how that sound assails me; I hear it now—as he went hurtling through already blazing seconds of space, and struck the ground, and was in smoke and fire. The building collapsed on him, and he was gone."

The next day Noah left for the yeshiva.

THE WAR DOCTOR

I

HE WAS AMONG THE FIRST TO COME OUT OF THE Soviet Union's post-Stalinist years in 1955. Trim, tight-shouldered, with cold hazel eyes and a straight nose and thin lips, the very picture of a KGB interrogation officer. Before the 1953 blowup in East Germany, the subsequent passing of Beria, and the coming of the Khrushchev era.

When he emerged from the taxi, it was to stand in front of the lower landing of the stone stoop and defer a moment to the cool September dust of a gray morning. Down 110th Street was Broadway, and six blocks to the right was the entrance to Columbia University.

A door opened on the top landing, and a young couple stepped out and went down past him. He lifted his bags unhurriedly and made his way up the steps through the wrought-iron front door to apartment 3-D.

He found the apartment to his liking. He removed his coat and jacket, unpacked, sat himself down on the couch and closed his eyes. At 8:00 A.M. he was awakened by a buzzer on his wristwatch. He reached for the telephone.

"Ilana Davita," he said. "This is Leon Shertov."

"I'm glad to hear from you," she answered. "There is a

restaurant on West 114th Street, two blocks and across the street from the university. We can talk over breakfast."

"That is fine."

"I'll be wearing plaid pants and a white blouse. I have shoulder-length blond hair, and I wear glasses."

He found her right inside the door to the restaurant. They shook hands. They followed the waiter to the far end of the restaurant and took their seats at a table.

In Western Europe, after passing almost imperceptibly across the East German border, he was asked what confidential and privileged information he might be able to provide. There was a man of lower rank there, and he kept asking was he a defector or a provocateur. How serious is he about being helpful, or is he a setup? They need bona fides, biographical data. He was passed from one intelligence group to another. In the States he spent a long time talking. They informed him that the CIA does settle defectors whom they have determined to be legitimate. They oversee them. They give them a stipend and, although they are not wards of the state, they do help them get employment, social security, a driver's license. They are usually settled in areas of high concentration of the Russian community. The San Francisco Bay area prominently is one of those places, as is of course New York. There is a cell, unnamed in the agency, a political bureau, whose responsibility it is to take care of these people. Congress monitors these activities. He himself had settled in the Washington, D.C., area. He had signed on with a firm organizing their lectures. This was his first time out: the University of Pennsylvania, Princeton, Columbia, Yale, Brown, Harvard.

He was fifty-eight years old. He did not know what else to do with his life. In so many ways his life was now over.

"Mr. Shertov, it's good to meet you. I asked the chairman of my department if I could be your escort."

The waiter brought their orange juice. She looked at him over the rim of her glass. The restaurant was crowded and noisy. He sat back, somewhat distancing himself from the crowd, as though afraid he would place too much of himself before this woman. He ordered scrambled eggs, bacon, and coffee. She ordered an English muffin and tea.

"You will be talking in the seminar about the Soviet psyche?" she asked.

"Yes," he said.

"We'll go from here to the university, and I'll introduce you to the chairman of the department."

The waiter came with their breakfast, and they ate quietly.

She opened a manila folder and pulled out a schedule. "Two days in seminars with students, morning and afternoon, lecturing on the Soviet psyche, and an evening lecture open to the public on the Soviet Anti-Fascist Committee." She handed him the folder, retaining the carbon copy of the schedule.

Ilana Davita watched him eating. She admitted to herself a hesitation: what should she say in the face of this KGB presence? "My parents were Stalinists back in the thirties. My father was sent to Spain by his newspaper, the *New*

Masses, to cover the civil war. He tried to save a nun during the German bombing of Guernica, and both were killed. I often wonder what he would say if he were alive today."

"Your father?"

"My father. If he were alive today, what would he be saying about the KGB and the Soviet system?"

"What was your father's name?"

"Michael Chandal."

"I thought your name was Ilana Davita Dinn."

"Dinn is my stepfather's name. He adopted me. My original name was Chandal."

He went on eating. When they were done, they left the restaurant, crossed the street, and walked the two blocks to Columbia University. They headed for the Russian studies department. She introduced him to the chairman, a tall, lanky man with a crew cut. The three of them went off to a small lecture hall where Leon Shertov was scheduled to conduct a seminar. The chairman introduced him to the waiting students. Ilana Davita, who was a teaching assistant, took her seat among them.

"Mr. Shertov is one of the more recent experts to come out of the Soviet Union and to work with the State Department on the Soviet Union's way of looking at the world. For more than twenty years he was an integral part of the Soviet regime. His topic is 'The Soviet Psyche.' This is a four-part seminar."

Leon Shertov spoke in a spare, riveting voice. Part of his talk he devoted to the Soviet Union's relationship with the foreign press. Later, Ilana Davita asked if he had ever heard of the journalist Michael Chandal. He paused, looked at her, and said that for two weeks in 1936 during the Spanish Civil War, he had worked for Tass in Moscow, and that that correspondent's articles had passed regularly through his hands. He would have them translated and then would reread them carefully. They became part of the daily briefing book for Stalin and the Kremlin.

After the public lecture that night he saw Ilana Davita and asked her when they could sit and talk. They arranged to have a drink in a nearby pub.

It was crowded, dim, and smoky. They followed a waiter to a corner booth, where each ordered a beer. Leon Shertov leaned back against the bench.

"What is your dissertation, Ilana Davita?"

"Babel and Camus: Twists of Fate and Faith. Babel's *The Red Cavalry* and Camus's *The Stranger.*"

"Interesting."

They talked at great length and with intimacy.

She talked about her early life. Her father was a foreign correspondent. Her mother, Channah Chandal (her father called her Annie), was an immigration social worker. Both were very active in the communist cause, holding meetings regularly at their home, which her mother continued even after her father was killed. Her mother broke with the party because of the Hitler-Stalin pact. Her close friend, the European writer Jakob Daw, spent time at their home in the early forties. He introduced Ilana Davita to literature and writing and stories. U.S. Immigration deported him to France, where he died of pneumonia.

They started a new life—as an observant Jewish family—
with her mother's marriage to Ezra Dinn, an immigration
lawyer who had offered help to Jakob Daw in his battle
with U.S. Immigration.

The next afternoon she came to his final seminar in the
series. His bags were packed and he was ready to leave at
its conclusion for his next university appearance. As she
accompanied him outside the building she asked him if
he'd ever written anything about his early life.

He said no, but there are stories he could tell, stories
about *his* Red Cavalry, stories about a war doctor. "But I
would never put anything in writing."

"Then your stories will die with you."

"So they will. Who needs stories of yet another Jew?"

"I need them. Without stories there is nothing. Stories
are the world's memory. The past is erased without stories.
When you get a chance, at least write about the war
doctor."

"I will not take that chance."

He hailed a cab, threw in his bags, climbed in, sat down,
and was driven off.

About the end of December she received a package
from him containing stories and accompanied by a letter.

"Dear Ilana Davita—I had not wanted to write these,
but hearing your words made me change my mind. These
are the first stories, and are true to the best of my ability to
recapture things."

The second stories followed within weeks. After a hia-
tus of a few months, she received the third and final stories.

74

2

IGREW UP IN A RELIGIOUS HOME IN THE UKRAINE, and during the First World War the army of the Tsar put me into a labor battalion. Probably because I was a Jew and those in command didn't trust us to be proper combat soldiers. That was all right with me, I wasn't eager to be in the front lines fighting the Germans. We loaded boxes of artillery shells onto wagons, and for a while I even drove one of the clattering wagons—it was always heavily laden and had a team of four strong horses—back and forth between the loading area and the front through marshland and along dirt roads. In a bad rain the horses slipped and strained and sometimes our wagons sank to their axles in the mud. One morning the Germans shelled us as we raced through a bog, and when the barrage lifted, only eighteen men were left. I was among them.

All around me in the marshy terrain lay pieces of soldiers and horses. I sat in shallow water leaning against the head of a wiry black mare and met the gaze of its dead eyes. There was a ringing in my ears and a trembling in my arms and legs. Through the ringing I thought I could hear the wailing of the wounded, though it may have been the cold autumn wind blowing past my ears. It made me sad to see our ammunition wagons in ruins, with shells spilled everywhere. Many of the boxes containing English artillery shells had exploded in the barrage, which is why so many were killed. I felt bad because there was a shortage of ammunition in the three lines of our trenches. Later that day the division retreated and I thought we were to blame for that and they would say it was the fault of the cowardly Yids.

They then made me an officers' orderly in a quartermaster battalion and I tended to their boots and uniforms and brought them lunches and suppers and sometimes cared for their horses. The officers used the foulest language, cursed their men, and were often drunk. Sometimes they beat the men with their swagger sticks and even with the knout, calling them lazy and stupid and wishing them dead. Nights they spent with women of the village where we were billeted. One morning many of the officers rode off to a division meeting and later we heard the rumbling of a distant thunder and some of the officers came galloping back in a sweat and we quickly packed up everything and joined a big retreat.

Retreating along dusty roads and barren fields, I heard men muttering to each other that the Yids were the reason for the success of the German army in Poland. I tried to find out-of-the-way places where I could put on my tefillin and pray the Morning Service, but some days I couldn't. We kept marching or waiting for hours on end, there was a confusion of jammed roads and lost units. We heard that the Germans had taken the city of Vilna.

One day we forded a shallow river and I saw two villages burned to the ground and along a road dozens of men hanging by the neck from trees, and an old toothless peasant standing by the side of the road, his hat in his hand, told us they were Jews who had been spying for the Germans. I think that was near the border of the part of Poland called Galicia.

We came to a region of low hills and rolling fields and dirt roads and there we dug lines of trenches and the Germans attacked and our soldiers drove them back and then we attacked and afterward all I could see in the fields were bodies. Amid the poppies and birch groves and flower-covered slopes—a rich harvest of torn bodies.

They gave me a shovel then and told me to help with the digging of graves. We dug them more than six feet deep and very long and wide and filled them nearly to the top with the bodies of our soldiers. For days we dug and filled graves. Bodies in odd positions stiff as wood, and gasses and eerie sounds coming from the wounds. We tried to keep their faces covered. The dead, the dust, the flies. Sometimes I saw from a partially naked body that it was a Jew I was tossing into a mass grave and I quietly said a psalm.

We were retreating again. Then my platoon leader told me to run forward with the others and if one was killed I was to take his weapon. I pulled a rifle from the hands of a headless soldier and ran alongside another soldier and fired when he fired, stopped when he stopped, fell when he fell. I saw he was dead and followed another soldier. For a while artillery was landing just behind us and I thought our own batteries must be firing on us to drive us forward into the attack. But I really could not figure out what was happening. Whining shells and erupting earth and the dry, distant rattle of machine-gun fire and lines of men falling and terrifying noises and the smell of gunpowder and blood. I had no idea where I was going and did what those around me were doing, running toward a forest. I kept slipping in blood and stumbling over parts of bodies and falling into dust and dry grass and getting to my feet. Abruptly, everyone stopped heading toward the forest and turned and ran back, and I with them. No one seemed to know where to go. Then I remember swamps, frost, icy winds. And many dead lying in strange positions everywhere. During all that time I was not seriously hurt—some cuts, a badly bruised foot, a wrenched back, lice, blisters, rotting skin between my toes, but never truly hurt—though on occasion I never slept without bad dreams and there was little to eat. We built fires in the open and in trenches and scoured the fields for vegetables and sometimes I ate the meat of pigs but never of horses.

Early one morning I turned a corner in my trench to be alone so I could put on my tefillin and pray the Morning Service. I was wrapping the tefillin around the fingers of my left hand when an artillery shell landed where I had stood minutes earlier and blew to pieces everyone there, six men. I stood amid the blood and pieces of flesh, and trembled and vomited.

Can you believe that for some weeks I was a machine gunner and killed many German soldiers? Then they found that I could ride a horse and they gave me the chestnut mare of a Cossack who had been killed and suddenly, feeling the eyes of the battalion upon me and insane with reckless courage and heeding the orders of an officer, I raced ahead into a forest where we lost most of our men but routed the enemy and they made me a platoon leader because there were almost no noncommissioned officers left after that attack.

All the time I followed orders and did what those around me said to do. One day I heard my men cursing the Tsar—my men, peasants mostly, actually cursing their own Tsar. Soon afterward there were new soldiers in our regiment. They looked like students—pale, thin, wearing eyeglasses and crimson caps. They handed out leaflets and talked about an end to this cursed war. One pushed a leaflet into my hands and said the country would soon belong to the workers.

That summer we took Lvov. But then we retreated again. Really it was a rout—I had lost most of my platoon and rode exhausted in a long cart with about a dozen others, pulled by four half-starved horses. We were in a dusty column of troops and vehicles that stretched ahead and behind as far as we could see. In late September the Germans attacked again and we withdrew through forests and marshes. I think we were moving back toward Riga and Petrograd.

I had been given a new platoon and overheard some of the men talking about being led by a Yid—Kalik the Yid, they called me—and that night two deserted. One day in the fall an officer informed us that there was a new government in Petrograd and it would make peace with the Germans. He then announced that he was going off to get drunk. I went out to a nearby field to pray the Afternoon

Service and to thank the Almighty for bringing an end to the war. Standing in tall dry grass, I heard a whisper of air go past my left ear and felt the small stir of a shock wave followed by a thin distant crack and knew that someone was shooting at me. Were my men firing at their Yid leader? There were two more shots from behind me, from my own unit. I ducked down and began to run. Something struck my left arm below the elbow. I looked and saw the sleeve of the gray uniform torn and awash in blood, and then I was clubbed across the head.

I EMERGED FROM THE DARKNESS AND OPENED MY eyes. "Don't move your head," a woman's voice said into my ear. But I moved it anyway. A stab of pain rammed through my head and down my spinal column into the back of my legs.

I lay still as a nurse tended to my head. She brushed something into my forehead that burned briefly, and put on a new bandage. Then she went away, taking with her the enameled pan into which she had tossed the old bandage and some swabs and a pair of scissors.

Slowly, I turned my head and saw I was in a large room with tall windows through which pale sunlight shone. A field hospital. The floor was strewn with straw. Three rows of men lay beneath blankets on the floor. Two attendants and a nurse moved among the men. Dust-filled air and the stench of urine and blood and the whining of the wounded.

At the head of the middle row close to the far wall stood a man with a long white beard and white hair. His face was ghostly in the pale light. He wore a long dark robe and a small dark skullcap. In his left hand he held a book and in his right a large cross.

A priest!

He was chanting from the book, blessing the wounded and the dying. Should I tell them I was a Jew and the priest's blessing could cause me harm? He was using the name of their god.

I lifted my head off the straw and instantly felt a wave of nausea. A terror fell upon me.

The priest stood chanting from his book under the raised cross.

I fell back into the darkness.

THEY MOVED ME TO A HOSPITAL IN PETROGRAD, where I lay in a narrow bed on a thin mattress. The walls of the ward were white and blue and the nurses padded about quietly. Many of the wounded died and were taken away and new wounded brought in.

The bullet that had creased my forehead left a reddish trench that angled upward from just above my left eyebrow to below my hairline. I had never gazed upon myself with pleasure, but after three years of war against the Germans, and the head wound at the hands of my own men, I looked grotesque.

The wound in my arm had turned septic soon after I

arrived in the hospital. I was burning with fever. I knew I would soon die.

Into the ward drifted word of disorder. Revolutionary upheavals in Petrograd and Moscow. The Tsar and his family imprisoned. Bolsheviks named Lenin and Trotsky and Stalin and Zinoviev and Bukharin in power. Some of the wounded muttered darkly that the Yids were taking over the Motherland. Yids wherever you turn, Yids running everything. Who's ready to take orders from Yids?

I lay with my face to the wall and was quiet.

Two doctors came over to my bed and talked about whether my arm should be removed from the elbow or a few inches above.

That was my very blackest moment. The doctors went away and some minutes later one of them returned. He was in his late thirties, tall, trim, with a reddish beard, a small mouth, and over his pale blue eyes a pair of round thin gold-rimmed spectacles.

He said to me in a quiet voice, "Tomorrow I will try again to clean the wound. It will be painful. But I will try one last time." He stood looking at me thoughtfully. Then he glanced around and asked in a low tone: "Are you by any chance a religious Jew?"

My heart froze.

In the bed to my right lay a Don Cossack who had lost his legs, and to my left a peasant from the south who had been shot in the throat.

I closed my eyes and turned my head away.

He asked me again: "Are you a religious Jew?"

I thought, my head burning with fever, Why is he asking, all he needs to do is—

"All right," he said. "Never mind."

I heard his receding footsteps and opened my eyes and saw him walk along the aisle between the beds and out of the ward. A tall man, carrying himself with utmost dignity.

THE NEXT MORNING A NURSE NAMED GELYA, BLOND-haired, pink-faced, and plump, washed my face and chest and left arm, but did not remove the bandage. "Tell them to fill you up with vodka," the Cossack advised as Gelya and an orderly started with me through the ward.

The orderly helped me onto the metal table in the small operating room.

"Do you want vodka?" asked the nurse. "I cannot give you chloroform. We save it for the very serious cases."

I shook my head.

"Good," she said. "It will only make you sick later."

The doctor entered. He wore a surgical gown. "Are we ready?" he said. "Good. You seem to be a brave soldier. We will proceed slowly and with care, and we will try to save your arm."

Gelya helped him cut away the bandage. The orderly stood by. The bullet had splintered upon entry, cut through flesh and muscle, chipped a piece of bone. The doctor adjusted the overhead light and bent over the arm with scissors and swabs. I watched with fascination his agile hands. As he worked, he talked to me softly.

"The hand is a marvelous creation," he said, "a thing of surpassing complexity and perfection. Of all the parts of the body, nothing so fascinates me as the hand. How smoothly the bones and muscles and tendons work together to accomplish the tasks they are given. The radius and the ulna. The bones of the wrist and palm and fingers. And the special miracle of the thumb with its extensor pollicis longus and flexor pollicis brevis, which enable it to straighten and to bend. And the long tendons of the arm— you are most fortunate no tendon was damaged, we would need a fishing expedition to locate the ends—that connect the muscles in the forearm to the wrist and fingers. A severed tendon is a serious affair."

I heard a small click and the pain was such that I jerked my head but did not cry out. He did that three or four more times. Then he poured liquid over the entire wound and over my hand. Then he cleaned the wound again and poured the liquid over it again; it smelled a little like iodine but I was dizzy and feverish and wasn't sure. I saw sweat on his forehead. His short red beard pressed against his surgical mask. He sprinkled some powder over the wound and signaled the orderly to release me.

Gelya put on the bandage.

The arm throbbing, I felt its pain in my chest and groin. I lost consciousness before they took me from the operating room.

When I woke, Gelya was at my side. She gave me some water. Soon the doctor came over and signaled her to leave.

"I think we cleaned it all out," he said. He leaned over close to me. "I know you are a devout Jew, because I heard you say a prayer in the operating room. Where is your home?"

I told him the names of my village and the nearby town.

"If the wound becomes infected again, you will be sent to Moscow. We will not do the surgery here. This city may soon fall to the Whites. If the wound begins to heal and the city does not fall, we will keep you here as long as possible." He was quiet a moment and tugged briefly at his beard. "I am aware that what I will now tell you is pointless, but I will tell it to you anyway. I feel a need to say it. I am unable to read or speak our sacred language. I envy you your ability and am regretful that it was not given to me in my childhood."

He straightened, regarded me sadly for a long moment, and went away.

The next day Gelya told me that the army of the Whites was now less than a hundred kilometers away, but there was no talk yet about evacuating the hospital. I thought they would probably wait until the last minute and leave behind those with serious wounds. My fever had gone down. Returning from the bathroom, I overheard two orderlies talking about how the Whites were blaming the Jews for the Revolution and were massacring any Jews that fell into their hands.

"You are doing well," the doctor said two days later as he dressed the wound in the operating room. His name was Pavel Rubinov, and his home was in Moscow. "I made some inquiries concerning your village. It was near the front lines for quite a while, but things are quiet there now." He gazed a moment into my eyes. "I have here a book." He removed from a pocket of his uniform a volume and showed it to me. It was a book of Hebrew prayers. "This was given to me some weeks ago by a wounded soldier who unfortunately did not survive. He was afraid it would be thrown into the trash. Is it possible, perhaps, you might teach me how to pronounce the letters and the vowels?"

I stared at the prayer book. It was very much like my own, which I had lost along with my tefillin somewhere between the field hospital and Petrograd: small, old, worn, stained. The doctor was asking me to teach him to read the sacred language. In this hospital.

"I understand your situation," the doctor said. "It would not be out in the open. Perhaps in this room," he said. "Only a few minutes each time. I am a very fast learner."

I said I would do that.

He slipped the prayer book back into his pocket and told me to walk around awhile for some exercise and then go back to bed.

IN A WEEK HE HAD LEARNED THE LETTERS AND vowels, and in two weeks he was reading. We sat in the small room, he would change my dressing, and I would tell him how to pronounce the letters and vowels.

I asked him, "Am I the only Jew here?"

"As far as I know, the only religious Jew. Are you aware that you speak the sacred language in your sleep?"

My mother's Psalms, I thought. I asked him why he had not learned to read before.

"There was no need. My family is very Russian. But now I am sure that I will die in this war, and I wish to die with certain words in my heart and on my lips. There is no point to running away anymore."

A few days later he said, "The White army of Yudenich is in Gatchina, about thirty kilometers from here. It seems they have British tanks." He paused. "I am experiencing some problems in connection with your travel documents. There is so much confusion everywhere. It will be pointless for me to try again today or even tomorrow. Now, please go over again this section of long words. I am having some difficulty with the vowels."

When I returned to my bed, the Cossack raised himself up on his elbows, glared at me for a moment, and hissed: "You Yid bastard, when the Whites come I myself with pleasure will tear your arm off." He fell back, breathing heavily.

The next day I said to the doctor, "Will they evacuate the wounded who can walk?"

"I don't know. We have received no orders yet."

"The Whites will kill all the Jews."

"I have been promised by a certain patient of mine that you will soon have your papers."

More days passed. I heard the name "Trotsky" repeated

in the ward. He had come to lead the battle against the Whites. The Cossack called Trotsky a Yid and cursed him. Two days earlier, one of the Cossack's stumps had become infected and Doctor Rubinov operated on him. Now he lay about four feet away from me, his hands over his eyes, his beard sticking up over his blanket. The blanket bulged over his chest and thighs and groin and then dropped and flattened awfully at his knees.

Some days later the doctor came over to my bed and told me that the army of the Whites had been defeated and was retreating. The danger to Petrograd was ended, he said. Outside the windows of the hospital a heavy snow was falling.

"Soon," he said quietly, patting my arm, "we will have you out of here. They will send you back to your village and there you will be reassigned. A new beginning for you. Come to my room this afternoon and I will have another look at your arm and then read to you some more."

Someone woke me in the middle of the following night. It was Gelya.

"Get dressed," she said. "Quickly and quietly. I will help you."

I went with Gelya through the dimly lit ward past the orderlies. At the doorway to the hospital, Gelya showed the guards a piece of paper with a signature. We went out the front doors.

Gelya handed me a packet of documents. "These will get you home," she said.

"Thank you," I said.

"I am a Ukrainian," she said. "The Jews in my village were our friends."

She hurried back into the hospital.

A horse cart stood waiting in the street. The driver motioned to me and I climbed on board. We rode through the snow-filled streets. Dark figures flitted among the silent buildings. The wagon squeaked, but its wheels and the hooves of the horse were muffled in the snow. Armed men appeared suddenly out of the darkness and rushed by on horses and in cars and trucks and vanished back into the darkness.

We rode to the train station, which was very dimly lit and crowded with troops. The driver tied the horse to a post outside and took me by the arm. He was a short man with a dark beard and a broken nose, and he carried his long whip over his shoulder. Inside the station he told me to show my papers to one of the guards. The guard looked carefully at the papers and raised his hand to his cap and returned the papers. The driver led me through the crowds to a train platform that was crowded with soldiers and civilians. He told me to show my papers to a train official and to some more guards and then pushed me into a crowded car. Then he removed his cap, bowed slightly in my direction, took a step back, and disappeared into the crowd.

I REMEMBER THE CAR HAD PAINTED ON IT THE number "322032" and below it "29.OKT.19." The numbers and letters were grimy but large and visible. I remember them because once the faint cold light of morning appeared in the winter sky we stopped often and sometimes we climbed down to relieve ourselves and I could see the numbers and letters when I got back on board. Some of the places where we stopped were thick with feces and so I assumed trains stopped there frequently. At some places there were crowds waiting, and when the train came to a halt they made a noise like the wind in the chimneys of my village, a kind of roaring and keening, and people would come rolling down the embankments and leap onto the buffers or try to wriggle through the passengers jammed in the doorways or force open the windows and climb in. Some got off at certain stops and a few managed to board. The cold air was dense with human smells. I slept standing, like a horse. Once, rolling slowly through the darkness of the early afternoon, I heard the ominous thunder of an artillery bombardment, but after a while the guns fell silent.

My arm hurt. Faint tremors began at the fingertips and ended as jabs of pain in my shoulder. I ate some of the bread and sausage Gelya had packed for me and gave some to an old man, who munched the food slowly with his toothless gums. Later, I stood pressed against a middle-aged woman. She was bulky in her padded clothes and shawl, but I felt her softness. The rhythm of the train, the small region of warmth now hovering over the bodies pressed together in the car, the years of war and homelessness, the weeks in the hospital, the haze of fatigue, the soft sinking into the woman's flesh, the smell of her hair gathered up beneath her coarse black shawl, images and visions and standing very still and the tightening of my flesh and finally the brief, shivering release. I felt sweat on my face. Now and then someone stirred, coughed, let out a moan. Slowly, the brief gray day turned into the long night.

LATER I DISEMBARKED IN A RUINED TOWN AND stood in the deserted station waiting for another train. Two hours went by. I ate some more bread and sausage and drank water from a stream in back of the station and then sat against a broken wall so the wind would not freeze my nose and face. About an hour before dark a train came. I rode the buffer until there was room for me inside.

At sunset we went past long columns of soldiers and soon the train stopped and everyone was ordered off. I showed my papers to an officer and he snapped to attention and gave me a salute. The passengers in my car looked at me and once back on the train they made a small but discernible circle of space around me. We rode through the night and I slept on the floor with my head on my rucksack.

Soon after dawn the train stopped and I disembarked in the town near my village.

THERE WERE TROOPS AND VEHICLES AROUND THE station. The town had suffered bombardment and buildings stood with walls blackened and rooms naked to the streets. I saw no fires, but people picked their way through the snow, looking dazed, as if the shells had only recently stopped falling.

Outside the station I asked the driver of a wagon if he would take me to the nearby village and he gave me a curious look and glanced up at the sky and spat into the dirty snow. His beard was gray and uncombed and he wore boots and a long coat and a fur hat. His black eyes gleamed with the tears that are brought on by freezing winds.

"Why do you want to go there?" he asked.

"It's where I grew up."

He gazed at me suspiciously. "Whose son are you?"

"I am Kalman son of Levi Yitzchok Sharfstein."

"I don't know him."

"He is the carpenter of the village."

"How long have you been away?"

"Three years."

He hunched his shoulders and peered up at the sky and stared at the horse and wagon. Fingers of frost had formed on his beard. I shivered inside my greatcoat.

"All right," he said. "Get on. But pay me first."

I climbed aboard the wagon. He touched the horse with his whip, and the beast stirred itself awake and flicked its ears and started forward.

We rode through the town. About a kilometer outside the town we stopped to let a convoy of trucks pass us. There were troops in the trucks, their uniforms tattered, some of the men sleeping on their feet. The trucks lurched heavily from side to side in the dirty snow, gears whining and grinding. They turned onto the road that led to the town about ten kilometers south, where a White regiment was still fighting.

The wagon driver clicked his teeth and the horse started again.

We rode in silence through the mist-laden winter day and I saw the fields farmed by the peasants, frozen now, and the pond, black with ice, and on the edge of the pond where the women washed their clothes the remains of a horse partly covered in snow.

"The Whites burned down the prayer house of the Yids," said the driver. "The Reds burned down the church. Then the Whites burned down everything that was left."

Splintered ends of charred wood stuck out of the snow, a portion of frayed white rope, the strap of a pair of tefillin, fragments of books, the pieces of a fence, a chair, a wall, a chimney, a brick stove.

"Between the Whites and the Reds, this is what's left," murmured the driver, blinking his eyes in the wind. "The same thing happened in other places around here. But here it was especially bad. The Whites took all the horses and shot the smugglers."

"Smugglers?"

"Those that dealt with the horses. The whole village."

"They smuggled horses?"

"Jews, peasants, everyone."

"You mean across the border?"

"The whole village lived off it. When did you say you left?"

"Why did they shoot them?"

"They said they were stealing White Cossack horses. Who knows if they were or weren't? In this war, you don't need an excuse to shoot anyone."

I climbed down from the wagon and stood on the road. The wind was cruel. I stood in the void of my past and trembled and shivered. Wasn't that the Rebbe coming along the road on a golden Karabakh horse, followed by a procession of Jews, my father among them, all on splendid horses? And peasants lining the road, their caps in their hands, and the village priest murmuring words of greeting. And the Rebbe raising his arms to the blue sky and a sweet song descending and gently bathing the village.

"They tore up the cemeteries too," said the driver from his seat on the wagon.

The procession vanished.

I felt in my heart a stone of anguish and a fire of rage. In my left arm a sudden terrible electricity. I clenched and unclenched the fingers until the tremors ceased.

"Like Tatars," the driver went on. "Broke all the stones, like crazy people, like there were demons inside them. People from the town came over and dug a big grave and buried all the villagers together."

"Were they all killed?"

"Everyone. A curse on their heads."

All dead.

"Do you want to go over to the grave?" asked the driver, shivering in the wind.

He brought me to a vast low snow-covered mound near

94

the forest. The tall silent trees stood bowed and shriveled in ice and snow. At the edge of the mound, I recited quietly one of my mother's Psalms and the Kaddish.

I climbed back onto the wagon.

"A bad business," the driver muttered.

"Take me to Red Army headquarters in the town."

We rode back in silence. He let me off in front of a dirty white building with green shutters. I had already paid him but I gave him a bit more. He put his fingers to his cap and drove away. I went inside.

A Red Army soldier sat behind a battered darkwood desk in the wide entrance hall. He looked closely at my papers, got to his feet, saluted, and directed me to a door. Inside the room a headquarters company major studied my papers and asked me to be seated. He went out and returned shortly, accompanied by a tall man with a leather coat, boots, and a peaked cap.

The major left and closed the door.

The tall man, my documents in his hands, walked over to where I was seated. He had black hair and brown eyes and a long narrow face. His boots creaked in the quiet room.

HE HELD UP THE PACKET OF MY DOCUMENTS. HIS fingers were rough, dirty, the backs of his hands chapped. "How did you obtain these papers?"

Together with the documents had come advice from Dr. Rubinov: respond with silence should I ever be asked that question. And so I said nothing. We waited in the silence between us.

Again, he leafed through the documents, holding them in his long, thin fingers, turning them, scanning them with care. And then he read again, slowly, the accompanying letter. The army papers, the release from the hospital, the travel orders, the health records, the internal passport, the letter with the signature. He tapped the sheaf of documents against the palm of his left hand and returned it to me. I stuffed it into my rucksack.

"You should get some rest. Tomorrow morning we move out. We will kick the Poles in the ass and then return and finish off the Whites."

"The Poles?"

"Wait here. Someone will find you a place to sleep."

His boots creaked as he left the room.

I slept that night in a church with Kuban Cossacks, squat, boisterous fellows who only recently had come over to the side of the Bolsheviks. They shaved each other's faces and talked about their horses and their recent engagement—the taking of a hill to prevent the outflanking of the division—in which five of their comrades had fallen, and about the women of the town with whom they had found pleasure. They invited me to share their beet soup and pork. All the pews in the church had been removed and chopped up and used for firewood, but a tall painted wooden statue of Jesus stood untouched near the altar, its arms raised as if in supplication, its haggard face wearing an expression of infinite sorrow. I put down straw on the wooden floor in a dark corner of the church and used my rucksack for a pillow and my coat for a blanket.

The next morning one of the Cossacks prodded me awake with a stick. In the cold light of the winter dawn, the brigade commander asked if my arm was well enough for me to ride a horse. I removed the arm from its sling, felt the slight quivering, and said yes. He gave me a horse that had been wounded some weeks back and was now healed—a shell had opened the face near the muzzle—and made me a troop leader.

I rode westward with the Red Army.

No one I talked to seemed able to figure out why we were attacking the Poles in the west when the counter-revolutionary Whites were in the south.

SOMETIME AROUND THE END OF MARCH WE WERE in Mogilev, and soon afterward in Minsk. There was no real war; it was all a lot of skirmishing. A world of marshland lay to our south, and below that were two more Bolshevik armies. Altogether, we were five Bolshevik armies marching on Poland, while the Whites were retreating into the Russian heartland.

I asked the brigade commander one day what we were doing, and he said, "Since you're asking, I'll tell you what I think. I think we're going to take Warsaw, link up with Comrade Pockmark, and give the Germans and the French something to lose sleep over." I had no idea what he was saying or who Comrade Pockmark was. He wore a short leather jacket and breeches and a pointed helmet. He was mounted on a white stallion and looked very official and very military.

The men in my troop were good horse soldiers, all loyal Bolsheviks. There were a few Jews among them, mostly from small towns and villages in the south, as boorish and bloody-minded as any Cossack.

We were moving through wet fields and forests, and the sodden remains of towns and villages. It was during the spring thaw and in the warming air were the smells of raw moist earth, sudden storms, animal manure, human dead. Everywhere, splintered trees, cratered earth, bones of men and horses. We moved westward and halted for a while, and suddenly the Poles hit us hard and we had to fall back, and they took Kiev.

Who would ever have thought that the Poles could fight with the cool ferocity and cleverness of the Germans?

Soon afterwards we returned to the offensive and got as far as the outskirts of Warsaw. But something went wrong with our southern armies—the brigade commander muttered darkly to me about the idiotic maneuverings of Comrade Pockmark, whoever that was—and the Poles hit us again very hard, this time on our exposed left flank, and again we fell back. By the end of August one of our armies was entirely destroyed and the other four were in disarray.

In September the war against the Poles was over and they told us we would be moving south to finish off the Whites in the Crimea.

THE COMMANDER RODE OVER TO MY TROOP THE next morning, looking sober and thoughtful. "Listen, I have something to tell you. You are being reassigned to a special unit. We think you can be of use to us."

I said nothing.

"Do you agree?"

I nodded.

About a week after the end of the Civil War I boarded a train to Moscow.

I RODE IN A FREIGHT CAR, AND THE CLOSER WE GOT to Moscow the more crowded the train became. A small cast-iron stove stood in the middle of the freight car but threw off little heat. We took turns sitting around it and slept in shifts. In the final hours we ran out of wood. Three of the old people were dead of the cold when we pulled into the station. It was night. A driving snow; the city ghostly with few lights and almost no traffic. Just inside the doors of the station, away from the winds sweeping along the tracks, a tall man emerged from the shadows and took a step toward me. "Comrade Lieutenant Kalman Sharfstein?"

Uniformed, wearing a greatcoat, boots, a pointed Red Army hat, and a wide leather belt with a holstered pistol. A lieutenant, young, blond hair, pale-blue eyes. I followed him through the crowd to where a black car stood waiting, with a uniformed driver behind the wheel.

We rode in silence through empty streets to a dimly lit, second-rate hotel. The lieutenant accompanied me inside to the porter, who took me to a tiny unheated basement room. The lieutenant said the driver would come for me in the morning, and left.

Early the next morning, the porter brought me luke-warm tea and a stale, misshapen roll. Waiting outside was the uniformed driver in the black car. It was still dark and snowing. The car creaked and rattled over the rutted roads. Long lines of people waiting outside shops, and at a ghostly intersection some old women tearing down a fence—for firewood?—with their fingers. The driver smoked, quietly cursed the road. The sky graying over the buildings; the snow whirling, falling. A gate, a guardhouse, a courtyard, a tall stone building; long, brightly lit corri-dors, an office; a bald, stocky, uniformed man with the rank of major seated at a mahogany desk and gazing at a file open before him. "The name will not do, no, no, it will not do, how will it sound if you go among our peasants or are ever with foreign diplomats?" Diplomats, I thought, astonished. "We change it to Leonid Shertov"—and he made a note in the file and sat back and looked at me. A short man, his face still glowing with his morning shave. Small, beady eyes, thin lips. "I see in your file the mention of a certain letter. Do you have it with you? Yes? Let me see it. Good. We will add it to the file. You come with a splen-did military record, Comrade Lieutenant Shertov. I will tell you what we have in mind for you."

And he leaned forward and put his elbows on the table

and brought the tips of his fingers together and told me
what they had in mind for me. I listened and nodded and
got to my feet. I saluted and he returned the salute and said
in Yiddish, "Go in good health and return in good health,"
and I tried not to let my face show surprise.

I walked back along the brightly lit corridors to the
front doors and outside, where the car and driver waited.
We rode through the city and I saw women in long coats
and dark shawls standing in the snow-filled streets, selling
artificial flowers and buckles and old medals. Elderly men,
one wearing the robe of a priest, were shoveling snow
under the eyes of a police guard. Later, in a hotel bar, I
found a woman and went with her to her shabby apartment. The next morning I boarded a crowded Red Army
train. The coal-burning locomotive was being fueled with
wood, which would surely ruin it. This time I had a seat.

SOMEWHERE IN THE HEARTLAND A BLIZZARD
halted the train and we waited a long while for the snow to
end and the tracks to be cleared. The windows were covered with snow and frosted over. I tried clearing my window from inside, but the blowing snow made a mirror of it
and I saw my face and turned away. The car was very
crowded and I gave my seat to a sergeant who had been
standing for hours.

We rode through the snow-muffled land. Frozen forests
and fields, frozen rivers and lakes, frozen hamlets and
towns. I was head of a special unit, a food detachment,

with a quota to meet and authority to take all necessary steps to meet it. We were to requisition grain from village peasants in order to feed hungry city workers, without whom the country would soon be bereft of industry.

We were down there a long time; saw the winter turn to spring and early summer; saw the most terrible of droughts; saw the mighty Volga turn into a narrow stream; saw the worst of harvests; saw people dying of hunger, become crazed, begin to eat one another. We slept in huts and barns and churches and on the ground. It was not pleasant to sense their hunger-darkened eyes upon us as we removed the hidden grain and carted it off. Twice they came at us with pitchforks and axes. A number of my men deserted. Once a screaming peasant woman came at us with a pistol and one of my men shot her in the arm and she sat on the ground moaning and bleeding until her husband came with a cart to get her.

My sergeant came over to me. "Another one for you. A tough nut, this one."

He was an old man and stood with his head between his shoulders, expecting to be beaten.

"The Revolution needs your grain," I said. "Where did you hide it?"

"The Revolution can go drown in its bowel movements," the old man said in a hoarse voice.

The sergeant, once a peasant himself, from the Ukraine, was ready to smack him, but I shook my head.

"One last time, grandfather. Where did you hide it?"

We were in his workshed. He was a farmer and a carpenter. I saw all around me familiar tools. The sacks of grain could be anywhere: buried in the floor of his hut, near a tree, under our feet.

"The Revolution is a trick and a swindle," said the old man fiercely. "Bad crops are from God, hunger is from man. The Yids have taken over and are ruining the country."

"We don't have time for this," I said. "Sergeant, find out if he has a grandson and bring him to me."

The sergeant went away.

The old man and I stood there in the workshed with three others from my detachment. It was a hot summer day. He smelled of sweat and fear.

"You're an old man and I don't want to hurt you," I said. He rolled his eyes. Then he gave me a piercing stare and proceeded to curse me, spittle flying from his dark lips. After a lengthy moment of that, he said, "Shoot me, why don't you? Better to die from a bullet than starvation. Shoot me, shoot me." But then the sergeant was back with a frightened flaxen-haired boy who ran quickly over to the old man, and the old man held the boy and lowered his eyes and told us what we wanted to hear, and we dug up the workshed and took the sacks of grain and went away, the curses ringing in my ears. The sergeant wanted to shoot him before we left, but I forbade it.

In Moscow they gave me a small one-room apartment on the first floor of a nine-story building near Gorky Street. Though it was early fall, the weather was warm. Outside the shops the lines were long. I ate my main meals at a government canteen on Gorky Street near Red Square. The food was ample and tasty. Through the large plate-glass window I watched as three elderly women stood on the sidewalk displaying trinkets from the time of the tsars.

I reported to the major. He seemed to have put on weight. He said he had read my report and the reports of others on my work. I had done a splendid job, he said with a thin smile, and was now ready for my next assignment. He told me I had one week of leave and was afterward to report to a Colonel Razumkov at a certain time in one of the buildings on Dzerzhinsky Square. Then he just sat there and said nothing more. I saluted and turned to leave. As I went out the door, I glanced over my shoulder and saw him sitting behind his desk still looking at me.

I ENTERED THE BUILDING ON DZERZHINSKY SQUARE through the proper doorway and reported to Colonel Razumkov. He was a tall, brown-haired, unpleasant man, with a nasal voice. He wanted to know about my village, my parents, my education, my years in the army of the Tsar and the Red Army, and even about my time in the military hospital in Petrograd and the doctor who had saved my arm, Doctor Rubinov. He gave me a lengthy questionnaire to fill out. I went to my apartment and worked on it through much of the night and brought it back the next day and he asked me more questions about what I had seen and done during my recent assignment among the peasants. Then he sent me to another colonel, who asked me the same questions. A doctor examined me and declared me fit. "Whoever treated your wounded arm did a fine job," he said. The final medical results, he went on, would be in in a few days.

A week later, after a morning of more questions by a third colonel, Colonel Razumkov informed me that I was being assigned to a certain school.

"You will need to join the Party, and we'll take care of that," he said. "To be candid, you displayed weakness and bourgeois sentimentality by ordering your sergeant not to shoot that lying old peasant. But you are still young, you will learn. We'll teach you everything."

3

THE SCHOOL WAS HOUSED IN A STONE BUILDING in a fenced-in forested compound outside Moscow. Amid tall wintry pines and spruce and oaks, near a frozen pond, and far from the view of outsiders, twenty-two of us studied the many weaknesses of the human body and mind. Day and night we trained in the rigorous science of investigation, arrest, interrogation, persuasion, confession; in methods of inducing helplessness, bewilderment; how to layer terror upon terror. In the kingdom of hope there is no winter, goes a Russian proverb. Well, from a tradition passed down for centuries, one generation of interrogators and torturers to the next, we learned how to dissolve that kingdom and bring to our prisoners the eternal winter of hopelessness.

From instructors who were demanding but not brutal

we learned to use sticks, whips, truncheons, and other such instruments. It was all taught to us in a professional manner, and we worked hard to master the various techniques.

As far as I could determine, no one among us could have been called a sadist. An elderly instructor spoke briefly once about the aesthetics of pain. "There are those who claim that suffering sometimes creates great beauty. They say that in order to take pleasure from causing pain, you have to torture people. Well, those who say such things are degenerate swine, they are rabid dogs who must be shot. We are not here for pleasure, but to perform a duty."

I had little to do with the others in the class, all of whom, except for three Jews from the Ukraine, were Russians. Of the twenty-two who began the course, four disappeared, one Jew and three Russians. One morning during our second month they were suddenly gone, and no one said anything about them.

We slept three or four to a room, had plenty of exercise and some weapons practice, but not much—it was rumored that there was a shortage of ammunition. We were not permitted off the compound. Evenings we had one hour free, and I took frequent walks alone in the forest. The tall, dense, snow-laden pines and spruces and oaks reached to the sky in pure and majestic verticalities as if hinting at something beyond the earth, the grave, the awful suffering and travail of the Motherland. They seemed to say that there was more than just this valley of darkness, this blood-drenched struggle to bring equality to the workers of the world. Walking on the black ice of the frozen pond, I remembered the women washing clothes beneath the willows along the dark waters of our village pond. Gone, gone, all gone into the void of a common grave. They owed me a restitution, those slayers of my past, those enemies of the Revolution, those killers of my family and destroyers of my village.

The winter was long and bitter. Wild, driving winds and dense snows and leaden, misty skies. And cold, cold. Rumors frequently penetrated the compound, moved through the corridors, reached our ears. Peasant revolts in the south, famine in the heartland. Lenin seriously ill. A name drifted through: Zinoviev, the Party boss of Petrograd, who had used military cadets to quell food riots in his city, because he would not trust the Red Army to do that dirty job. *Zinoviev!* That was the name, the signature, on the letter once given to me in Petrograd by Doctor Rubinov. But it is possible that the Petrograd food riots occurred earlier. Still, I remember that the name Zinoviev did come up for some reason while I was there.

Three women, all widowed by the Civil War, cooked and served our food—abundant, tasty—in a common dining room. We chopped and hauled our own wood. The house was run by a dour-looking man with the rank of major, who had under his command a squad of special troops. No one in all my subsequent years in Moscow ever spoke of that house in the forest. When we left after five months we were ordered not to mention its existence. I don't know if it is still in use today or even if it is still standing. I remember the rooms smelled strongly of antiseptic cleanser and were always kept warm.

THE DAY LENIN DIED, IN JANUARY 1924, THE people I saw in my apartment building—I lived now on the third floor—and in the offices on Dzerzhinsky Square were all grim-faced and spoke in low voices. No one wept. The phone in my office rang: I was to head up a security squad for the funeral.

That was an uncommonly cold day, even by our standards, as if nature had drained all warmth from the world and joined with us in mourning. The crowd was enormous, respectful. We stood in the cold for hours while factory whistles blew and cannons thundered. The bier carrying Lenin passed quite close to me. I could not figure out why he had been mummified, why they had made a holy relic of him—filled him with alcohol, glycerin, formalin to preserve him as a sacred object—when everywhere we were knocking down churches and demolishing relics and confiscating icons and church treasures. I wondered why Trotsky was not at the funeral. Would he be the next leader?

One of the pallbearers was Stalin and I got a close look at him. About five feet four inches in height; his face sallow, pockmarked, a gouge in the flesh below the right eye; his left arm deformed. He seemed like a cat, eyes slitted, yellowish. Pockmarked that way. During the failed offensive against Poland, the brigade commander had several times mentioned a Comrade Pockmark.

I didn't know much about the political maneuvering that then went on inside the Politburo. I remember, of course, that Trotsky was sent into exile, and in mid-1927 Stalin rose to sole power. In the meantime, I was rising in the ranks, and eventually was able to move into the fifth floor of a huge new apartment building with large wooden front doors, a marble entrance hall, and an inner courtyard with benches. An elevator took me to my apartment. I had no lack of women friends but did not marry. Many Gentile members of the Central Committee and the Politburo had Jewish wives; but no Jewish woman would come near me once she got wind of what I did, and I did not want a Russian wife. Very few among us were unmarried, and the head of my department often urged me to find a wife. I would greet his words with a nod and a smile. After a while he stopped mentioning it.

I had plenty of work and I was very good at what I did. My left arm was quirky, would go numb at odd moments. I did not want to injure my right arm, would use it only on rare occasions, used instead the science of persuasion, intimidation, endless interrogation, threats of harm to the family. I had no regrets. Those who came before me were enemies of the people, swine, mad dogs, saboteurs, degenerates. The older ones were the hardest of all; during their Revolutionary years, they had already been through the worst—so they thought. The Party people I now saw were well fed, most of them in fairly good health. Weeks and weeks of work: letting them sit and stare at the instruments; then the lengthy days of interrogation; then take away their sleep and force them to stand for hours at a time—what that does to the legs; then, only if necessary, the truncheon. Weaken them, wear them down. It worked; they would sign the one hundred pages or so of testimony in their own trembling hand.

Whenever it was possible, we suited the treatment to the individual: the diabetic wife of a prisoner would be deprived of insulin, a heart patient's nitroglycerin might be carefully withheld. I got to be so adept at my work that I even wrote a long interoffice memo—a sort of handbook—on interrogation techniques I perfected, and to my astonishment the minister saw it and showed it to Stalin, who commented on it favorably. Word came down that he wanted to meet me and I had awful night sweats over that. But the murder of Leningrad Party boss Sergei Kirov in December 1934 distracted him, and nothing came of it.

A strange pall of fear descended upon Moscow. Many of the inhabitants of my apartment building worked in the various offices on Dzerzhinsky Square, and we would pass one another in the marble entrance hall and the corridors, or stand packed together in the elevator—and avoid eye contact and remain silent. In the neighborhood shops, where I would always go straight to the head of the line, the clerks continued to serve me—but without conversation. Like a pervasive gray mist as fine as powdery snow, the fear hung in the air, clung to light poles and tramlines, fell upon the streets, and stopped up mouths. It was well that people were cautious: more than the walls had ears. We were running so many informers that it was difficult to keep up with their reports, many of which were outrageous lies: people getting even with unfaithful lovers, despotic bosses, authoritarian teachers; husbands looking to get rid of wives or hateful relatives.

During one of those winters, in the early or mid-1930s, I went about Moscow trying to find a pair of socks and could not find any in the entire city. No socks in all of Moscow. I couldn't quite figure out why Stalin was expending so much time, energy, and money cleaning out the enemies of the people from the cities and the rich peasants from the villages, when all the while no one was thinking to bring socks into Moscow. Maybe the enemies of the people were sabotaging the supplies of socks the way they were ruining everything else. The country seemed to be brimming with saboteurs.

I did not like some of the things I saw. The unnecessary use of force on prisoners; the occasional crude interrogation that bordered on sadism; the haste with which at times, on explicit orders from above, investigations had to be conducted, confessions obtained. Also, some of our men acted badly, would confiscate the possessions of a prisoner's family and divide the clothes and furniture among themselves; others would move with their wives and children into the apartments of families that had been arrested. We had unpleasant fellows in our midst. In the end, about twenty thousand of *them* were arrested. No great loss to the Motherland.

One day in the mid-1930s, when I had begun to think that I could not take on any additional work—I labored deep into the nights, I slept fitfully, I had frequent night-mares about my parents and sisters moldering in their grave, my left arm troubled me endlessly—I came into my office, read through the previous night's special arrest list always placed on my desk by one of the secretaries, and noticed what I thought was a familiar name.

I checked; it was the correct name. A prominent member of the Central Committee. But hardly the first of that august group to have been arrested. And he was assigned to me—my old brigade commander, Semyon.

"Well," I said, after the guards had left and we were alone.

I extended my hand. He stared at me, blinked, squinted his cold brown eyes.

Hesitantly, he shook my hand. His fingers were cold. He looked at me narrowly, a deep wedge between his pencil-line eyebrows. "I wondered what had become of you. Here of all places."

"Sit down."

He reached for the back of a chair and slid stiffly into the seat. He seemed to be suffering from a bad back and sat very straight, his hands on his knees. He had gained weight. His once long and narrow face was now jowled and ended in the beginning of a double chin, and he had the start of a paunch. The frenzied look of the new believer, which I recalled from our time together in the Red Army, was still part of his bearing, but only distantly discernible, windowed over now by a fragile defiance that was intended to conceal the disbelief, the helplessness, the desperation all prisoners felt when they were brought into this building—as if to say: Surely a mistake has been made! Surely there has been a bureaucratic mixup somewhere! Surely you will soon discover the error and have me released! He wore a gray suit, a shirt, no tie. Already the jacket was crumpled, the trousers creased. He would lose weight fast; his clothes would droop; he would need to hold up his pants with his hands because his belt had been taken away; he would become a shell, a bundle of sticks, like the peasants I had encountered on that assignment more than ten years before—and whose starved, dark-eyed faces I sometimes saw in dreams.

"Perhaps you could let me have a cigarette?" he asked, sitting stiffly in the chair.

I was perched on the edge of the desk, my legs crossed. "We don't permit smoking in our offices."

He looked at the pale-green walls, at the closed window, at the linoleum floor.

"Tell me, if you will, exactly what am I being charged with?"

"You of all people know I can't discuss that."

"I've done nothing wrong."

"Others will determine that. I'm not in charge of your case."

He closed his eyes and took a deep breath and sat very still in the chair. His lips went rigid, vanished entirely into his face, leaving only a vague line of mouth. He opened his eyes.

"You have no influence here?"

"How much influence does a major have?"

"I repeat, I have committed no crime."

"Well, comrade, either I believe you or I believe Comrade Iosif Vissarionovich. Whom would you have me believe?"

He trembled then, quite visibly. I pictured him on his horse, urging men on for our cause. Yesterday an influential member of the Central Committee; today a traitor, to be interrogated and made to confess—by any means. "Beat, beat, and then beat again," Iosif Vissarionovich had repeatedly ordered concerning others. Over the phone someone had given me the list of the comrade's transgressions: enemy of the people; petit bourgeois deviation; Trotskyist opposition; membership in a terrorist organization; Polish spy; plotting to assassinate the head of state. They would be merciless with him.

He knew what awaited him. He ran a trembling hand over his flat hair.

"Listen," he said suddenly. "I have a wife and children. A boy and a girl. I plead with you that they be spared."

"Comrade—"

"What happened was that somehow he must have learned I once called him 'Comrade Pockmark.' Maybe I told that story about Comrade Pockmark recently to a friend after a little too much vodka. That's what happened, I'm sure of it. Otherwise this makes no sense. No one could be more loyal to him than I was—than I am."

I looked at him.

"Listen, Comrade Major, ask them if someone can assure me that my wife and children will be safe. I will say anything and sign anything if I am given that assurance."

"I'll pass that on."

"Tell them, if you will, that I embrace Comrade Iosif Vissarionovich and I embrace the Party, no matter what happens to me. Nothing can stand in the way of the Party."

"I'll tell them."

There was a pause. I buzzed for the guards and they led him away.

I called Colonel Razumkov on the interoffice phone.

"I can't speak with any authority about his wife and children, and I don't want to know about his love for them. There are certain things he must do and say for us, regardless of what is to happen to his wife and children, and he will do and say them even if we have to stick twenty needles up his ass. Do you understand me?"

"Yes, Comrade Colonel."

He hung up.

It took some while for my left arm to stop throbbing.

Those who were assigned to deal with the brigade commander reported that his interrogations were lengthy and thorough. But he would say nothing until word came down from on high that his family would be spared. Then he gave them names, accused others, and signed the 128 pages of confession they put before him.

He went on trial, was found guilty, and two days later was executed with a single shot to the back of the neck. He was an enemy of the people and got what he deserved.

Soon afterward we received orders to arrest his wife. She was given ten years and sent off to one of our labor camps in the Far East. I don't know what happened to their children; probably relatives took them in.

About two or three years later, we began to arrest Red

Army and Navy officers. Some generals came through my office, a cool professional lot, who thought they knew how to take interrogation. On a number of them we used what we called the "conveyor": teams of interrogators that went at it for days without stopping. Most of the time, one or two weeks of that was enough; they confessed to the crimes we put before them and then incriminated themselves in court.

About the time the Germans invaded us in 1941, the arrests had almost come to an end. By then I was a colonel.

EARLIER THAT WARM JUNE NIGHT, THE NIGHT OF the 21st, I was with a woman. By the beginning of the forties there were fine restaurants in Moscow and even some nightspots. I got back to my apartment after midnight, sated and in a good mood. But I slept restlessly, woke and slept again, troubled by dreams.

For weeks some of our departments had been receiving secret dispatches from our overseas agents, from certain other reliable sources, from our embassies, from our commanders in the field, about a German troop buildup along our western frontier. We knew that Luftwaffe reconnaissance planes were constantly overflying our border and photographing our airfields. British intelligence kept insisting that Hitler was planning a June invasion. But we were at peace with the Germans: tourists arrived regularly from Berlin by commercial aircraft to take in the sights of Moscow, and ships and trains laden with food and raw materials moved from our ports and our heartland to Germany. I couldn't figure out why Stalin had made a non-aggression treaty with Hitler, the most hated enemy of Communism—unless he thought the Germans and the English would exhaust themselves in war and we would then emerge as the dominant power in Europe. All those heated warnings about German activity along the frontier were repeatedly dampened by explicit orders from the top that we say and do absolutely nothing that might be interpreted as even the slightest provocation against Germany.

Our country was in an awkward situation. Many of our marshals and generals had been shot by order of Stalin. Most of our officer corps—dead or in labor camps. Our forward border units—pulled back. On Dzerzhinsky Square we were reasonably sure we understood what was going on: the Germans were getting ready to move against us. But we had been told: "Don't panic. The Boss knows all about it."

I dreamed that night that I had stepped through a massive wooden door into a world of pure silence. Not Russian silence, which is the silence of terror, or of reverence for those taken by age or illness or murderous events. Rather, the silence that was the absence of all light and sound, the silence of an emptied globe, a planet without people, without life, without air, a world of naked rock and dormant sand distantly seen by indifferent stars.

I woke with a sense of dread.

Someone was banging on the door to my apartment. They were coming to arrest me.

I opened the door and saw my driver.

A redheaded twenty-year-old lad from a village south of Leningrad. He lowered his arm, his face went scarlet. "My apologies, Comrade Colonel. They tried to phone you but could not get through. I have orders to wake you."

He informed me that the German army was crossing the border and we were at war. All department heads were ordered to report immediately to their offices on Dzerzhinsky Square.

My instinctive reaction as I absorbed that news—a flood of relief that I was safe. Then—cold dread. We were at war with that monster from the west—and nearly naked before its murderous teeth and claws.

THERE IS A RUSSIAN SAYING: EVERY DAY LEARNS from the one that went before, but no day teaches the one that follows.

How we stumbled and staggered about during the weeks that followed! Three million men were marching against us—Germans, Rumanians, Hungarians, Italians, Finns. With thousands upon thousands of aircraft, artillery pieces, tanks. They had split their force into three huge army groups: the northern was to take Leningrad; the center, Moscow; the southern, Rostov and the Crimea and the oil deposits of the Caucasus. How we bled! Millions of lives, vast stretches of the Motherland—quickly lost to the teeth and claws of the enemy.

The Dark Tyrant was not in Moscow when the Germans struck but in his dacha at Kuntsevo. And Comrade Zhdanov, the chief of Leningrad, toward which an enemy army was now advancing as if the roads were greased— Comrade Zhdanov was vacationing in the Crimea on the shores of the Black Sea.

In our building on Dzerzhinsky Square a rumor began to creep through corridors after four days of silence from the leadership: Stalin had returned to Moscow, gone for a briefing at the Commissariat of Defense on Frunze Street, been stunned by the realization that our entire central front had disintegrated, exploded with anger and insults, left the briefing room with his head down and stooped over, like a peasant shrinking from an arm raised to strike him, climbed into his car, and gone home. Now, in a mood of black despair, he was hiding in his dacha, with no idea what to do. Drunk on vodka and awaiting imminent arrest for his disregard of all the warnings, his misreading of Hitler's intentions, his immense political miscalculation. The Politburo was trying to keep the country from falling to pieces. Then came the rumor that the foreign minister, along with two or three others from the Politburo, had gone to the dacha and urged Stalin to establish an emergency defense committee, with him as chairman. He had immediately regained his self-confidence, was now back in the Kremlin. And some days later we heard his calm voice over the radio:

"Comrades! Citizens! Fighting men of our army and navy! Brothers and sisters! I turn to you, my friends."

Comrade Stalin calling us *his friends!* An astonishment!

He told us what we had lost to the Germans: Lithuania, Latvia, western White Russia, much of the Ukraine. He said, "Our country is in serious danger." Everything that could be moved was to be sent eastward; all that could not be moved was to be burned, destroyed, wherever retreat proved inevitable. The struggle against the German enemy was to be relentless.

The town near my village—in German hands! German troops and tanks treading upon the unmarked mass grave of my parents, my sisters, the Rebbe, the others in the village. Heavy German boots marched over their bones.

NO REST FOR ME EITHER.

Moscow was warm, windless. Long days, short nights. The atmosphere tense, silent. During the day we went about our work; at night the city lay dark, blacked out. People seemed to be straining, listening, waiting for the first sounds of approaching tanks and artillery. I rode through the city, thinking, Moscow is now a pleasant place. Different from when I had arrived twenty years before. Almost no food or fuel then. Cold gray skies, freezing mists, filthy ice in the winter, mucky puddles in the spring. Buckets, pitchers, rags during my brief stay in that basement room; I sawed wood for the stove, washed old potatoes in icy water, boiled them in a battered pot. I remembered: One year in the early thirties there had been no socks in the entire city; that was a year or two before Kirov, the Leningrad chief, was assassinated, and we thought they would start on all of us in Moscow after they finished with nearly the whole leadership in Leningrad—for carelessness, inadequate vigilance, negligence in connection with our duties. But they stopped with the Leningrad bunch and only started on us in Moscow a few years later when our minister got scooped up and put away. Somehow I survived. Moscow had become a fine city in which to live—and now a lot of us would be dying in it.

In early September we began to evacuate children under the age of twelve. A few days later word came down to our departments that the German northern army had completed the land encirclement of Leningrad. Then Kiev fell; we lost five armies there, more than half a million men. I lay in bed nights listening to the city: silence, darkness, millions of Muscovites holding their breath, waiting.

Three weeks later the order came to disassemble factories for evacuation eastward. Then the government fled the city—to Kuibyshev, about five hundred miles to the east. But Stalin remained behind and set up headquarters in the marble cavern of the Mayakovsky Metro station. I say that to his credit. He could have left with the others, but he chose not to.

In the meantime there were things our departments had to do. Much of our army was demoralized, units in disarray not only because of casualties but also on account of a general breakdown in discipline and sudden doubts about directions, plans, loyalties. We reinforced our security troops. And once again we began to attach political commissars to the army; we had stopped doing that in

1940. Then we started to shoot people for any act of sabotage or defeatism. You tell soldiers that being taken prisoner by the enemy is an act of treason, it stiffens their resolve, makes them think four or five times before they throw down their weapons.

I myself volunteered to go to the front as a political commissar, and my commanding officer sent it through channels to the minister. But the minister gave me one of his thin smiles and said he needed me close by, there would soon be a lot of work to do.

I began to understand what he meant when we started to arrest the high-echelon officers of the western front where the Germans had broken through. They were charged with having taken part in a military conspiracy against Stalin.

"Please have the decency not to insult my intelligence with such nonsense," a general officer said to me when I asked him for his signature to a prepared confession of high treason and conspiracy against the head of state. He was a tall, thin, graceful man in his fifties, from a noted family of officers that went back to the armies of the tsars. He had pale-blue eyes, a deep, musical voice, and long, delicate fingers. "You were not there," he added. "You cannot have the slightest understanding of what went on."

"Must one always be present at a crime to know that a crime has occurred?" I asked. He looked very tired. He had seen many thousands of his men die. I didn't think it would take long to bring him around.

"This is complete nonsense," he said. "It is garbage for goats and pigs. I was the one who, two days before the German attack, asked to alert my forces, asked to move units forward, and was repeatedly ordered not to."

"None of that is of any significance here. Surely you understand that."

"Comrade Colonel, have you no sense of honor, no shame?"

"What has any of that to do with this? It's your future and that of your wife and children we are talking about here."

"I should be on the front lines fighting Germans rather than in Moscow fighting you and your people. Tell them to send me to the worst part of the front. To Leningrad. To the Crimea."

"You know where you're going."

"Comrade Stalin is the culprit here, not I and not my officers."

"I will pretend you didn't say that."

"Pretend whatever you wish. Do me the simple favor of putting an end to this nonsense. I will not sign my name to rubbish."

I regretted having to subject him to the "conveyor"; he was a man of considerable dignity and had fought the Germans with courage. But I had my orders: it was necessary to fix blame for the debacle in the west; and clearly it could not be placed on Comrade Stalin, who had unified the country and was guiding it through this war.

It took three weeks to wear him down. A stubborn man. Two days after his trial they shot him in one of our execution cellars.

I felt a twinge of regret when I heard that, but it was

quickly forgotten because we were very busy then watching the American and British delegations that were in Moscow meeting with our officials about our defense needs. We discovered two of our Foreign Commissariat people trying to use the meetings to establish connections they thought might help get them out of the country. Contemptible traitors.

Those were terrible months in Moscow. Half a million women, teenage children, and old men labored day and night to build the defense lines around the city: antitank ditches, troop trenches, miles of barbed wire. Mobs roamed through the streets, panic-stricken people, often drunk, crazed with terror over the advancing Germans, over spies, over what they were certain was the approaching death of their city. I saw a mob one night from the window of the car in which I was riding with the minister and two of his aides: a raging crowd of teenagers surrounding a woman on crutches. Probably accusing her of being an enemy spy who had broken a leg while parachuting out of a German aircraft. Inside the car, I was briefing the minister on some matter and could see his pince-nez glinting. There were no electric lights anywhere, only the light of a full moon, and his spectacles somehow glinted in the darkness of the car's interior. An odious man, dwarfish, probably syphilitic, with a penchant for deflowering virgins. Later I walked with him through a long underground corridor and waited out of earshot while he approached the man who sat behind a large writing table on which stood more than half a dozen telephones. They spoke quietly. At one point I heard the man behind the desk say, "Calm your-self, calm yourself," and a moment later he turned and I saw a small round bald patch on the back of his head, and then the two of them looked at me and I saw the mous-tache, the pockmarked face, and the prominent nose. I felt his dark eyes, *felt* them upon my face, and could see even from a distance the gleam of yellow in them and thought he would motion me over to him. It was, I knew, danger-ous to be in his company: you could not be certain when you left where you might end up that night, at home or in a prison cell. But, to my great relief, they both looked away and went on with their quiet conversation.

I don't wish to continue here with too many additional accounts of that terrible war, because it is what took place *after* the war that is of true importance insofar as the rest of my story is concerned. I will tell you that I spent part of the war in Leningrad, where I was sent during the siege to take care of a matter involving some troublesome writers, and saw that the military hospital where I had recovered from the wound to my arm—when the city was called Petrograd—had been almost entirely destroyed in an air raid. The ceiling had collapsed onto the large room where I had lain after the doctor saved my arm. The Germans were bombarding the city and trying to starve it into sub-mission, and the only access was the road we built across the thick ice of Lake Ladoga—the "road of life," people called it. All the dogs and cats had been eaten; there were no chickens, no pigs; there was no heat or electricity; peo-ple walked to work and back in freezing cold; they were eating carpenters' glue and leather; some, crazed with hunger, ate the corpses of those who had perished. Not in all my years in the army of the Tsar and the Red Army was I so cold, so helpless. It was as if the sun had died and now lay buried in the bleeding soil of that city. I felt I was a dweller on the planet of death. I left burdened with guilt that I was unable to remain and be of help.

Toward the end of the war some of our departments took on the task of deporting hundreds of thousands of people from the Crimea and elsewhere to Central Asia, Siberia, and the Arctic north—because they had welcomed and collaborated with the German invaders. Many of the stories I heard about those deportations were unpleasant, but I had nothing directly to do with any of that.

I also had no connection with the small group of Jews that Stalin sent to America in 1944 to gain us the sympathies of rich anti-Fascist American Jews and to raise money for our war effort. There had been some talk that I would head up the security police team that would accompany them, but I was ordered to Tashkent instead, where we were facing a problem with some of our intelligentsia. It was fortunate that I was not sent to America, because after the war everyone who went on that mission was arrested and shot.

When the war ended there was a victory parade in Moscow and a night of fireworks. Drunks staggered about the city, pissing on the sidewalks. I was a little drunk myself for a few days, and enjoying the company of a lovely Russian woman, who kept admiring the furniture in my apartment. I told her I had made many of the pieces myself. Some of the chairs, the coffee table, the end tables. Did you make the bed, she wanted to know. The bed is from the time of the tsars, I said. Come back to the bed, she said.

The war was over. The Motherland had been ravaged. Blood had seeped into every level spot of ground. But I had survived. I was forty-eight years old.

It meant nothing to me that we were soon arresting all the members of the Jewish Anti-Fascist Committee who had gone to America. The charges against them: They had become Zionist agents in the pay of American intelligence; they were trying to weaken the Motherland, establish a separate Jewish republic in the Crimea from which they could threaten the very heart of the state. In the end we arrested nearly the entire committee—writers, poets, actors, musicians, journalists, composers—and found all the evidence we needed to put them away. We even arrested the Jewish wife of our foreign minister for talking in Yiddish to Golda Meir, the Israeli foreign minister, and shipped her off to a camp in Central Asia. It seemed the Boss was returning to his old suspicions about foreign influences corrupting the Motherland and weakening his rule. All it meant to me was more work.

Nor did the heated newspaper campaign in *Pravda*, *Trud*, *Izvestia*, and elsewhere against "rootless cosmopolitans" and "traitors within" cause me any concern. True, a few dozen Jews in our departments were quietly transferred to police work in the provinces. But that had nothing to do with me. In fact, General Razumkov—he had recently been promoted—told me that they had no complaints against me, I had worked very well and had nothing to worry about. And so I continued to wake in the mornings, dress, eat my breakfast, and go to my job—and my work was the same as it had been for years: interrogation.

And it continued that way until we began arresting and interrogating doctors.

4

DO YOU REMEMBER THE RUSSIAN SAYING I mentioned some while ago? Every day learns from the one that went before, but no day teaches the one that follows.

Well, sayings are as often wrong as they are right. One day *can* teach the day that follows. . . .

One day early in November 1952 General Razumkov handed me a file and said: "Look for a group. The Boss says that it's impossible he acted alone."

More than forty of us, from senior lieutenants all the way up to two major generals, had been working on the Jewish Anti-Fascist Committee case since late 1948. For a while, in 1949, we were sidetracked by a conspiracy against Stalin in the Leningrad Party, and I went over there with a team of security people to arrest most of their administrative and management leaders. Then I became busy with the interrogation of another member of the Politburo, one of the leaders of that conspiracy. When we finished with them we suddenly found that we had a problem with our Lubyanka leadership right here in Moscow, a struggle for power. Finally, early in 1952, we got ourselves back to the Jewish Anti-Fascist Committee case, brought it to the military collegium of the Supreme Court of the USSR, and were finished with it by the end of July. The newspapers were calling the committee members a "vile gang that stank unbearably" and urging the judges to show "not a drop of pity for the rabid wolf pack." Some were shot, others were sent off to the camps.

I was very tired, went away to one of our security police resorts on the Black Sea for a long-overdue vacation, walked along the beaches, and wondered what lay on the other side of all that water. The sun got to me one day and I ran a high fever. I lay in my seaside room hallucinating.

The next morning the fever was gone but the scar on my left arm had a vivid pinkish hue. I was careful with the sun the rest of my time there.

About a month after I got back to Moscow, General Razumkov handed me a file.

"Find a group," he said. He had gained a lot of weight. His brown hair had begun to thin. "There's talk the Boss got a letter about Kremlin doctors in Zhdanov and is getting ready to finish off the whole leadership. This business is going to make or break careers here. Talk to this Doctor Koriavin and find the group. And, listen, we're in a hurry. It's got to be done quickly."

Doctor A. M. Koriavin turned out to be a man in his early seventies, of middle height, heavy-shouldered, silver-haired, with a high, smooth brow, thoughtful gray eyes, and a generous roundish face. He stood before me in my office wearing a brown suit and a white shirt, not a flicker of fear in him.

"I am Colonel Leonid Shertov," I said. "I will be in charge of your investigation."

"Comrade Colonel, I am prepared to answer truthfully every question you put to me."

"Then we shall get along very well. Please sit down."

He took the chair.

"It says here that you are retired."

"That is correct."

"Why then were you recently in the Kremlin clinic?"

"I was consulted on a matter of highest importance."

"And what matter was that?"

"It had to do with the health of Comrade Stalin."

"Who called you?"

He gave me the name of a doctor whose reputation I knew.

"And why would such an esteemed and active doctor feel the need to consult with you, a retired doctor, on this matter?"

"Because until my retirement two years ago I was the leading specialist in our country on this particular ailment."

"What ailment is that?" I asked. The very moment the question was out of my mouth, I regretted having asked it. Instinctive curiosity; poor judgment.

But Doctor Koriavin answered without any hesitation,

as if eager to have others made aware of the diagnosis: "Comrade Stalin is suffering from maniacal aggressive psychosis, aggravated by high blood pressure and arteriosclerosis of the brain."

The small office we were in was overheated; most of the building often lay awash in steamy air that coated the windows with vapor in cold weather and was at times raised to nearly suffocating temperatures inside some of our punishment cells in the internal prison. But a blast of the coldest Siberian air seemed suddenly to have entered the room. I thought the window had blown open, but it was closed, barred, its outside netting coated with snow.

The doctor sat very still, gazing at me out of his gray eyes.

"I am not asking you to commit suicide," he said quietly. "If you do not wish me to answer, please do not ask the question."

I said, "Very well, since you are so eager to answer questions, tell me who among the Kremlin doctors has joined in the conspiracy to assassinate the leadership of our country?"

He lost his composure for a moment. "I beg your pardon?"

"Who among the Kremlin doctors is conspiring to murder our leadership through incorrect medical intervention?"

He pursed his mouth and sat gazing at me. "So *that's* what this is all about," he said finally, shaking his head. "Now I understand. He is absolutely fiendish."

"I warn you again, be careful what you say here."

"Oh, I am very careful, Comrade Colonel. I am a doctor, I am always careful with words. 'Fiendish' is what I said, and 'fiendish' is what I meant. This is how he is finally going to solve his Jewish problem."

I asked in surprise, glancing at his file, "Are you a Jew?"

"My nationality is Russian." He looked at me keenly. "And you?"

"I am not a Jew, I am a Communist."

"Ah, yes? I am glad. Or I would ask what you are doing here."

"There are many Jews here."

"Indeed?"

"Many."

"Not for long."

He had somehow managed to throw me entirely off balance. *I* was answering *his* questions. A clever man. My head had begun to ache and my left arm tingled.

"Enough," I said, getting to my feet. "Sit here for a while and think about my question. We'll continue when I return."

"I am not a young man and will soon need a toilet," he said quietly.

"Sit and think. I want the names of everyone in the group."

I left him with a guard and decided to go to the dining room for some lunch. The small elevator with its iron prisonlike door was crowded. Six of us stood inside, silent and sullen. The dining room was nearly full, everyone tense, avoiding conversation. One heard clearly the clink of dishes, the thin sliding sounds of silverware. Something enormous was brewing; after so many years of this, you learned to smell it in the air and feel it on your skin. The arrest of Jewish and Russian doctors, which had begun in the early summer during the trial of the Jewish Anti-Fascist Committee, was now taking on the proportions of a tidal wave. Our people were out almost every night hauling them in. Mostly Jews, some Russians. Bewildered, terrified; trying for some semblance of dignity; lords of medicine, unaccustomed to being treated that way. Surgeons, internists, neurologists, pediatricians, ophthalmologists, pathologists, psychiatrists, urologists, laryngologists. Word had come to us from on high: The Jewish doctors were killers in white coats; they were murdering people on the operating table, poisoning them with drugs, had even drawn some Russian doctors into their conspiracy. Our prison cells were becoming crowded with the great names of Soviet medicine. The Boss wanted confessions, a trial.

Riding the elevator back to my office, I wondered who was now caring for the patients of all those imprisoned doctors. I felt tired, sweaty. My left arm throbbed, the fingers cold, as if emptied of their supply of blood.

When I returned to the office, I found the doctor still in the chair, looking a little fatigued. I dismissed the guard.

It was hot. I removed my jacket, loosened my tie, and sat on the edge of the desk.

"Well?" I said.

"It is necessary that I use a toilet," he said quietly.

"It is necessary that I get an answer to my question."

"I will not help you fabricate a group."

"One way or another you will sign a confession and give

us names. I would rather not have to subject you to our various forms of persuasion. You have a wife, children, grandchildren. Your refusal to cooperate with us will fall heavily not only upon you but upon them as well. What I will do now is let you go to the toilet and then return you to your cell so that you can have more time to think."

"Comrade Colonel, you appear to me to be ill."

"What?"

"Your eyes are toxic. I believe you have a fever."

"Comrade Doctor-Prisoner Koriavin, go to the toilet."

I buzzed for the guards and they took him away.

Alone in the office, I sat behind the desk for a while doing paperwork, then signed myself out of the building and went home through a heavy fall of snow.

I had no appetite, slept poorly, but was back at my desk at nine the next morning. I scanned the newspapers, opened the safe, took out my papers, looked briefly at the arrest list, placed Doctor Koriavin's file before me on the desk, and called to have him brought in.

I motioned the guards out of the office. The doctor sat straight and poised. A Russian worried about anti-Semitism, warning me. Strange. Stubble on his face now. The tired look. No picnic, those cells. Before the Revolution his family might have been members of the nobility. Now, a hated enemy. I must finish this quickly.

"Good morning. I trust you are being treated reasonably well in our hotel."

"I have lived and eaten in worse places." His voice had weakened. It was dry, hoarse. The heat in the cells did that sometimes. But his eyes were bright and his features still wore their look of open generosity. "I was in Leningrad during the siege," he said.

I was about to ask him where he had served but drew back from further conversation. No more time for small talk. The general was pressing me for results.

"So were about two million others," I said. "We will now resume our talk."

"As I told you yesterday, Comrade Colonel, every question you put to me, I will answer truthfully. I have nothing to hide."

"Very well, then. Tell me if you know the following people."

We went through lists of doctors. He knew most of them professionally, some socially.

"Is it not true that you, together with these and these, were involved in a conspiracy to assassinate our heads of state through the use of improper pharmaceuticals?"

"My duty is to heal, not to kill. I leave the killing to soldiers and police and politicians."

"I suggest that you stop this talk, otherwise it will end badly for you."

"I have no expectations that this will end well for me."

"You have a family."

"Comrade Colonel, if you must know the truth, I do not want my family to grow up in this country. Now that I can see what is really about to happen here, I know that this country has nothing to offer them."

"You don't care for the health and safety of your own children and grandchildren? Who has the sick mind here?"

"Are you telling me that you can guarantee their health

and safety? Why should I even *want* their health and safety? So that in twenty years one of my grandchildren can sit where I am sitting now and be put through another such experience?"

I removed my truncheon from a desk drawer and held it in my right hand. He stared at it.

I said in a low voice, "I will strike my desk a number of times and shout at you. Cry out in a loud voice each time."

He stared at me in amazement.

"A loud voice," I said through clenched teeth.

He nodded, still staring.

I struck the desk repeatedly and he cried out. I shouted, "You will confess. Save yourself and your family and confess!"

I struck the desk again. His face was flushed. Astonishment and amusement played about his mouth and eyes.

I stopped. A sharp pain had lodged above my eyes. I stepped back to my chair and sank into it.

"Think about that on your flesh," I said after a moment, feeling the tightness in my left arm. "Go back to your cell and think about what it will feel like on your arms and legs."

The guards came for him.

I made some notes in his file and closed my eyes.

They brought him back later that day and he sat quietly in the chair. He was beginning to look scruffy. His trousers and jacket lay upon him creased and rumpled. He gazed slowly about the room. On one wall hung a framed picture of Stalin; on another, of Dzerzhinsky. He said softly, "Is it permissible for me to speak?"

I nodded.

He paused, regarding me intently out of his calm gray eyes. "I mean, is it permissible to *speak*?"

I felt myself mesmerized by him, and nodded again.

"I know his mind," he said in a low voice.

Stop him, I told myself. But I said nothing.

"I was his doctor for years. No one knows him better than I do. I know the inside of his head."

We sat there looking at each other in silence. Outside the window it was growing dark. An icy gale blew snow in white waves through the streets.

He said quietly, "I will offer you a conjecture as to what he is planning."

I felt myself staring at him through the cloud and the buzzing noise in my head.

"At best, he regards doctors as bourgeois intellectuals; at worst, he looks upon us with psychopathic dread, because he stands naked in our presence. He is afraid that we will know him too well. And he is absolutely correct. I would conjecture that he plans to do away with all of you."

"All of—?"

"The Jews."

"All right," I said.

"Every last one of you."

"Enough."

"Sooner or later, he will finish what Hitler started."

"I said, enough!"

"I speak as a Russian who cares for his country."

"None of this can be of any help to you."

"Probably through deportation. He has already deported more than half a dozen nationalities. He will deport all of you too."

"Listen to me—"

"A hue and cry throughout the country over the diabolical Jewish doctors, and then a mass deportation of all the Jews—"

"*Enough!*"

"—with the support of the entire Soviet people."

"What you just told me can get you ten years in a camp!"

"Comrade Colonel, I am repaying you for your kindness to me this morning."

"I'll give you one more night to think about my question. Tomorrow there will be no charade."

He said abruptly, "You look decidedly unwell."

"I'm fine."

"Are you in any discomfort?"

"I have a slight headache."

"You should see a doctor," he said with a faint smile.

The guards took him back to his cell.

I ate without appetite that evening, went with a woman to the theater, but left her shortly afterward and returned home to a night of bad dreams, none of which I remembered clearly the next morning.

I had the doctor brought to one of our more austere interrogation rooms. He looked weary and less sure of himself. His face was sallow, his gray eyes blurred.

I said, "Doctor Koriavin, the preliminaries are over."

He said, "With all respect, Comrade Colonel, for you they have just begun."

"Give me the names."

"There are no names. There is no group. The man is old and sick. He sees conspiracies everywhere. He refuses to take the medicines prescribed for him."

"The names!"

"I tell you there are no names. He is delusional. With medication, he may live another two or three years. Without—who knows?"

"Listen, you're a doctor, I have great consideration for doctors, and I don't want to raise my hand to you. But you're leaving me with no choice."

"I am grateful. You leave me with some hope for our country. Please consider this. He recently mobilized all of Soviet medicine to find a cure for his hypertension. Then he has his best doctors arrested. Tell me, is that the act of a sane person?"

"Enough!"

"Where did you get that scar?"

"What?"

He was looking at my arm. I had removed my jacket and rolled up my shirtsleeves.

"It's an old war wound. The first war."

"Was it recently exposed to the sun?"

"Yes."

"I will give you some medical advice. Don't expose an old scar like that too long to the sun."

The arm was strong, ridged with veins, the scar like a

white-and-pink range of low hills about six inches long and in some places half an inch wide.

"You're very fortunate that you didn't lose that arm. In war it's more practical sometimes to remove an arm than to take the time to treat it."

"A Doctor Rubinov treated it."

"Rubinov?"

"Pavel Rubinov."

"Indeed? The hand surgeon."

"You know him?"

"Of course I know him. For years I referred patients to him. He is probably in one of your cells."

I stared at him.

"He treated the arm of Comrade Stalin."

After a long moment I said, "Listen, you will cry out and scream, just as you did yesterday in my office. Understood?"

Later I sat at my desk, looking through the arrest lists of the past days, which I had scanned too quickly before, and found his name. Pavel Rubinov. The one in charge of his investigation was Colonel Rudenko, a methodical and ruthless man. There would be no charades in his interrogation room.

My head throbbed. I looked at my left hand, saw with alarm the way the fingers trembled, and left the office and went home.

I drank myself into a stupor that night and fell asleep in my clothes in one of the easy chairs, and woke suddenly in cold terror to the sounds of someone knocking on my door. "One minute, one minute," I called out, straightening my clothes and running a hand through my hair. I opened the door.

The hallway was deserted. Blue-black shadows clung to the walls and doors. I stood there a long moment staring into the darkness. I closed the door and collapsed back into the chair and fell asleep.

The next morning I went to our infirmary. The doctor who looked me over said I had the flu. "A mild case, two, maybe three days. Take aspirin, go home, sleep it off." Four days later I was still sick but returned to work, and the next day went again to the infirmary. The first doctor was not there and a different one examined me and asked some questions. "Probably you picked up something on your vacation," he said. "A Black Sea bug." He gave me some pills.

That day we started Doctor-Prisoner Koriavin on the "conveyor." There was nothing I could have done to prevent it.

In a room nearby, Doctor-Prisoner Pavel Rubinov was undergoing interrogation at the hands of Colonel Rudenko. Not yet the "conveyor" for him. Shivering with fever, I went home early.

I lay in bed two days, sweating, then saw another doctor, who said I had a minor blood disturbance that would resolve itself by the end of the month when a certain constellation in the sky reached a certain alignment. By then we were in the dead of winter, Moscow lay deep in snow, Doctor-Prisoner A. M. Koriavin was writing his confession, and Doctor-Prisoner Pavel Rubinov was on the "conveyor."

It was January. My headache and fever had disappeared for two days at the end of December and then returned; the fever was now low-grade, annoying, on occasion causing me the shivers. We were still arresting doctors. The work felt endless, exhausting. In the provinces they were purging Party people—most of them with Jewish names, I noticed. There is an old Russian saying: When fingernails are being pulled out in Moscow, fingers are being chopped off in the provinces. That saying one can take at full value.

On Dzerzhinsky Square there were chilling rumors of an impending major shakeup of our department because we hadn't detected the plot by ourselves and had begun to act only after receiving a letter from some informer, an X-ray technician, a woman. Someone I knew who worked in our archives told me they had started to review old files. "Winnowing and threshing," he said, giving me a sad look. Back in my office I phoned General Razumkov. "Don't get heated," he said. "I won't ask who slipped you that piece of information, but it has nothing to do with you. You get the highest commendation, especially after the job you did with Koriavin." I had no idea what he meant and later learned that he immediately called for a meeting of the archives personnel and the next morning raged and stormed at them for their big mouths. Then I remembered with a thunderous shock that decades ago he had put into my file the old letter signed by Zinoviev. Zinoviev, whom Stalin had hated as much as he did Trotsky and who'd been executed after his public trial back in the thirties. A favor from Doctor Pavel Rubinov to get me back safely to my village; a payment of a sort for having taught him to read some Hebrew prayers. I had no idea if the letter represented a threat to me. Doctor Pavel Rubinov. I pictured him in his white coat and trim red beard and gold-rimmed spectacles, and I wondered if he had continued to read Hebrew.

After three days of normal temperature my fever returned, along with the headache. I did not go back to the infirmary but took aspirins instead.

Black ice and filthy slush encumbered the streets. On a freezing day in mid-January I opened a copy of *Pravda,* saw the large headline, ARREST OF A GROUP OF SABOTEUR-DOCTORS, and slowly read the story about the recent discovery of a "terrorist group of doctors who had made it their aim to cut short the lives of active public figures of the Soviet Union through medical treatment involving sabotage." The story went on through ten paragraphs. It listed nine doctors, six of them clearly Jewish, and claimed that "documentary evidence, investigations, the conclusions of medical experts, and the confessions of the arrested"—I paused over that, and had a vision of Doctor Koriavin—"have established that the criminals, who were secret enemies of the people, sabotaged the treatment of patients and doomed them by wrong treatment." The editorial referred to the doctors as "monsters and murderers," as a "gang of anthropoid animals," and pointed out—I turned cold reading the words—that "some of our Soviet organs and their leaders abandoned vigilance and became infected with gullibility. The Agencies of State Security did not detect in time the existence of a saboteur-terrorist organization among the doctors."

In the building on Dzerzhinsky Square, we walked around avoiding one another's eyes and kept busy: more doctors were being brought in. They were busy in the provinces, too. Then some of the Jewish personnel in the building began to disappear. One day here, the next suddenly vanished. No one talked openly about them. I bumped into General Razumkov in a corridor. He looked enormous, bulging out of his clothes. "Don't worry so much," he told me. "After the job you did on that Russian doctor, why are you worried?" I stared at his corpulent back as he waddled away and had no idea what he was talking about.

The weather was terrible in Moscow that winter. Sleet, wind, snow. Unending snow. Air so bitter cold it felt solid: ceaseless blasts from a frozen hell.

My fever and headaches kept reappearing and vanishing. The newspaper reports about Jewish doctors had become nearly frenzied. Nine time zones of papers and journals were writing day after day about "monsters disguised as doctors," about "counterrevolutionary wreckers," about "people we don't need in Russia," about "child murderers." In a marketplace in Moscow I heard a drunk shouting: "The Yids tried to poison Stalin!" A Russian woman I invited out to dinner one night kissed my fingers one by one, put my hand on her heart, and pressed it against her. She was telling me she didn't believe what she was reading about the Jewish doctors.

Strangely, five or six times in the weeks between the middle of January and the middle of February I heard banging on the door to my apartment. But no one was ever there. Only the deep blue-black darkness in the hall-way. And the pounding in my chest. And the cold metal taste of terror in my mouth.

In our building on Dzerzhinsky Square we began to hear about a letter that leading Jews were being told to sign. The letter was in the office of *Pravda*. Something about an appeal to Comrade Stalin to save the obstinate and unruly Jews of the Soviet Union from the deserved wrath of the Soviet people by shipping them all to a distant region of the Motherland where they could dwell in peace and learn to become proper Soviet citizens.

The day I first heard that rumor, I was interrogating a Jewish doctor. "When did you enter the espionage service of the Americans?" I shouted at him. He was a small, slightly built man in his sixties, an eminent cardiologist, and he sat before me, bewildered and trembling. "Who recruited you? Who are your collaborators? We have all the proof against you that we need. We can make you confess to anything. Your life is hanging by a thread. You had better come to the correct conclusions." We had lowered the heat. It was cold in the room; he sat naked to the waist and shivering. "You are destroying my health," he murmured. "And for no reason." He took the pen and paper I gave him and began to write down all his contacts with enemies of the people. "You won't need to invent anything for your trial," I told him. "We'll provide you with every sentence of your testimony. You'll have to memorize it. Your case will be ready in a month, at most two." I let him put on his shirt.

Later I was in the elevator with an old friend, and he whispered to me the names of those who had already signed the letter to Comrade Stalin. A famous novelist, a violinist, a historian, a physicist. All Jews, of course. There would be many more, he said.

That night I asked my driver to take me to an apartment building where one of my women friends lived. He left me in front of the building and drove off with a grin on his face. I waited in the entrance hall until he was gone, then took the Metro to one of the Moscow railway stations. The huge station was crowded. I bought a ticket to a suburban stop and boarded the train. It was jammed with weary-looking, expressionless people heavily bundled against the cold. The train rolled out of the station and along the rail yards and after a while I saw the freight trains through the windows, silent and sealed, lining the side tracks for miles. I got off at a stop and took the next train back to Moscow. Another Metro ride brought me to a different railway station. Again the freight trains standing deep in old snow, waiting. I did that two more times. By then I was very tired. It had begun to snow again. I waded through drifts, my face raked by the crystalline flakes, and later sat in a drunken stupor and heard the knocking on my apartment door and did not get up to answer it.

In the last week of February one of our agents, an old friend, returned from the east and told me over dinner and vodka of the camps he had heard were being constructed in the desert region of Kazakhstan—a vast flat lunar wasteland—and all along the rail line to distant Biro-bidzhan. "They're all waiting for the Jews," he said, quite drunk but instinctively careful to talk in a low voice. "But don't worry, not you," he added, patting my arm. "You're one of us."

Later that night I walked through the elegant marble entrance hall of my apartment building and instead of going up the elevator went on ahead and took the stairway down to the basement. At the end of the long, dimly lit corridor was the office of the building committee, its door closed. The lock presented no difficulty. I opened drawers, scanned lists, and after a few minutes found what I had come for: a new list for the local police of the Jewish families in the building. My name was not on the list.

Carefully, I replaced the list and locked the door.

The next day I asked to see Doctor-Prisoner Rubinov.

"What the hell for?" Colonel Rudenko, his interrogator, asked, immediately and understandably suspicious.

"He was the one who saved my arm."

"You're going to kiss his ass?"

"A visit for old times' sake."

"Stubborn piece of shit. Get him to sign his confession and I'll owe you a big favor."

I went through the building and down many flights of stairs and through dimly lit corridors and past many guards. A guard let me into the cell and closed the door behind me. The flesh on the back of my neck crawled as the door slammed shut. Odd thoughts entered my mind: Comrade Stalin has never seen the inside of one of these cells; Comrade Stalin has never visited a labor camp. I stood blinking in the light shed by a single bulb in the tiny cell. Stone floor, bare walls. A single bucket. The cold air reeking of urine and feces. No windows; nothing on which to lie down. An icy tomb.

Near one of the walls sat an old man, naked to the waist. He wore loose gray begrimed trousers with no belt and battered black shoes with no laces. On the lower part of his gray-white wrinkled face was a short disheveled white beard. Gold-rimmed glasses lay crookedly over his large dark-rimmed eyes, both earpieces bent. His hair was thin, scraggly, white. I could see the ugly welts on his arms and ankles. The bones of his chest and shoulders and rib cage protruded grotesquely: sticks trying to push through the drum-tight cover of dry, yellowish skin. He looked starved, shrunken. He sat hunched over, shivering, his head between his shoulders, moving his hands slowly through the air, thumbs and forefingers extended. I watched him and realized after a moment that his hands were performing a tremulous dance with invisible instruments, vague echoes of operating-room procedures: cutting, snipping, swabbing, cleansing, suturing. Then he stopped and lowered his hands and slowly, tremblingly, ran the digit finger of his right hand over the tips of each finger of his left hand, touching them lightly in a flickering caress.

He ran his fingers back and forth across his palms, closing his eyes and then opening them as he raised his hands and his fingers began again the surgeon dance.

I said quietly, "Comrade Doctor Rubinov?"

He ignored me and went on swabbing, cleansing, suturing.

I said again, "Comrade Doctor Pavel Rubinov?"

He looked up at me then, blinked, narrowed his blurred, unfocused eyes, and turned away.

I could not recognize him at all.

He sat there moving his hands in that surgeon dance, now murmuring something in a reedlike voice. A vile smell began to rise from him. He sat in a slowly widening puddle of water, waving his sticklike fingers through the air and moving his dry, caked lips. It took a moment longer before I realized he was reciting a Psalm. "O God, do not be silent; do not look aloof; do not be quiet, O God," he murmured in Hebrew.

I got to my feet and banged on the door and the guard came and let me out.

"What is he on?" I asked.

"They put scopolamine in his potatoes."

I nodded. The drug would keep him sedated, close to a hypnotic state. I returned to my office and some time later checked out of the building.

I was with a woman that night and we both got drunk and I didn't return to the apartment until after two. I switched on a lamp and sank into an easy chair. Slowly, the room began to spin. The lamp flared, dimmed, brightened, burned steadily. There were deep blue and purple shadows in the corners of the room near the desk and the windows. I owned a few books, mostly cheap novels, and many inexpensive reproductions of old Russian paintings of horses and some statuettes of horses and a large reproduction on very good paper of a painting by Degas of horses racing, their jockeys urging them on. Sitting in the easy chair, I thought I saw the Degas horses actually moving, and quickly shut my eyes. Drunk. I was drunk. And frightened. And angry.

I opened my eyes, startled.

Someone had tapped on the apartment door. There was a brief silence and then, again, the tapping. One two three four.

Dazed, I rose to my feet and went to the door.

I saw only the blue-black darkness.

I stood staring into the darkness and reached out to it and touched it and felt the cold, hollow night emptiness of all the hallways in this enormous building and stepped back and closed the door. The lock clicked loudly into place. I switched off the living-room lamp and went into the bedroom, turned on the lamp near my bed, got into pajamas, quickly washed, and lay in the bed gazing at the wall opposite me, on which hung a large oil painting by a Ukrainian artist of a Russian village. A small village, with a wide dirt road running through it and peasant houses on both sides. Fields and a forest and a pond. A blue sky. Horses feeding in the fields, chickens and piglets playing on the road. No church, no synagogue. It was the only original work of art I owned. Inexpensive. Bought during the thirties when Razumkov, then still a colonel, had sent me to the Ukraine to assist in the purge of some local intelligentsia. An ordinary village. Except for the missing church and synagogue, it resembled closely the village of my early life.

I lay there looking at the painting and must have fallen asleep with the lamp still on and woke groggily to turn it off. As I reached for it, I heard again the knocking on my apartment door and nearly jumped with terror.

It ceased, and then came again: one two three four. Knuckles or fingers rapping on the door. I put on slippers and padded out of the bedroom and switched on the living-room lamp on my way to the door.

The corridor was a dense blue-black void. I downed some vodka and switched off the lamp and went to bed.

The next day a number of men in our various departments did not report in. We knew better than to ask about them. It meant more work for everyone. We were preparing for the trial of the doctors.

I went to the infirmary. "A kidney infection," said the doctor. "Nothing to worry about." He gave me a liquid medicine named after one of the Jewish doctors in our prison. No order had come down to change the name on the bottle.

Later that day I saw Doctor-Prisoner Pavel Rubinov again. He had confessed to nothing, signed nothing. He sat shivering in his urine, leaning his skeletal body against the stone wall and murmuring inaudibly.

"Cover their faces with shame," I said quietly as I stood in the cell looking at him. "May they be disgraced and doomed forever."

Day after day we waited to see who among us would pay for our lack of vigilance, for our not having detected in time the terrorist organization of doctors.

Suddenly, in the last week of February, there were no more orders for additional arrests. We sat in our offices, walked through the corridors, rode up and down the elevators, ate in the dining room—in an atmosphere thick with fear and silence.

The minister was nowhere to be seen, could not be reached by phone.

One afternoon I came upon General Razumkov in a corridor. His face was white, the rolls of fat on his neck quivered. He said nothing to me.

I sat at my desk on the first day of March, a snowstorm raging outside my window, and read carefully through the day's *Pravda*—and saw no mention of doctor-poisoners. For the first time in months. Not a word. I looked through the newspaper again and then put it down and sat staring at it. Murmurous voices filled the air and I felt my flesh crawling. I looked quickly around and saw I was alone.

Nor was there anything in *Pravda* about doctor-poisoners during the days that followed. Work in our department seemed to have come to a stop. As I sat reading *Pravda* in my office one morning, the phone rang. General Razumkov wanted to see me. Immediately.

We were alone in his office. He spoke quickly, tensely,

without preliminaries. "Stalin croaked. A stroke. Our old boss is back."

I stood there gaping at him. The room whirled. Outside his window the freezing air seemed crowded with faces peering in, listening.

"Start cleaning up the doctors."

I found myself standing outside his office and taking in great gulps of air. My left arm tingled and throbbed, its muscles in spasm.

A great gulf of terror opened before me. Stalin is dead! What will happen to the Motherland?

Anarchy!

The world will devour us!

Then, slowly, came composure. And a soaring elation. *Stalin was dead!*

"Start cleaning up the doctors," General Razumkov had ordered.

That meant we would soon be releasing them!

I went along corridors and down dim stairways, rushing now, ignoring the thunder in my head and heart and the pain in my arm, and discovered that Doctor Pavel Rubinov had died during the night.

IN THE WEEKS THAT FOLLOWED I FOUND THAT HE had entered me and become a permanent dweller in my memory. It was as if memory were a large hotel and he resided in one of its better rooms. He would emerge often and I would see him not as he was in his prison cell but as he had been in Petrograd during the war: a tall, trim man with a kind face, a short reddish beard, and pale-blue eyes covered by thin round gold-rimmed glasses.

I would hear him say, "Tomorrow I will try again to clean the wound. One last time."

And, "We will proceed slowly and with care, and we will try to save your arm."

And, "The hand is a marvelous creation, a thing of surpassing complexity and perfection. Of all the parts of the body, nothing so fascinates me as the hand."

And, "I have here a book of Hebrew prayers. Is it possible you might teach me how to pronounce the letters and the vowels?"

My memories of Doctor Pavel Rubinov would not fade. I see and hear him often to this day.

Various rumors drifted our way about how the Dark Tyrant had died. One described a drunken party at his dacha with a few of his cronies, after which he had lost consciousness; another, a meeting of the Politburo—or Presidium, as we now called it—when the normally submissive members had strongly and unexpectedly opposed his plan to deport the Jews, and he became so enraged his eyes rolled and he collapsed.

All the great Kremlin doctors who might have saved his life were in prison.

The second-rate doctors who were called arrived, diagnosed a stroke, and said there was little they could do. He was still breathing but could not talk. At one point he raised his left hand and pointed it accusingly at those gathered around him.

Then he began to suffocate.

His face slowly turned dark, his lips blackened. It took him hours to die.

Our minister, we were told, did a little dance around his body. "We are free!" he cackled. "The tyrant is dead! Rejoice!"

Another Politburo member had the final word. He said, "Tonight, the mice have buried the cat."

They embalmed him. He lay in public view in the Hall of Columns, waxen, mummified. Millions came to his funeral. Hundreds were crushed to death. We had our security troops everywhere. One of the pallbearers was his son, who was drunk. I saw him up close; he kept drinking from a flask and openly cursing our minister.

The next day I drove past the Hall of Columns. Workmen were taking down the huge painting of Stalin that had covered the facade of the building. One of the workers released the ropes too quickly and the face tumbled into the street below. They seemed in no hurry to retrieve it.

OUR BORDERS, SOME WILL INSIST, WERE EVERY-where tightly sealed. But do you know how many times I went back and forth across borders—crawling, sliding, cutting, running—in the two wars in which I fought during my life? In a time of war, one must necessarily act quickly. But in a time of peace, one makes a plan; one waits with patience. A year, two, five. And then one moves. And trusts to skill and luck.

I could not figure out all the maneuverings that went on

in our Politburo during the months that followed the death of the Dark Tyrant. The arrested doctors were ordered to speak to no one about their time with us and were sent home. Doctor Pavel Rubinov was buried in a Moscow Jewish cemetery. I attended his funeral, observing from a discreet distance. A cold day in March. I heard as if from another time a bearded old man chanting the Kaddish and then reciting a Psalm. Icy winds blew among the silent gravestones.

The fever and headaches came and went. None of the staff doctors seemed to know what was wrong with me. I didn't want to see a Jewish doctor privately. That may have been foolish of me, but I felt too ashamed.

General Razumkov had clearly taken me under his wing, and I couldn't figure out why. He would smile at me, wink, poke me in the ribs, share with me his vulgar jokes and political stories, slip me confidential information. After many weeks of conversations and allusions, I began to understand that my interrogation of Doctor Koriavin had been so successful that he had spent almost no time at all on the "conveyor" before confessing, signing, offering names. He had then remarked repeatedly to his interrogators and to General Razumkov that his acquiescence was entirely due to my interrogation. I had convinced him of the wisdom of yielding, he said. Apparently, that had saved General Razumkov's head, which had been on the verge of being cut off because of our negligence and the slow pace of the investigation. I could not figure out what Doctor Koriavin had had in mind. Unless he knew how near the Dark Tyrant was to the end. And with all the doctors he

had named now locked up, there would be no one of sufficient skill around to tend to him, pull him through so he
could wreak another two or three years of havoc, murder
thousands more. And why not reward me for the charades
we had played, for sparing him pain? Maybe. But I have
never been able to figure it out.

The Moscow weather slowly turned warm. General
Razumkov's glee increased with every passing day. He put
on more weight. "Our man might be the next Boss," he
said to me one day in his office. "You know what that
means for *me,* for *you.*" His porcine features flushed and
quivered with anticipation. I thought he would do a little
dance around his desk. It astounded me, how closely he
had linked our two destinies.

In the late spring, warnings started to come in from our
agents in East Germany that there could be trouble there
during the summer: demonstrations of dissatisfied workers and maybe riots.

Our minister, the possible future Boss of the Motherland, who was responsible to the Politburo for the stability
of East Germany, immediately ordered up a security police
team and put General Razumkov in charge.

It surprised no one that the general insisted I accompany him.

"If we do this right, it puts him in the front seat," he said
to me, barely able to contain himself. He was talking, of
course, about our minister. "And if we put him in the front
seat, you know what he'll owe us? You'll make general. I'll
see to that myself."

The flight to East Germany was tedious. Razumkov sat

next to me, drunk on vodka and eager to get started breaking German heads. We would be purging the Party, smash-
ing secret nests of workers. Nothing we hadn't done many
times before. I had no compunctions about tearing into
the Germans. It was only eight years since the end of the
war.

The opportunity to move, to act, to depend totally
upon one's skill and luck, came much sooner than I had
anticipated. You quickly realize that you can get the guards
accustomed to your odd comings and goings. Who would
dare to question the movements of Colonel Leonid Shertov, the right arm of General Razumkov, himself the right
arm of the possible future Boss? You have your car, which
on occasion you now drive alone, ready at all times. You
have a map, food, a versatile knife, heavy-duty wire clip-
pers, civilian clothes, good hiking boots. You wait for a
night of the worst kind of weather, lashing rain, mist, fog,
wind. You know the exact hour before the change of the
border guards, when they're most weary, least alert. You
know where to ditch the car, what roads to avoid. You
mime the rise and fall of the ground with your body as
you run in the rain through fields and forests. You lie flat
in puddles of muddy water, ford cleansing streams, are
drenched to the skin by the chilling rain.

I had told my office that I was experiencing a recurrence
of my fever and headache and would probably be sleeping
late. I don't know when it finally dawned on them that they
now had a headache of their own.

East Germany to Czechoslovakia to West Germany.

I emerged from a forest beyond a village road and crossed in a deluge of rain two hours before dawn.

The West Germans and Americans listened with interest to what I had to say. I was not the first to cross over—nor the last.

There was no doubt a big noise made about it in Moscow and a lot of talk concerning enemies of the people and how one can never trust Jews. But they probably forgot about me when East Germany exploded with violent demonstrations a short while later. Our minister, blamed for that, was either shot or strangled at a meeting of the Politburo—that was the word I got, though the world heard about a trial.

I don't know what happened to General Razumkov.

Now let me say this, though it would not surprise me if it cannot enter the hearts of those who suffered at my hands. All the anguish I caused others in my zealous protection of that once splendid dream; all the emptying of hope and civilization I inflicted upon those who stood before me; all the many questions I asked as an act of wounding and all the answers I received through another's screaming; all the worlds I permanently altered in the hearts and minds of people—for all those deeds and a great many more, I uttered, as I stepped into freedom, a Russian word, *"Proschay,"* which means "Good-bye forever." And also means "Forgive me."

For a long time afterward I wondered who had moved into my Moscow apartment and what had become of my painting of the village.

The fever and the headaches? An intestinal parasite I picked up during my months with the Red Army in the Crimea.

"Treatable," says my American doctor, "but not curable."

It comes and goes. It is tenacious, like memory.

THE TROPE
TEACHER

I

THAT MELANCHOLY APRIL, TWO WEEKS AFTER Benjamin Walter's wife fell ill, a woman moved into the Tudor on the other side of the rhododendron hedge. The postman, the gardener, and the owner of the local bookstore made it a point to inform him that the woman was the noted writer I. D. Chandal. Benjamin Walter, pre-occupied with scholarship and in the midst of struggling for months with his memoirs, had little time for fiction. But he knew the name I. D. Chandal.

He was sixty-eight, and ailing. A tall, lean, stately man, with thick gray hair, a square pallid face split by a promi-nent nose, and large webbed eyes dark with brooding behind old-fashioned gold-rimmed spectacles. His long, large-knuckled fingers swollen at the joints, the dry, papery hands flecked with age spots; his lips thin and turned down at the corners; his body fragile, bones prone to breaking.

At times, in the company of intimate friends, he referred to the memoirs as his deathwork.

Much to his wonder and disquiet, when he'd begun the task of remembering his early years he discovered that his

zone of deep memory was, as he put it to himself, well for-
tified and resistant to frontal assault. Only reluctantly did it
begin to yield to determined probing, surrendering now
and then a tiny territory of uncertain value: a narrow city
street deep in snow; a parental voice quivering with anger;
a man's pale eggplant features spectrally detached from
name and frame; a wisp of odd melody curling and fleeting
as a morning mist. He barely recognized those fragments
from his past, was unable to locate what he single-
mindedly sought and uncovered in his scholarly tunnel-
ings: the linking trails of cause and effect; the cords of
connection, as he labeled them, that invariably led him to a
unified chronicle.

He would sit in his oak-and-leather desk chair or lie
back on his worn recliner, brooding, searching, writing,
discarding. He had for fifty years not reflected much about
his very early past, believing always that he could retrieve it
with ease. How very disconcerting, the obsidian face that it
now presented to him.

Especially as memory was what he was best known for;
most notably, his remembering of war. War was his subject: war in general, the two world wars in particular. He
was foremost among the sociologists of war, celebrated,
esteemed. His monographs were studied in universities
throughout the world, at West Point, in the Pentagon. Put
to him an inquiry about the rise of the knightly class in
Europe, and he would trace it to nomadic incursions from
the steppes and to Viking raids; about the causes of the fall
of Constantinople to Muhammad II in 1453, and he would

connect it to the horrors of the Fourth Crusade 250 years earlier; about the rise of the cannon and firearm, and he would begin a discourse on the crossbow, its stock and recoil; about the connection in the First World War between tranquil English town, hamlet, club, and pub to the ghastly stench and slaughter near Ypres, Wytshaete, and Messine, and he would respond with a lecture on the speed of the British postal service. Query him on these and similar matters of war, and you received unambiguous replies delivered in the rhythms and accents of exquisite Oxford English, with not the vaguest trope to indicate his New York beginnings.

His current reputation was vast; his embryonic years clouded. Information found in the usual brief biographies of notables yielded only bare bones: born in New York City in the 1920s; a void about his early years; then, in the Second World War, to England, France, and Germany with the American army; a decision to remain in England after the war; a bachelor's, master's, and doctorate from Oxford; marriage to an English woman of the aristocracy; scholarly articles and reviews for estimable American and international journals of sociology and military studies; a member of various august scholarly societies; abrasive essays in the *New Republic* and the *New York Review of Books;* the first major work, published when he was thirty-five, *Clausewitz and War: The Birth of the Battle of Annihilation;* and seven more books, among them the much-honored *The Triumph of Thanatos: War in the Twentieth Century* and the disputatious *Why So Late: America's*

Entry into the Second World War. And his return to the United States.

Now, in near-old age, perpetually in the limelight, regularly approached, noted, quoted. In *Time, Newsweek,* and *Vanity Fair,* he was the Professor of War. The reason, no doubt, behind the *New York Times* report, in its "Friday Book Notes" column, of the impressive six-figure advance for his memoirs, and the widespread anticipation of their appearance.

In the third week of that unhappy April he sat laboring at his desk one morning, his wife ill in the adjoining room, the nurse at her side, and after a futile inroad into early memory, he raised his weary eyes and gazed out the window at the rhododendron hedge that was part of the border between his home and the Tudor, and saw I. D. Chandal, the new owner of the neighboring house. From a distance of about forty feet his weary eyes let him see narrow hips garbed in tight dark-blue jeans, and breasts covered by a light-blue, short-sleeved jersey. She stood gazing at the hedge, looking surprisingly young and trim for a woman said to be in her middle years.

He put down his pen and closed his eyes. Nothing was happening with the work that morning. Barren wells, puerile words. Might as well meet the new neighbor, clear the head of the long night's frequent wakings.

He informed the nurse that he was stepping outside for a while. Fresh air, a walk in the woods. His wife lay asleep, breathing shallowly. White hair uncombed on the white pillow; beads of sweat on her pale forehead and cheeks;

bluish half-moons under her eyes. She lay diminished, her chest nearly flat. Once robust, moist, and wondrous with love in bed. His heart throbbed with grief. How recapture the past when the present exhausted him so?

But no, he told himself as he left the house and started along the flagstone path to the lawn and the hedge, it was not the accursed illness that had drawn up the blockade to memory; it was something—and here the warm air of the sunny morning fell upon his eyes and face—no, someone, some being from the past itself, a creature elusive as waning shadows and morning mist.

Well, he thought, approaching the figure by the hedge and feeling the heat of the late-morning sun rising from the young spring grass on the lawn, she is a good-looking woman, indeed. Change of neighbor, change of luck?

The hedge was about thirty feet in length, extending from the tall spiked wrought-iron front fence to nearly halfway up the lawn. Beyond the hedge the lawn ran smooth and straight, vanishing into the shadowy dead-leaf interior of dense woods. Three or four feet deep, the rhododendron hedge was situated on a section of the border line between the two properties, and I. D. Chandal stood on the Walter side, peering intently into its leafy interior, her back to Benjamin Walter. Close up, a woman small and dainty in stature, jeans tight, without the revealing curve of panties, he couldn't help noticing; sandals and thin ankles and bare toes; he felt the beat and drum of his blood.

She must have sensed his approach, for she straightened

and turned. He noticed immediately the bony shoulders and small, firm breasts and the nipples beneath the blue jersey. She was not wearing a brassiere. Pretty face, oval-shaped, high cheekbones, blue inviting eyes. How old is she? Forties? Fifties? Face astonishingly unlined. How long has Evelyn been teaching her work? Five years, maybe longer.

A singular fragrance, richly sweet and warm, rose from the hedge. Strange. These rhododendrons have never before given off a scent. More likely blowing in from the woods behind the house. Trees and wildflowers stirring and the two water oaks budding and the grass in the cemetery rising after the storms of the winter.

"Good morning, Ms. Chandal," he said. "I hope I'm not disturbing you."

"No, no. Not at all."

"I saw you through my study window and decided to come down and welcome you to the neighborhood."

"Why, thank you," she said, and added, "Professor Walter."

A demure smile. Lovely Cupid's-bow lips. And the smooth face so white, set off by blond hair in a pageboy cut. And a long slender neck, white, alabaster white.

"Ah," he said, with a slight bow.

"Those who informed you about me informed me about you." A throaty voice, musical.

"We are a close-knit community."

"And gossipy."

"Gossip is a way communities protect their values."

"I remember reading that in one of your books. Was there gossip on the street when the Tudor fell vacant?"

"It was expected to be a difficult house to sell. Indeed, it stood empty for more than a year."

"It's vast. I love it."

"You live in it alone."

"Entirely alone. And relish it."

"Never married?"

"Once married. A recent mutual parting. Two children, grown, long gone from the nest. And you?"

"Married, three children. My wife is home ill."

"I'm sorry to hear that. About your wife, I mean."

"Otherwise she would have brought you some of her English things by way of welcome. Cakes she likes to bake, and teas. She is from England. Does literature. Formerly at Oxford, now at Princeton. She teaches your books. Big fan, as they say."

"I'm flattered." A faint crimson tide rising to the white cheeks, a diffident smile, averted eyes.

"I regret I read no fiction these days, experiencing a bit of a bottleneck with my own work, my memoirs, difficulty locating certain memories tucked away, you might say, tucked away somewhere quite deep. Do you encounter similar problems on occasion?"

She turned her eyes fully upon him. Almond-shaped, with a dark gaze. "On occasion? No."

"Ah."

"Always."

"Always?"

"Incessantly."

"And how does one manage under the circumstances?"

"One sits and ponders."

"Ah, my dear Ms. Chandal. If I could tell you of the hours I have spent sitting and pondering—"

"Relentlessly, pitilessly."

"Yes, indeed."

"Pondering, probing, prying."

"Ms. Chandal—"

"Please. We're neighbors. We've been engaged in conversation now for more than, what, five minutes. Call me Davita."

"Well. Indeed. Davita. And you must call me Benjamin."

"Benjamin."

"The hours I have spent at my desk—"

"Try talking. You know, the way you learn a language. Out loud. Tell it to the air. See how it begins to unravel."

"It is more like attacking a fortress."

"Memory is like a ball of woolen thread, Benjamin. If the pen cannot unravel it, the voice can. All my books are unravelings of voice and pen. Would drive my poor husband to distraction, not to mention the children. They thought I had multiple personalities. A loony wife and mother. He's a very uncomplicated man, my Donald. I would've left him sooner but for the kids. He owns a headstone business. For graveyards. Very fancy carving, and very expensive. Benjamin, I think you're standing too long in the sunlight. It's nice to have met you. May I shake your hand?" She rubbed her right palm on her jeans. "A bit grubby with earth, I'm afraid. Sizing up a flower bed."

Fingers short, slender, dry. Tendons ridged along the underside of the thin wrist. Smooth.

"You write by hand, I see," she said, gently turning his hand as it lay against hers and rubbing the tip of a finger over the small hillock of callus on the first joint of his middle finger. He felt her finger through the dry mound of dead skin. "Same thing with me." She showed him a callused finger.

"Everything, monographs, letters, books."

"Your *Why So Late* I read in college and wrote a term paper on it. Memorable. The book, I mean."

"Thank you."

"Your account of the final German offensive. Frightful."

"Indeed."

"Were you there?"

"Oh yes, I was certainly there."

"Benjamin, you're perspiring, you should go inside. First really hot day, beware too much noonday sun. I will invite you and your wife over one day soon."

He looked toward the woods behind the house and at the cemetery visible through the trees. The air thrumming with birdsong.

"I doubt my wife will be able to join us."

"I'm genuinely sorry."

In another month the trees will shield the cemetery from view. The sun on the Revolutionary War gravestones, white, sparkling.

"I believe that there is always a ram in the bush," he heard her say.

He turned to face her. Small white expectant features. Wide unblinking eyes overlaid with a transparent yellowish film flecked with pinpoints of golden light, probably from the sun. A serpent's eyes, they almost seem. The eyes of a story writer?

"A ram in the bush, you say."

"I believe that."

"How very nice to think so."

THE FOLLOWING DAY HE FLEW TO CHICAGO. A graduate seminar on Clausewitz; an interview with the Op-Ed page editor of the *Tribune;* a private lunch with two deans and the provost; an afternoon colloquium on the Persian Gulf War.

High piercing noises emanated from the speakers and rendered the large audience restive. He stood helpless behind the podium. Why am I here? Why am I doing this? A sudden vision of his house, his study, and the rhododendron hedge in the sunlight. The nurse waiting patiently until he returned. Once again he spoke into the microphone, but it hurled back his words in fierce electronic resistance. He leaned heavily against the podium, his legs aching, a twinge in his right arm below the elbow. Bones beginning to hurt. When did I take the medication? A scruffy ponytailed young man in slovenly jeans hurried down the aisle and onto the stage, and checked plugs, wires, outlets. Proper sound and order restored, the audience again focused on him. Benjamin Walter spoke for an hour, detailing his position on the war, his voice a rich baritone, his tone properly ironic and dry, his Oxford English echoing faintly off the high walls of the crowded auditorium. He invoked Weber, Durkheim, Freud; he cited Churchill, Fussell, Janowitz. He analyzed roots and causes and drew tight the cords of connection. Nevertheless, during the question-and-answer period, contentious voices were raised: Was this not antiquated gunboat diplomacy? Regressive, imperialist, colonialist, favoring oil interests and decadent regimes? How could he be so certain of the causal lines he had drawn up when one might easily see it this or that other way? Why did there have to be cogent causal lines at all, why could it not all simply have, well, happened? Someone cited Kuhn; another, Rorty. He felt himself growing weary. This young generation, nothing sacred to them, reduce everything to a postdeluvian shambles. He held his own, he thought, gave far better than he received, he was certain, and afterward one of the younger faculty, a bright assistant professor of English, who knew Evelyn's work on Virginia Woolf and I. D. Chandal, accompanied him to the university bookstore and then drove him to the airport.

Seated in the airliner, the huge jet airborne, he removed from his briefcase the collection of stories he had purchased in the bookstore, the most recent book by I. D. Chandal. Its title, *Calling Upon Hell,* and the photograph on the back of the dust jacket displaying an I. D. Chandal quite different from the one he had met near the hedge: gray-haired, plump, wearing a man's shirt and tie, a tweed sports jacket, dark slacks, and with a strange fierce look in her eyes. Round-faced, heavy-bosomed, the early traces of a second chin, tiny lines biting at her lips. The jacket unable to conceal the hefty endowment of hip and thigh. Apparently, between the book and the hedge she had dyed her hair and lost a lot of weight.

He turned to the epigraph in the front of the book.

There was nobody left who had not experienced more misfortunes in four or five years than could be depicted in a century by literature's most famous novelists: it was necessary to call upon hell to arouse interest.

The words were the Marquis de Sade's.

He sat reading.

Strange stories. Many situated on the Upper West Side of Manhattan. Old World men with threadbare dreams entering the fearful midnight of their lives. Elegant pre–World War I apartments, tall ceilings, paneled rooms, dark-wood tables, upholstered couches, tasseled lamps. In the first story, "A Rainbow Costs 50 Cents Extra," an elderly man orders a birthday cake from a bakery for his dying wife, and is infuriated by an unexpected fifty-cent-extra charge for the decorative rainbow he has requested to be added to the icing as a symbol of love and peace. He recalls rainbows he and his wife have seen in skies churned by storms, returns to the bakery with a .22 revolver, and shoots the storekeeper dead.

In the story "Spring Gardens Only," an aging artist who is also a gardener lives in a brownstone in the midst of the city, and in a patch of ground behind the house plants the gardens he paints. His watercolors are exquisite, famous. He starts his gardens in April, abandons them in July. One spring a visitor from his past appears, a male lover from a distant hungry winter before the time of fame. They renew their affair; they quarrel bitterly; the lover leaves. The artist, overwhelmed by memories of the original affair, installs a fountain in the garden wall. The water attracts songbirds, one of which on a lightning impulse he kills with a stone. He sketches it, paints it, a male cardinal, gorgeously feathered, and buries it in the garden.

Some of the stories were about women. "Fresh-Cut Color" was a monologue by a once-famous lesbian film actress about to find out if her adopted daughter has been accepted into the first grade at a highly prestigious private school. The child is rejected. Memories flood the actress: her early rejections, her successes, her current fading career. The vengeance she wreaks upon the school. . . .

A renowned architect returns to Cracow on a search for Holocaust memories; a former colonel of the KGB recalls his years as an interrogator and torturer; a professor of Western intellectual history faces a plagiarism scandal; an aging homosexual goes on a Russian roulette of cruising in the wake of the death from AIDS of his young lover—all nearing the end of their active lives, all tangled in memories of the past, which come to them too late and return nothing, not an echo, not a whisper, not a hope. Relentless, the cold tone of the tales; exquisitely baroque, the lush, alliterative language, the exuberant figures of speech. A grandeur of style painting lives sown with salt.

Enough. Slightly unhinged by the language and dismayed by the lives, he closed the book and proceeded to pick at the food placed before him by the flight attendant. But the book, which he had inserted into the seat pocket before him, seemed to be sending forth tendrils that were sliding toward him. The stories were a *presence*. Quite understandable that Evelyn was teaching her work.

He fell into a troubled sleep and was awakened by the bump of the landing gear on the tarmac. That late at night Newark Terminal was nearly deserted. He retrieved his car and drove along a foggy parkway and country roads to the town; the roads littered with branches, here and there dark puddles in the headlights of the Saab. Tired, very tired. Legs and arms aching, and now the back of his neck and his eyes.

It was shortly after ten o'clock when he turned into his driveway, and saw the asphalt wet and strewn with branches. Lights burned in the living room and master bedroom. Oddly, the Tudor stood dark: no interior lights, no outside lights. The previous owners—elderly people, he an investment broker and she an interior decorator, who had gone to live with their only daughter in Phoenix— would set the house ablaze at night. "Tudors are built to be dark," the man had once remarked to Benjamin Walter.

"Spooky place without lights." Advise her to put the exteriors on automatic. Not good to leave the house dark at night. The exterior floods had switched on each evening and off early each morning all through the year the Tudor had stood unsold and uninhabited.

He parked the car in the garage behind his house and climbed out from the front seat, pain flashing in his legs, then went to the trunk for his travel bag and briefcase. The storm had done nothing to cool the air, which smelled of mist and sodden earth. The night was sultry, waterlogged, stirred by moist winds.

A voice startled him. "Welcome back, Benjamin."

His heart skipped, raced. He looked around, saw no one.

"Over here."

He spotted her then, about thirty feet away, near the rhododendrons.

"Hello," he called. What was she doing there outside in the dark? And wasn't the lawn sopping wet?

"We had a very bad storm, Benjamin. Lost two trees over on the next street. No damage to your trees, though."

No damage to his trees? Had she walked through the woods, inspecting? The previous owners had never entered his section of the woods, not to his knowledge.

Carrying his bag and briefcase in one arm, he stepped out of the garage, pushing the button that lowered the door.

"A long trip?" he heard her ask.

"Chicago." She stood just beyond the rim of his exterior

house lights, her face seeming to hover like a dimly lit globe beside the hedge. "I read some of the stories in your current collection on the flight back."

"Did you?"

"An eagle's language, a scorpion's bite, if I may say so. You depict a unique hell."

"We live in a strange time. A different hell is called for, most definitely, wouldn't you say?"

"Aren't you standing in a very muddy lawn?"

"Oh, I don't mind the mud. Actually, I'm watching the fireflies."

The lawn was ablaze with the tiny low-flying creatures, lending the dark air the appearance of a star-sprinkled sky.

"Light without heat," he heard her say. "Since early childhood, fascinated by fireflies. Did you deliver a talk in Chicago?"

"On the Persian Gulf War."

"Ah, of course, the Professor of War discoursing on war. You must tell me what you said. Did you use anecdotes in your talk?"

"Davita, it's quite late."

"Like all writers, I am eager for good stories."

"I teach tomorrow."

"I didn't mean right now. Over coffee, one day soon?"

"It will be my pleasure."

"Good night, Benjamin."

He went along the side of the house and the flagstone front walk to the porch. Climbing the three steps, he looked briefly to his left and saw across the lawn the vague globe of her head still suspended in the darkness near the hedge.

Inside, the nurse sat waiting. They talked briefly about the day—Evelyn's progress, her response to the medications, her frame of mind—and the nurse then slipped quietly out of the house with a murmured good night. He turned off the lamps, leaving only the night-light burning, a faint greenish glow near the foot of the stairs. The house, once resonating with the buoyant mayhem of children, now sepulchral with silence. Slowly, he climbed the well of carpeted stairs.

A wedge of yellow light from their room spilled onto the dim second-floor hallway. He entered the room, set down the bags. She opened her eyes.

"Benjamin." An effort, her whisper.

"My dear," he said softly.

The pneumonia was deep this time, exhausting, but still treatable at home. Large shadow-rimmed gray eyes in a thin long face drawn pale and tight across the temples and cheekbones. The warm acrid odor of her sweat.

"Is there anything I can get you?"

She replied tonelessly, "Dear Benjamin, how about a dill-and-yogurt soup?"

He lowered his head.

"Don't forget to add a generous grinding of pepper." Her voice matter-of-fact, a near-whisper. "And veal alla marsala. Again, don't forget the pepper."

"My dear—"

"Rice Creole, once again the pepper. And ratatouille."

"Dear—"

"Shall I have a salad? Perhaps a string bean salad with vinaigrette?"

"Dear, dear Evelyn," he murmured.

"It is all still very astonishing," she said, and closed her eyes and turned her face to the wall.

She lay very still, breathing with difficulty. He turned off the light and stood gazing into the deep blues and purples of the darkened room. The partly open windows faced the rear of the house and he distinctly heard the trees: the oaks and pines, the cedars and elms.

Arms and legs throbbing, he undressed and slipped into pajamas. Skeletal underpinning slowly but irreversibly splintering and fracturing; Humpty-Dumpty in slow motion. In the bathroom he washed and took his medications and gazed at himself in the medicine-cabinet mirror. Not yet the ravaged midnight features of W. H. Auden. He thought of the face of I. D. Chandal. The two faces, the one on the lawn and the other in the book. It occurred to him that his wife's library must have old hardback copies of works by I. D. Chandal, and he went quietly through the bedroom and crossed the hall into her study. Undisturbed the past two weeks, the air inside musty. Six novels by I. D. Chandal, and two short-story collections. He found her photograph on the back of only one of the books, a novel four years old. The same photograph as the one on the book he had purchased in Chicago—and which, he now realized with dismay, he had forgotten on the airplane! Annoyed over that. He put back on the shelf the novel with the photograph and, as he turned to leave, glanced out the study window, which faced the side of the Tudor, and noticed a ground-floor room, the kitchen, earlier dark, now lit. At a table sat a woman, her face concealed by her hand. The rhododendron hedge did not extend that far down the length of the lawn, and he was able to see clearly her pale-blue nightdress and portly form and graying hair.

Fatigued now beyond easy measure, and the sleeping pill he had earlier swallowed beginning to take hold, he returned to the bedroom. Cool sheets, moonlight on the windows, the trees murmurous. Evelyn breathing steadily. She'll wake at least once. From the woods the hooting of an owl and before his aching eyes the sudden image of the picked-clean skeleton of a squirrel on the front walk one morning. The children gaping at it, shrinking back, fascinated, horrified. Tiny, delicate, glistening bones: spinal column, feet, all neatly splayed, as if pinned for dissection. Owls do that, he said, pick you clean to the core. Evelyn said, No, dear, that was not an owl, owls eat everything, even the bones, and if it's eating a bird it will leave only the feathers. More likely the work of our neighbor's cat, she added in that wondrously amiable way she had of imparting knowledge without the least display of conceit; the Tudor people'd had a white tabby in those days. He scooped up the skeleton of the squirrel with a shovel and tossed it into the garbage bin near the garage, the children watching, shocked, unnerved. Were they thinking: Will this happen to us too, one day reduced this way to bone? Should've talked to them about it afterward but they went off to school and the incident was never brought up and why was he remembering it now, oh, yes, the owl. He thought, woozy from the medication: How tedious and commonplace, this business of mortality. Infrequently considered, and when considered, too quickly put aside. What returns it to remembrance is irony. A war trench repeatedly shelled is soon lost to recollection. But bomb a sleepy town—the irony will nail it solidly to memory. There, the owl again, from the woods or the cemetery. Oh, yes, an explosive device ravaging an innocent airliner is the very guarantor of memory. Is that the reason we remember forever the biblical Amalekites who attacked Israelites during the exodus from Egypt? The assault upon helpless, fleeing people a bitter irony. What would that strange man, the trope—cantillation—teacher, have said to that? The trope teacher! Why have I suddenly recalled the trope teacher? A quickening beat of the heart in the swiftly gathering clouds of sleep.

His wife woke him later that night, and he went to her. Feverish again and soaked with sweat. Gently, he raised her, dried her with a towel, helped her into a fresh nightgown. He murmured to her reassuringly: she would come out of this as she had before. She coughed and belched. He helped her to the bathroom and supported her so she would not tumble off the toilet. She lay on his bed as he changed her sheets.

"Actually, dear, I would prefer lunch in Davy Byrne's with Leopold Bloom," she said.

He laughed softly.

She murmured, as he helped her into her bed, "One can hardly believe that one's own body could become such an awful enemy."

She fell asleep.

He remained starkly awake and after a while went to the bathroom for another sleeping pill. But he decided not to take it; the aftereffect would smother him in a wooly blanket of exhaustion that would linger into the morning and he had a full day awaiting him at the university. Spend an hour or so now working on the memoirs, fall asleep over that.

He entered his study and, looking out the window at the Tudor, saw I. D. Chandal in her kitchen, yellow-lit, framed by the window, obese. All the rest of the Tudor had melted into the darkness. She sat hunched over a pad, writing. He watched until he grew sleepy and then returned to his bed.

The nurse arrived punctually, as always, in the early morning. A hot, cloudy day, more storms predicted. His wife was still asleep when he left the house. The oaks behind the house, silent. And hushed, too, the woods.

He went along the driveway toward the garage and saw I. D. Chandal, shovel in hand, bent over a wide length of raw earth she had dug from the end of the hedge to the border of the woods. Her blond hair was covered with a bright-yellow bandana. Firm breasts, shapely hips. A dizziness came over him.

She said, straightening, "Good morning, Benjamin. It will storm again today."

He was fighting off the sensation of being slightly unhinged.

"Benjamin?"

A pause. Two or three deep breaths. Then, "Good morning. You're up early."

"A wonderful day to plant. Earth soft from yesterday's rain, and put the flowers in before the next rain."

He climbed into the Saab.

She said, "How is your wife?"

He closed the car door, rolled down the window, and started the engine. "My wife had a bad night."

She raised toward him slightly the hand that grasped the earth-encrusted shovel: a gesture of sympathy.

"Davita," he said through the open window of the car. "Your ram in the bush?"

"Yes?"

"Where is it?"

She gazed at him without expression.

He moved the car along and glanced at her in his rearview mirror. She stood, shovel in hand, watching him turn onto the street. Even from that distance he could see clearly the look of ferocity on her face.

HE DROVE CAUTIOUSLY ALONG THE WINDING COUN-try roads and the curving corrugated parkway, sticking always to the right lane, watching out for the potholes, aware of the cars in the center and left lanes racing past him. On both sides of the parkway tall trees with infant leaves silhouetted against the cloudy sky. Broken patches of road jarring the steering wheel and his fingers and hands. The upper deck of the bridge nearly lost in a yellow fog and the wide river dull gray and running into mist and the city endlessly bleak beneath a blockade of low, dense clouds. Tiresome this drive. Still, the Max Weber Chair in Sociology sufficient reason to have moved here. But to live in the city—unthinkable. Yet the travel time. And Evelyn's commute to Princeton. And the costly private schools for the children. Poor choice in the end? Maybe. Hindsight always the winner in the war of wits. Hardly the streets of Oxford and the bike rides to Balliol. Destitute England like a wheezing invalid then, my mother secretly sending the food packages, my father utterly mute. That old bike with the basket in front and the dead metallic sound of its warning bell. Riding down the road and turning left and passing the playing fields of Magdalen. Cool sweet-scented air and flowers spilling over onto the sidewalks, houses pink in the early light and the gravel path to the residential street and on into the park with the broad fields and the cricket matches on Saturdays. And just inside the entrance to the park the tall thick-trunked tree with the haven of greenish shadows beneath its branches. How I loved that tree. And flowers lining the gravel path and the river running narrow and slow to my left along the water walks until it opened out into the wide water where Evelyn taught me to punt. Trees green and dense along the banks and the shadows of leaves on the dark mirror surface of the water. Putting the pole in, feeling it slide into the muddy bottom, pushing, punting. And Evelyn reading aloud from Auden about seas of pity lying locked and frozen. Why am I suddenly remembering *that?* Seas of pity locked and frozen. She taught me a great deal, my Evelyn: how to truly read and write, how to blissfully forget. And the gravel path led to the road that ran past the museum and the Bodleian and the pub and into Broad Street and Balliol, the quadrangle, the stone archway, the dining hall, the dorm rooms, the open green with the garden outside the chapel, and trees, lovely trees. Evelyn on her bike; long russet hair trailing in the wind. Color on her high-boned flushed cheeks and sweat on her face even in winter and the musky smell of the sweat between her breasts and under her arms. And the perpetual look of surprise in her eyes; surprise that she and her parents and her two brothers had survived the war; surprise that she had gone from nursing soldiers to reading literature; surprise that she had fallen in love with a Yank, an ailing Yank, a Jewish Yank, she being vintage Church of England stock and a descendant of William of Waynflete, who had been Bishop of Manchester, a loyal minister of Henry VI, and founder of Magdalen College. True, I wore a different face then: lank and pallid from the illness and not a little apprehensive, but handsome, and eyes glittering with a hunger to take in the world. And the infinite wonder each time the seeming fragile thinness of her would turn fiery and tumescent during the turbulence of sex.

The car lurched and plunged and climbed through a dip in the cobblestone street. Europe cobbled with the bones of war dead. Where did I read that? So tired this morning.

All that anger in Chicago, exhausting. Is that rain? No, street grit on the windshield. His eyes swollen with fatigue; his fingers tight on the wheel, aching.

He steered the Saab into the side-street garage and left it with an attendant. Umbrella in one hand and briefcase in the other; he had a gangly, flat-footed walk. Dark homburg and charcoal-gray suit; starched white shirt and icy yellow tie. Curious glances from the jeans and T-shirt crowd. Evelyn tells me that I bring to mind T. S. Eliot walking to his bank. Big fuss in academe now over Eliot's wretched anti-Semitism. Suddenly discovered America, as my father would say.

He took one of the pedestrian paths into College Walk.

The paved center lane was crowded with cars. Water splashing in the fountains of the plaza. Steps thronged with students. The sunless air strangely still; the flags drooping on their tall poles. Security guards: alert for the rites and tumults of spring? Posters announcing meetings, films, plays, demonstrations. Gays. Lesbians. Afro-Americans. Asians. Women's rights. Pro-Lifers. America Balkanized. *E pluribus plura.* What is this? A colloquium on Heidegger. Repellent philosophy from a damnable man. And another on Derrida. That too shall pass. All this academic cacophony, with the city as backdrop. Beginning to rain.

He rode the elevator up to his office and some while later sat before a microphone lecturing to nearly one hundred students in a large, stuffy hall whose open windows seemed to suck in the noises of the cars, buses, trucks, and pedestrians on the four-lane street. A steady background of sound during the fifty minutes of the class. Some of the students slept. One kept rolling his head: probably on drugs.

Before lunch a dissertation conference with a graduate student: a nervous, balding young man from India, too anxious to please. Then a lengthy telephone conversation with Stuart Fox, the head of the history department, about a candidate for a recently vacated professorship. Replacing the telephone, he turned to his mail. Invitations to conferences in Washington, D.C., Berlin, Tel Aviv, Amsterdam. Keynote a State Department think tank in Aspen. A request from a prestigious journal of American history for a piece on his army experience in Europe during the war. A catalog from a rare-book dealer in London. Behind him a sudden rumble of thunder. Turning, he saw through the tall window a whitish-green sky and, after a moment, a flash of lightning. Again, thunder. A light rain falling.

He ate lunch alone in the faculty club—a bowl of soup, a green salad, coffee. Many called out greetings as they moved past his table; none offered handshakes; nearly all knew of his fragile hands. It was raining steadily when he left the club.

He detoured to the library, entered the stacks, and in a cool, silent corridor lined with books discovered half a shelf of critical works on I. D. Chandal: one by an Oxford scholar, another published by Harvard, yet another by Chicago; a volume in the Twayne's United States Author Series; a number of UMI-printed dissertations; and a Modern Critical Views volume, with essays by Alfred Kazin, Harold Bloom, Robert Alter, Elizabeth Hardwick, Susan

Sontag, and Cynthia Ozick. He took with him the work by the Oxford scholar and the collection of essays.

Leaving the library, he ran into Robert Helman, who was standing in the doorway, looking forlorn and waiting for the rain to let up.

"Robert, share my umbrella."

Robert Helman murmured his thanks and ducked under the protective cover.

Together they walked in the rain, Benjamin Walter tall and mannerly, Robert Helman slight, in his mid-sixties, graying beard and hair, red bow tie, rumpled dark suit.

The rain was suddenly wind-driven, heavy, drumming upon the umbrella. Students rushed by. On the paths were miniature dark seas made turbulent by the wind and rain.

"Your wife?" asked Helman under the umbrella.

"Not well, I'm afraid."

"So sorry. A difficult time for you." His small voice, with its Middle European accent, sounding breathless, barely audible.

Benjamin Walter thought: Theresienstadt, sixteen months. Twelve months in Auschwitz. Helman an expert on difficult times.

"Your trip to Chicago?"

"Be careful of that puddle. Stormy opposition to the war. Saddam Hussein sitting on our oil flow an insufficient reason for interference in a regional quarrel."

"They favored appeasement?"

He knows about appeasement, too. Prague his provenance. "Inclined toward waiting."

"Evil feeds on waiting."

The wind gusted, the rain slanted, the umbrella jerked and pulled.

They entered their building. Benjamin Walter shook the rain from the umbrella. Puddles formed on the floor.

Helman delicately raised the bottoms of his trousers, tapped the rain from his shoes. He said, clearing his throat and adjusting his bow tie, "The candidate for the position in history, did you hear?"

"Oh, yes, the news reached me."

"And did you hear that she does not have the necessary language?"

"That I heard too, yes."

"Don't you think it strange, Benjamin, for the university to hire someone to teach the history of a people who doesn't know that people's language?"

"Fox told me this morning that he is taking the position that she was deprived of a proper language education because she's a woman."

"Oh, really? Well, I was deprived of a proper education in physics because of my genealogy. Am I therefore now able to teach physics?"

"Fox claims that her dissertation is outstanding."

"Benjamin, permit me to tell you a little story about dissertations and doctorates. In my current research on the Wannsee Conference I have discovered that, of the fifteen men who sat around the table establishing the bureaucracy for the murder of European Jewry, eight held doctorates."

"Fox wants this woman and will turn it into a war."

"How sad if he does that."

"You'll lose even if you win."

"And what is your position on this?"

"I've written on war in Japan, and I don't know Japanese. Good translators are more than adequate."

"I don't know about the Japanese. I know about Jewish history. No language, no historian. This will be a war worth waging."

"Fox won't forget, Robert. He'll make you pay in a thousand ways, and war will be the winner. War always wins."

Robert Helman shook his head and sighed. Pale forehead creased, eyes deeply furrowed at the corners; premature aging and permanent sadness, wearing visibly his years in the German factories of murder. A great historian, hard-nosed, public and private opponent to Benjamin Walter's notion of underlying cords of connection, a proponent of what he called the three laws of the chaos theory of history: chance, chance, and chance. The haphazard, the accidental, the arbitrary, the contingent; discrete events banging randomly against one another, with humans creating the fiction of connection. "Historians record, clerics connect"—an oft-quoted remark of his, uttered in exasperation one day at a conference. His wife taught art history at the university, they lived in a nearby apartment building with an exquisite view of the river, and there were four grown and lovely children.

Robert Helman thanked Benjamin Walter for the sanctuary of his umbrella, asked to be remembered to Evelyn, and went off to meet with Stuart Fox.

Some minutes later, Benjamin Walter stood at the tall window between the floor-to-ceiling bookcases in his office, watching the rain. The quadrangle, dripping and depleted of hues, lay deserted. A diagonal streak of lightning ripped across the sky, followed almost immediately by drumbeats of thunder that rattled the windows. In the ensuing silence he thought he heard someone at the door.

"Come."

The door opened and a young man entered and closed the door. He wore rain-stained blue jeans and a soaked white T-shirt and sandals with no socks. Muscular arms and chest, veins and tendons clearly showing. Blond hair tied back in a ponytail, wet strands on his forehead and ruddy cheeks. A small gold earring.

The young man said in a matter-of-fact tone, "Professor, I can't take the exam, I've got to go home right away."

Benjamin Walter recognized him. A senior, infrequently present in class, with a show of indifference to the subject, but very bright those few times he'd spoken up. His parents of western Pennsylvania aristocracy.

"I do not give makeup examinations."

"Professor, I was just on the phone with my mother. My best friend, the friend I went to school with from third grade on, is very sick."

"That's of no—"

"I mean, it's pretty serious. He's in some kind of a depression or something, and he's asking for me."

Benjamin Walter said, "In such matters, the department requires corroboration."

"I can get that."

"Where does he live?"

"He's at Yale." Blue eyes chilly even in this distress. Features blank. Flat, glacial voice. Bred for self-control. "So can I take a makeup exam?"

Benjamin Walter nodded.

The young man left the office without another word.

Outside the rain had come to an end. Water dripped from the branches of the scrawny street trees. Patches of blue sky shone above soaring gold-rimmed clouds.

He sat for some while, working on his memoirs, filling the margins of the manuscript with notes in his minuscule handwriting. Two hours went by, the phone did not ring, no one knocked on his door. But it was futile; he had already set down most of the middle and more recent years, but nothing of the beginning, nothing to which he could connect his later life—and how does one write a life without a seed, a source, a commencement? His mother and father and sister and brother, he remembered. But there was someone else he could recall only in dim outline, a teacher, yes, a teacher of trope, but, more important, also of, of—elusive, a phantom of some kind. Why am I not able to resurrect him?

He put down his pen and sat back, exhausted, his fingers aching. No more work on the memoirs today. Thus far, the memoirs a book without a beginning.

Umbrella in one hand, briefcase containing the manuscript in the other, he walked to the garage and retrieved his Saab. The air smelled of dank streets. Late-afternoon

sunlight cast a pale-pink wash across the walls of tall buildings. Traffic inched along the streets to the parkway. He
drove with his windows open, staring fixedly at the road,
ignoring the horns directed at him.

The sky was barely lit when he entered the town. Street-
lights shone upon the debris-strewn wet roads. When he
turned into his driveway he was momentarily startled, certain he had erred: this was not his home.

Jagged fragments of raw wood lay everywhere, on the
lawn and the driveway and near the garage, some small,
others the height of a man and thrust deep into the earth.
Blocking the end of the driveway just beyond the entrance
to the garage, was a huge tree limb. Beyond the rhododendron hedge stood the Tudor, all its windows ablaze. And
emerging from the line of trees and hurrying toward him
was I. D. Chandal.

2

THE TWO OAKS AT THE EDGE OF THE WOODS
were nearly as old as the core of the house, and the
cemetery beyond the woods was older still, with some
gravestones from colonial times. And the woods between
the cemetery and the house—the wild, cool growth of
trees and underbrush with their greenish whisperings and
murmurings—the woods predated all.

From the first moment he'd set eyes on the house more
than thirty years ago he'd silently accepted it as an echoing

link with a moment in his past from which he no longer felt a need to flee; the woods and cemetery seemed to possess a kind of welcome enchantment. The history of the house—recounted by the realtor—contained a beguiling mystery.

Built originally as a farmhouse during the Revolutionary War, said the realtor. Whoever owned it around the time of the War of 1812 knocked down an outside wall and added a room that doubled the size of the ground floor. The one who owned it during the Civil War built a new staircase: dark oak steps and a carved banister smooth and warm to the touch. Near the end of the First World War, before the winter froze the earth and the influenza epidemic began its murderous rampage, the then owner put down a patio of brick and flagstone outside the kitchen. And during the Second World War the people who owned it had a den built in the space between the rear wall of the parlor and the back lawn.

When Benjamin Walter had stood in the driveway gazing at the house that first time, an odd shiver had coursed through him, a pull of memory, and he asked the realtor if he could take a walk alone through the woods. He went about for a while in the cool green interior, the earth soft and moist beneath his shoes. Insects buzzed in the lacy patterns of sunlight that shone like shimmering water on the leaves. A rhythmic hum of cicadas and the sweetly piercing sounds of birdsong and the rustle of animal life in the underbrush. Trees tall and old, thick-trunked, bark like the hide of elephants, bulging roots deep and gnarled. Beyond

the woods lay a gently rising sward, a cemetery, gravestones ancient and recent. The trees were still that day. The
trees were merely trees that day.

Evelyn had wondered if the Tudor next door might be
for sale. Closer to her heart, that sort of house. Keen
memories of her family's country home before the war,
before she'd met and fallen in love with her Yank, before
the years at Oxford, before the wrenching move to the
United States.

The realtor had made inquiries. No, the Tudor was not
for sale. Its owners were quite content and had no intention of selling, thank you very much.

So they made an offer on the old farmhouse and
accepted the counteroffer and signed the settlement papers
in November 1963, four days before the assassination of
John Kennedy.

Five years later, they had completed major books: he on
war, she on Virginia Woolf. The children young and active:
the house untidy, crowded, and clamorous with their
friends.

Evelyn loved to give dinner parties. People came from
New York and Princeton. Scholars, poets, writers, artists.

He and Evelyn decided to expand the kitchen. The
country was then at war in Vietnam. He was at a sociology
conference organized by Philip Rieff at the University of
Pennsylvania the day workers broke through the outside
wall of the kitchen and found the old newspapers. Six-year-
old Kevin mentioned it the next day during dinner.

"Which newspapers?"

"Old newspapers, Daddy."

"What are we talking about here?"

"Stinky old," said Kevin.

"You are a stupid little fellow," said Laura, twelve, the older daughter. "Newspapers from the First World War, Daddy."

"Where are they?"

"Mother threw them into the trash," said Beth, nine, the younger daughter.

He looked across the table at Evelyn.

"Ben, they were falling to pieces."

After dinner he went outside and brought the trash can into the kitchen and hauled out crumpled brownish newspapers, which he set down on the floor and opened carefully. Pages dry and brittle. A local newspaper, the *Nyack Eagle,* no longer in existence. Its masthead an American flag draped around an eagle; headlines black and bold. Probably stuffed into the wall for insulation. Evelyn and the children stood around watching quietly as he spread the newspapers on the floor in proper sequence. The headlines read:

AUSTRIA DECLARES WAR,
RUSHES VAST ARMY INTO SERBIA

BRITAIN ON VERGE OF WAR WITH GERMANY

LUSITANIA SUNK BY A SUBMARINE,
PROBABLY 1,260 DEAD

WILSON BREAKS WITH GERMANY; WAR IMMINENT

WAR IS DECLARED BY U.S.

GERMANS TAKE MOST OF MESSINES RIDGE

GERMANS GET CHEMIN DES DAMES IN NEW DRIVE

OVER 1,000,000 U.S. SOLDIERS SENT ABROAD

AMERICANS DRIVE GERMANS BACK OVER MARNE

GERMANS AGREE TO SIGN; NO CONDITIONS

GERMANY GIVES UP; WAR ENDS AT 2 P.M.

One of the pages disintegrated as he unfolded it. He set out its bits and pieces on the kitchen table:

M RI NS TACK B TWE   SE D AR ONNE   OREST

" 'Americans attack between Meuse and Argonne For- est,' " he said to his wife and children, feeling a sudden drumming in his chest. Argonne. Ardennes. Memories of his own war.

The kitchen had begun to reek of rot and mold. He scooped up the newspapers and carried them to his study.

In the days that followed, he'd cut out the headlines, had them mounted and framed—four frames in all—and hung them on the wall in his study, which held memora- bilia of his life: degrees, awards, accolades, photographs with distinguished colleagues, university presidents, sena- tors, and Presidents John Kennedy, Lyndon Johnson, Richard Nixon, Ronald Reagan. He had a skilled craftsman

glue the headline fragments to a heavy gray matte card-
board and enclose it all beneath nonglare glass in a black
frame, which he hung on the wall over his desk. The
framed headlines cast an odd imbalance over the room, as
if dwarfing everything else on the walls and even the glass-
enclosed floor-to-ceiling bookcases with their rare and pre-
cious volumes and folios on war.

"They are quite overpowering," Evelyn said.

"Part of the history of this house."

"But that wasn't our war, darling."

"Oh, yes, it was. One long war with a brief respite
to facilitate recovery from the influenza epidemic and re-
arming. It was certainly my parents' war."

"You never talk about them, but you'll put their war on
your walls."

"Nothing to talk about, my dear. They lived, they died.
Unremarkable people."

"But they were your mother and father."

"Recollection very vague now. Retrieve it all if I must
one day."

"How can you be so sure of that, Benjamin?"

All this—returned to memory by a felled tree limb. In
their years on this property the woods had been struck by
lightning five times, though this sixth time was the closest
it had ever come to the house. Astonishing to have so
much come hurtling back into memory, as if an electric
switch had been turned on: the blasted oak, the awful
war, the shattered woods; the history of the house, the
resurrected headlines, the Argonne and the Ardennes, his

parents, and—yes!—the trope teacher. A long cord of connection.

He sat behind the steering wheel of his car, staring in shock at the huge tree limb that lay across the driveway and in the same moment seeing I. D. Chandal, coat and hat stained dark with rain, emerge from the woods and come hurrying toward him along the wet rear lawn.

SHE SAID, "ONE OF YOUR TREES TOOK A DIRECT hit."

"Which?"

"One of the oaks. It probably saved your house."

"One of the oaks?" He felt dazed.

"You'll need a tree person."

"A what?" What was she saying? She seemed so calm amid this devastation: a shattered tree, splinters everywhere.

"A specialist. To assess the damage."

"One of the oaks," he said, looking toward the trees.

"Benjamin, I'd love to stand here and talk to you, but I have to go to the bathroom. Listen, come over later for a cup of coffee, if you're so inclined."

He watched her move off behind the rhododendron hedge and head toward the Tudor. He parked the car and walked over to the oak nearest the house.

The tree was nearly one hundred years old. It stood illumined by the sodium floods. There was a faint smell of freshly splintered, charred wood. The limb had been hurled onto the driveway. And all those shards. Some like spears and swords with their points buried six inches in the earth. He shuddered at the image of a shard embedding itself in human flesh. Deep darkness lay upon the branches facing the woods.

Very still, the woods.

The silence chilled him. He entered the house through the back door.

The nurse sat waiting for him in the kitchen.

"Oh, the storm was something fierce. Mrs. Walter, the Lord bless her, is so brave. The lightning frightened her. Scared me too. Like the Last Judgment, it was. The hand of God. We thought the house was hit, but it was only a tree. I gave her a pill, and she'll sleep four, maybe five hours."

"Thank you."

"You should get a night nurse not only for when you're away."

"I can tend to her."

"For the next time, I mean."

"I'll worry about it then."

"I can recommend someone."

"If it becomes necessary."

"I'll let myself out."

He ate cold chicken, reading and half-listening to the news on NPR. Merciless bombardment of Sarajevo. Centuries of hatred surfacing. Tenacity of memory. An image came to him and he looked up from the book: I. D. Chandal hurrying across the rear lawn in her raincoat and hat. She'd worn sandals and no socks. An odd woman.

Upstairs, his wife lay sleeping. In his study, he removed from his briefcase books and papers and the manuscript of his memoirs. He sat down at the desk and opened the manuscript and stared at his writing. Lackluster words lay heaped on the pages: dead leaves. Amid the words he saw a man dressed out of fashion, giving off the stench of morgue and carnage; spittled lips and a diabolic grin; a blizzard of ashes and vile coiling hair. He trembled, his heart thundering. A sound from the wall on which hung the framed headlines. The house did that at times: moaned and creaked and sighed. Through the window he saw the Tudor, all its windows lit.

A moment later—it seemed a mere instant—he was standing at the door of the Tudor, ringing the bell.

THE DOOR OPENED. SHE STOOD THERE, SMALL, face white, hair shoulder-length and blond, and smiled openly and warmly.

"Why, Benjamin. How nice."

"That cup of coffee you so kindly offered." His voice with a slight quiver in it; hesitant, vulnerable.

"Your wife?"

"She is in a deep sleep."

"You're sure?"

"The nurse gave her something."

"All right, then." She stepped back, opened the door wide, motioning him in. He stepped inside and heard the door close behind him.

"The kitchen is this way."

He followed her through an empty center hall with a curving carpeted stairway into a large octagon-shaped room. Walls bare; floors bare; not a chair or a table anywhere. Dull lights from naked oval-shaped bulbs in antique brazen wall sconces. Their feet on creaky oak planks.

"There's furniture on the way. But I can really make do without much furniture."

He thought of Evelyn's exquisite taste in furniture, and remembered the apartment of his childhood: heavy mahogany tables and chairs; horizontal hanging mirrors nearly as long as a wall; floor lamps with tasseled shades; upholstered sofa and easy chairs; blue oilcloth on the floors, white shades on the windows; the chicken, fish, potatoes, and vegetable soup smells in the kitchen. Of all things, why was he remembering the apartment? The dismal light. His father's penchant for low-wattage bulbs. Save money on electricity and spend it on more important things. Give an extra dollar or two to the teacher. The trope teacher.

They went through a dim hallway lined on one side with floor-to-ceiling dark-wood cabinets and entered the kitchen.

It was a drab space with old cherry-wood cabinets, a sink and refrigerator and stove that seemed of 1950s vintage, and an overhead light fixture that emitted a cheerless yellowish luminescence. A rectangular brown-wood table and four wooden chairs near a window. On the table two stacks of newspapers. In the sink a heap of dirty dishes.

Reddish tiles covered the floor; faded light-green paint on the walls. And the walls bare—not even a calendar.

He noticed immediately the large open writing pad and the black fountain pen on the table near the newspapers and stood watching as she quickly flipped the pad shut, smoothly scooped it up together with the pen, opened a cabinet drawer, slipped the pad and pen inside, and pushed the drawer shut.

"I've interrupted your writing."

"No, no, I hadn't begun."

"I'm so sorry. I should have called."

"No, really, it's all right. Please excuse the mess. I'm not the tidiest person. One of the things my husband always complained about—the lack of tidiness, I mean. His funeral business he kept very tidy. Well, now, coffee. I have, let's see, hazelnut, Irish cream, espresso, Swiss mocha. Regular and decaf."

"Espresso regular, please."

She busied herself at the sink. "Sit down, Benjamin. Relax. Push the newspapers to one side."

He sat at the table near a window that offered a view of the oaks and the woods. Looking to the right, he saw the gray fieldstone side of his house and the window of his study. He had left the lights on.

"You want a donut, Benjamin? I love donuts."

"Thank you." What am I doing here? Evelyn so sick and me in this woman's house. Keeps herself neat and trim. No doubt dyes her hair. Good-looking woman. Seems a different person when she writes. Puts on weight somehow:

window-glass distortion? But the gray hair. Didn't she just say something?

"Please excuse me, my mind was elsewhere."

"I asked, Benjamin, if you wanted a single or a double espresso. I'm having a double."

"A double for me too, please."

"Here we are. Two double espressos and two donuts."

She set down the tray and sat across from him, gliding lightly onto the chair. Her sudden close presence. Smooth cream-white face; long neck; the clear outline of her breasts beneath the jersey. Hungry, glittering eyes. Moist lips. He felt a momentary dizziness; heart pounding, palms sweating.

The coffee hot, black, bitter; the donut stickysweet.

"Are you all right, Benjamin?"

"A little faint."

"Can I do anything?"

"A slight vertigo. Comes and goes."

"You should see a doctor about that."

"Davita, I see many doctors. I have an illness of the bones, which medications deftly control."

"And the dizziness?"

"As I said, it comes and goes. Tell me something, Davita. During supper I read an essay on your work by a noted critic who marveled at your memory, which he called, if I remember correctly, 'the memory of a sealed well, filled with water and leaking nothing.' A quaint metaphor. How do you do that?"

"I can't presume to know what he means."

"I am encountering a great deal of difficulty remembering certain matters."

"For your scholarly writing?"

"For my memoirs."

She bit into a donut.

He sipped espresso. His fingers trembling slightly, the beginning of a headache. How strange! Inside the kitchen of I. D. Chandal, drinking espresso, eating donuts. The downed limb of a lightning-struck oak across his driveway. Huge and deadly pieces of wood strewn about his property. His wife in a drugged sleep. Newspapers on the table.

SARAJEVO CLASHES IMPERIL RELIEF EFFORT,
DRAW U.S. WARNING

LEADERS IN MUNICH WARN RIVAL FORCES
IN BOSNIAN STRIFE

The vertigo again. What year was this? He read:

PLAN TO TIGHTEN EMBARGO ON IRAQ
SUGGESTED BY U.S.

NUCLEAR ACCORDS BRING NEW FEARS
ON ARMS DISPOSAL

"You see, I have no idea how to continue. I have a book without a beginning."

She put down her cup, patted her lips with a napkin. She gazed at him guardedly, seeming to be calculating, measuring.

"Well, Benjamin, I start from the zero point of memory."

"The zero point?"

"From the very least bit of memory."

"I'm not sure—"

"From the involuntary memory that comes like a bolt out of the blue. From the memory that is your aura."

"My what? My aura?"

"Listen to me, Benjamin. When I say the word 'war,' what comes immediately into your mind?"

"I don't—"

"The word 'war,' Benjamin. *Immediately!*"

" 'Why?' "

"Why what?"

"The word 'why' comes to mind."

"And who speaks that word?"

He hesitated.

"*Who,* Benjamin?"

A wildly careering search. "An old teacher."

"What is he doing and saying, your old teacher?"

"I can't—"

"*What,* Benjamin?"

Still he hesitated.

"You'll excuse me, Benjamin, but I see in your face that you have a story to tell. So tell me the story, get down to your zero point of memory. Or call it a night, go back to your wife, and I'll get on with my work."

A desperate effort. "Let me try."

"Good. Another espresso? Another donut?"

WHY, I'D HEAR MY CLASSMATES ASK, DID MR. ISAAC Zapiski wear those dark clothes? Fall, winter, spring, and summer: dark double-breasted suit, dark wide-brimmed hat, dark wool coat in cold weather, dark high shoes, dark tie. He wasn't a rabbi; he wasn't even a teacher in our school. Their somber garb accorded well with their sober calling: the handing on of an ancient tradition. But, as far as we knew, Mr. Zapiski eked out a living solely from the teaching of trope. Why, then, the dark clothes?

And the same dark clothes at that. Weekdays, holy days, sabbaths, festivals—the same seedy suit, the same shabby coat, the same shabby hat. We were all poor—those were the ghastly years of the Great Depression—but each of our fathers owned at least two suits, two pairs of trousers, two shirts, two ties. And the same pair of high black shoes, scuffed, misshapen, bulging out at the toes and down at the heels—why did Mr. Zapiski own only one set of clothes and shoes?

And why did he walk moving his left foot forward in a shuffle and his right foot trailing? Shuffle and scrape, shuffle and scrape, an awkward drag-footed gait. A small, bumbling, stooped man who wore his hat low over his eyes and his jacket or coat collar up, his neck squeezed into his shoulders, looking to all intents and purposes like a turtle in the act of withdrawing into its shell. He had a habit of shaking his head in a sort of nervous twitch, jerking it from side to side, as if trying to disentangle himself from some web in which he had been caught. He didn't do that often, but when you saw it, it was frightening, because the pupils in his eyes would slide up to the top and all you saw was the white, and his lips would become flecked with spittle, and you were sure he was going to faint. But he never did, it only lasted some seconds and it was over, and he seemed never to remember what had happened.

In the corner store on our street, where he bought his newspaper, I'd see him sometimes counting out his money with shaking hands from the small black pocket purse he carried, the sort with the little metal knobs that snapped shut. I'd have come in on an errand for my parents and he'd acknowledge my presence with a nod and a cough—he had a nervous little cough, a kind of perpetual need to clear his throat—and he'd be standing there with his cane under one arm, slowly counting out his money. He smoked endlessly, with enormous intensity, holding the cigarettes between his thumb and forefinger and sucking in the smoke as if his life depended on it. He went about beneath a weight of darkness save for his short white beard and frayed white shirt.

I remember asking my mother, "How old is Mr. Zapiski?"

"Mr. Zapiski and your father were born two days apart."

"Why does he look so old?"

"He went through a great deal in the war."

In the winter my heart would go out to him whenever I saw him picking his way through the snow on our streets, stopping before a patch of ice or at a corner heaped with snow as if to muster the strength to venture forward, while the wind lashed at his hat and coat. Once in a storm I offered to help him and he took my hand. I felt his weight as we made our way across the street in the snow and, climbing to the opposite sidewalk, he slipped and we both went down, and his cry when he fell haunted my dreams.

Some of my classmates would mockingly imitate his hobbled walk, his rasping voice, the way his face would twitch as if it had a life of its own. Most were indifferent. We all knew that he would inevitably enter our lives at a certain time and become a sort of teacher to us for a period of months.

It was inevitable that someone like Mr. Zapiski would give rise to tales and rumors. All the talk about him seemed connected to the Great War. Some claimed he had once been a Bolshevik general. Others insisted that he had served as an officer in the army of Emperor Franz Josef of Austria. Still others swore that he'd been a secret agent of Kaiser Wilhelm; a machine-gunner in a Polish regiment of the Austrian army; a courier in Switzerland for Lenin.

To me he was the least likely person to have qualified as a great warrior. He seemed to have been born broken.

He was, as far as I could then tell, my father's closest friend. Friday evenings and Saturday afternoons he would eat at our table. Though he rarely spoke more than a few words to me or to my younger brother and sister, he seemed unquestionably a member of our family. I learned early on that he was the only one in his family who had left

Europe. All the others—parents, brothers, sisters, uncles, aunts, cousins—had chosen to remain behind, and for reasons I could not fathom were now unable to come to America. During our meals, there were often long periods of silence; when he and my father talked, nearly always in Yiddish—we talked Yiddish among ourselves, English on the streets—their conversation invariably turned to politics: labor strikes, socialism, communism, Roosevelt, Hitler, Stalin, Franco, Trotsky. In my presence they never spoke about the Great War. My mother served and sat in silence, listening, sighing from time to time as memories of her life in Europe returned to her.

None of the talk interested me. I'd play word games with my brother and finger-rope games with my sister. When I was young I often sat on Mr. Zapiski's lap; but, growing older, I found him discomfiting, and I came to dislike intensely the cigarette stench in his clothes and the yellow stains in the beard around his moist lips. His mouth emitted fetid vapors.

The years went by. Eventually the time came when I was to be given over to Mr. Zapiski.

"Listen to me," my father said after supper one evening when he and I were alone in the kitchen. "I am going to tell you something, and I don't ever want to hear from you that you didn't hear me say it. Mr. Zapiski and your father grew up in the same town in Europe. We served in the same regiment in the Great War. For months we lived in the same trenches. We ate together, slept together, fought together, and suffered together. No one can ever be closer to you than the soldiers with whom you shared a trench during a war. Mr. Zapiski is my closest and dearest friend. Do not let me hear from him that you are not learning everything that he is teaching you."

My father leaned forward across the kitchen table and put his fleshy features and dark eyes close to my face—and I had a clear image of him hunched over his worktable in the window of the shoe repair shop where he now labored as a repairer of clocks and watches, his sweaty balding head gleaming in the yellow light of his work lamp. How abruptly he had fallen from a successful dealer in antiques to an indigent fixer of timepieces!

And so I began, twice a week in the evenings, to walk from our apartment to Mr. Zapiski: a gauntlet of gritty Bronx streets. Old red-brick apartment houses; scrawny cats and emaciated dogs around the garbage cans in foul alleyways. Trucks and automobiles rattling past on the cobblestones. Rectangles of yellow light behind drawn shades and sometimes a partly dressed man or woman in a window, smoking a cigarette and looking down at me as I went by, a bony, too tall kid, walking very quickly even though this was my neighborhood and I need not have been frightened; but my mother's fears had somehow attached themselves to me, her real terrors were often my imagined ones. And under the elevated train and up the street past an enormous red-brick brewery, whose hot, pungent stench was the plague of our neighborhood.

Mr. Zapiski lived in an apartment house at the top of that steep, narrow cobblestone street. The heavy metal-

and-glass front door creaked as I pushed against it. I'd walk up four flights of badly lit marble stairs, voices and cooking smells—beef, cabbage, potatoes—drifting through the closed doors, and I'd cross the hall to a wooden door, one of six on that floor, and twirl the knob on the old doorbell, which made the lifeless noise of a clapper striking lead.

Through the door I'd hear his shuffling gait as he came along his hallway. "Who is there?" he'd say, and I'd respond, "Benjie Walter," and hear him pull back the bolt and unlock the door. His face would appear in the narrow space between the door and the jamb. "Go into the parlor," he'd say, and I'd pass through the dimly lit narrow apartment hallway, while behind me he'd busy himself locking and bolting the door. I'd go past his kitchen—invariably, dirty dishes in the sink, a teakettle on the stove, Yiddish newspapers on the table, and often roaches on the walls— and into the parlor. There I'd sit in an easy chair: upholstery worn and grimy to the touch, springs hard against my rump and spine, an odor of dust rising from the fabric.

The first time I went to him was a bitter-cold evening in late November. I was uneasy; my father's words still echoed in my head. We sat in silence for some while in the dimly lit kitchen, drinking the tea he set before us. On the table lay Yiddish and German newspapers. I had the sense I was going to be put through some sort of initiation rite.

"Tell me, Benjamin, these days what do you really like?"

I told him I liked baseball and movies.

He wore a tall black skullcap. His head was balding. I knew that under the skullcap a four-inch vertical scar and a two-inch horizontal scar ran across his head and inter-sected above the right temporal lobe. There were tiny pockmarks on the parts of his face not covered by the beard. His face was pale and gaunt, almost bloodless.

"You still like to read, Benjamin?"

"I like adventure stories, sea stories, war stories."

"Yes? Well, there are plenty of war stories in the Torah. And a big war story in the section you will learn to read."

That was all he said, though he kept glancing at me over the rim of his glass. He had pale-gray pupils and his eyes bulged somewhat in their sockets and were encircled by bluish shadows and webbed skin. Though I had known him for years, I understood that we were now entering upon a distinctly new relationship: I was no longer merely the son of his closest friend. He was about to become my teacher, I his student. A wall of unspoken expectations was rising between us; it would be my obligation to sur-mount it.

He slurped tea from his glass, coughed, and wiped his lips with a not-very-clean handkerchief. I counted four roaches on his kitchen walls before we were done with our tea. He put the glasses into the sink and told me to follow him.

In the doorway to Mr. Zapiski's parlor hung worn pur-ple portieres. On the windows were run-down curtains and shades. Cracked brown linoleum in the hallway; faded carpeting in the parlor; peeling light-green paint on the walls and ceilings. Books lay on end tables and chairs, some facedown and open. The walls were entirely bare, without even the traditional velvet picture of Jerusalem. He seemed to fit the tatterdemalion apartment perfectly: his dark clothes threadbare, his beard unkempt, his shoes cracked, with his right foot resting on the floor at an odd angle to the other.

He motioned to an easy chair and I removed two books and took the chair, feeling myself sink deep into the seat. The chair seemed to seize me like one of those flowers that snaps shut on unwary insects. He dropped down into the sofa, from which rose little tendrils of dust. He stretched his left leg out in front of him, leaned forward with a low grunt, placed both hands on the trousers of his right leg below the knee, and swung the leg up, then lowered it so that it lay limp across the left leg.

"Now you will begin to learn the trope," he said in his hoarse voice, and coughed. He lit a cigarette and tossed the match into an ashtray that was close to overflowing. "First, I will teach you the notes and the grammar of the notes. Then I will teach you the meaning behind the grammar. And if I see that you have truly mastered that, I will teach you the magic of this music, things few people know."

At that point, because I'd always been inclined to pry into matters that aroused my curiosity, I said, "Excuse me, is it permissible to ask a question?"

"Without questions there is no learning."

"Why do you have so many books about war in your apartment?"

In my world we sized up people by the books they read

and by the libraries in their homes. Walking through the hallway to the parlor, I'd noticed bookcases filled with volumes, in Yiddish and English, about the Great War.

His face twitched with annoyance. No doubt he'd expected a question about grammar and trope.

"Because I was in the war, and I am trying to understand it."

"What did you do in the war?"

"I was a soldier like your father."

I have no recollection why I put the next question to Mr. Zapiski. Remember, I was not yet thirteen years of age; why would anything about that distant war have remotely interested me? Overheard private conversations between Mr. Zapiski and my father, perhaps; or that curiosity of mine boiling over. The answer is lodged in deep memory to which I have at present no direct access. In any event, abruptly, for no clear reason, I heard myself ask Mr. Zapiski, "Whose side were you on?"

My query startled him. His pale features turned crimson. He did not answer for a moment. Then he asked, in a tremulous tone, "Why do you ask me that question?"

The word he used for "why" was "warum," which is both German and Yiddish. He pronounced it "varoom."

I told him I was just curious.

He said, after another silence, "Your father and I fought in the army of Emperor Franz Josef of Austria, on the side of Germany, against England, France, Russia, Italy, and America."

On the side of Germany! They had fought on the side of

the enemy! Was that something to worry about? It had never occurred to me that my father had fought against the United States. How had he and Mr. Zapiski managed to get into America if they had once fought against it? Perhaps they had been asked and had lied. What if the American government should ever find out? Would Mr. Zapiski and my father be sent back to Europe?

Mr. Zapiski stirred and coughed. His head shook briefly from side to side and the skullcap slid from it, revealing the two intersecting scars and the curls of thinning white hair on the nearly bald scalp. How could he and my father be the same age? They looked thirty years apart. The skullcap tumbled to his lap and he put it back on his head.

"Enough about that cursed war. That is not why you came here. Open the book and we will study what your father sent you to learn."

He began to chant the notes in his hoarse and rasping voice, and I followed along in the adolescent quavering that would after some years change into the baritone you now hear.

He taught, and I learned. The weeks passed.

Regularly, my father would test me and nod, satisfied by my progress.

All that winter I trudged through snowstorms and frozen streets and studied trope with a man who had fought against my country in the Great War.

He drilled me in the complicated grammar of the sacred writings: long and short vowels; open and closed syllables; soft and hard dots of emphasis; the reasons for the placement of primary and secondary accents; the meticulous rhythms and trills of the musical notations. To grind the grammar and the music into memory, I'd walk home from Mr. Zapiski singing into the icy winds of the winter, and in the darkness of my small room I'd repeat to myself rules of grammar and take apart and put together lengthy verses of sacred text. He taught me the music of the book written by the Creator God. I am not now a believer, but I was then, and felt certain that I was learning the music chanted by God Himself whenever He opened the pages of the sacred narrative. And the angels, too, used that melody each time they told that story to one another. So Mr. Zapiski informed me one evening. Sweetly the celestial choir sang the sacred trope, and the music ascended through all the heavens and reached to the seventh heaven wherein was the Throne of Glory on which sat the Creator God, and the Creator God would hear the chanting and be transported with joy, and the joy would overflow and drift downward from the Divine Presence, down like an invisible benevolent rain through all the lower heavens and the fiery stars to our troubled Earth, and brush humankind with its radiance, and for a time there would be peace in the world and an abundance of happiness.

Often, about halfway through our hour, he would drop off into sleep. It was a strange and fearful thing to see: one moment he'd be wide awake, the next his head rolled forward onto his chest. He seemed then a helpless rag doll of a man. Wrinkled dark pants and jacket; stained white shirt, disheveled white beard; pale pockmarked features; the bad leg lying on top of the good one as if it needed more than the floor for support. Perhaps he slipped into a trance of some sort, the way his eyes were open to slits with only the whites showing; the occasional twitching of his face as he slept; and sometimes a low, deep snoring. None of my classmates ever saw him like that; they studied with him only in the school, during recess or after classes, where he would never fall asleep. I was the only one he taught in his apartment, because of his friendship with my father.

The first time it happened I sat frightened until he woke. Then I realized he would sleep about fifteen minutes each time. I began to use those minutes to browse through his books about the Great War.

Most were too difficult for me to understand. Some were in languages other than English and Yiddish and had horrendous pictures of blasted trees and fragments of human bodies and torn-up trenches and ravaged countrysides in which nothing remained except the sky. As a result, I began to have dreams of Mr. Zapiski and waves of faceless men climbing out of their trenches and attacking over duckboards laid across knee-deep mud and machine guns rattling and cutting them down like scythes leveling fields of wheat and rye.

One day in January I asked my mother, "What happened to Mr. Zapiski during the war?"

She said, not looking up from the kitchen sink where she was peeling potatoes, "About such matters, you speak to your father."

"Can it happen to me if I fight in a war?"

"Pooh pooh pooh! Don't say such things. Go talk to your father."

I asked my father.

His angry response startled me. "You little snotnose, why do you keep poking into matters that are not your concern? Turn your curiosity to more important matters. Your business is to learn Torah."

Standing before Mr. Zapiski's door one night in early February, I set down the bag of food my mother had told me to take to him and wondered how he climbed all those stairs. He must exhaust himself. No wonder he slept during the trope lessons.

And indeed he fell asleep that night and I turned to his books and opened a volume of photographs on the war between Austria and Russia and was leafing through it when he woke suddenly from his trancelike state and without preliminaries proceeded to speak to a point in the air behind me. He said, speaking rapidly in Yiddish, "Hear me out on this, Victor. I want you to hear me out. Not everything that sounds like music is truly music." There was a wildness in his eyes, a hollowness to his voice, as if some unbridled creature were speaking from inside him. "The tyrant Phalaris roasted his prisoners in a huge bronze bull, in whose nostrils he had his servants place reeds in such a way that the prisoners' shrieks were transformed into music. The sounds came out as music, but were they indeed music?"

There was a pause, a resonating silence.

"What do you think of that, Victor?"

I sat stupefied.

"Victor, what do you think?" he asked again, staring into the air behind my head and speaking now in a reasonable tone that was somehow more frightening than the previous wildness.

I didn't know what to do or say and thought of getting up and running from there, but just then his head dropped forward onto his chest, and after two or three deep, snorting breaths he was again asleep.

Frightened and bewildered, I went quickly on tiptoe and left the apartment, my ears reverberating with the imagined screams of those burning captives. I asked myself: Should I tell my father what happened? I didn't want to embarrass Mr. Zapiski. Besides, it would make no difference, certainly the lessons would not come to an end merely because Mr. Zapiski had experienced a bad dream in my presence. Also, in truth, I rather liked the lessons, I savored being with Mr. Zapiski, I was as intrigued by his strange behavior as I was by his books on the Great War. Indeed, as I hurried past the brewery and under the trestle of the elevated train, massive and monstrous in the night, I realized that much of my revulsion toward Mr. Zapiski had left me, and in its place had come an irresistible curiosity. Who was he? How could I find out more about him? And at that moment I sensed someone walking behind me, and I looked quickly around but saw no one.

At home that night I asked my father, "Was Mr. Zapiski a teacher in Europe?"

"In Europe Mr. Zapiski was both a teacher and a student."

"Where did he go to school?"

"In a university in Vienna."

"What did he study?"

"He studied history. Then history caught up with him. What did he teach you tonight?"

I told him.

"That was all he taught you?"

"He was tired and not feeling well."

My father, his face stiff, turned away.

Some days later I brought Mr. Zapiski a copy of my bar mitzvah speech, which I had carefully researched and written over a period of three weeks. This, my first public address, I was to deliver before the assembled throng of celebrating relatives, friends, teachers, and classmates as an example of my maturity in years and proficiency in learning.

"I want us all to be proud of you," my mother had said, watching me labor over the talk. "That's all I ask."

I read the talk to Mr. Zapiski.

"WELL, MY DEAR DAVITA, I DO HOPE I AM NOT boring you. I must tell you that many of the details of this story have been entirely forgotten by me until now, hence the story may lack the refinement of narrative and no doubt has thus far some dull and trying moments to it. But please accept my assurance that you will be recompensed, if memory serves, by what is soon to follow. In the meantime, I must use your toilet. I shall only be a moment."

"WHERE WAS I? AH, YES. THE TALK I HAD WRITTEN and was now reading to Mr. Zapiski. Indeed, a refill on the coffee will be appreciated.

"First, three or four sentences by way of introduction.

"My *rite de passage* was to fall on the Saturday morning when the biblical portion that is read aloud from the sacred Scroll of the Law deals with the war waged by Amalek against the fleeing Israelite slaves. Joshua organized the Israelite troops and fought off the Amalekites, aided by Moses, whose arms, raised heavenward, brought about the help of the Lord and spurred the Israelites on to victory.

"My little talk was about loyalty in war."

I SAT SUNK DEEP IN THE TATTERED EASY CHAIR AND read in a shaking voice a brief essay, which—how astonishing!—I think I will now be able to recall in detail. I began by asking: Why do people wage war? Would people kill and let themselves be killed unless there was a very convincing reason for doing so? If conquest is the only reason for a war, conquest from which only the ruler stands to gain, then people should refuse to fight. If, however, a war is to be fought for the defense of one's family and property, then men should fight with all their heart and might. The war against the Amalekites was a war of defense. In such a war, *all* must participate; no one has the right to refrain from taking part. And the cowards and deserters, all who would benefit from the courage of the brave, they have no right to share in the victory, and should be punished. Deserters most especially should be punished, because they run away in the face of danger, they leave it to others to fight and perhaps die in their place, they are the lowest of men, they—

My little talk, I must tell you, contained a splendid array of proof texts from sources both sacred and secular, over which I had labored long and hard. But that was as far as I got with it. For a sound had begun to emanate from Mr. Zapiski, a noise that sounded like *"What? What? What?"* in Yiddish, and I looked up and saw that his normally pallid features had turned crimson, and a blood vessel had risen and lay like a vertical ridge along the center of his forehead.

"What are you saying?" he shouted.

I stared at him.

"Who told you this? Surely not your father or mother!"

I hadn't the vaguest idea what he was talking about.

He leaned stiffly toward me and winced with pain as his hand inadvertently struck the knee of his right leg. The pain seemed to make him angrier still. I thought he might suffer a stroke and die of rage; I had heard about such things. He rubbed the knee, grasped the trouser with both hands, raised the leg so that it hung a moment suspended, lowered it onto the left leg, adjusted it. He took a deep, tremulous breath.

"Why did you choose this subject, eh? Is this what you intend to tell the people who will come together to celebrate your entering into adulthood? *This?* What do you know about it? Go fight in a war, God forbid, and then see what speeches you make. It isn't enough that your father suffered the way he did? Why must you now add to it with your cruel words?"

He fell silent, breathing heavily, glaring at me out of swollen eyes. He coughed and wiped his sweating face with a ragged handkerchief. The chair, the air, the room, the rage—I felt myself being stifled.

In a trembling voice I told him I did not understand what I had done wrong.

That seemed to infuriate him even more. "Don't play the ignorant innocent with me, you smart aleck! I know you. I see right through you. Nothing escapes you. You want to wage war against your father, do it another way. Erase those sentences from your talk!"

"Which sentences?"

"I told you not to play the dummy with me! You should know that I was once a candidate for a doctoral degree in a great European university."

"But I don't know which—"

"Read it quietly to yourself and then read it to me again!"

I stared at my notebook, swiftly searching through the talk. Which words was I to omit?

And here, Davita, we come to a moment of memory that is still unclear to me. Hastily scanning my words, I decided to drop all mention of desertion, and I cannot remember why I did that—perhaps because it was the only part of the talk that had come from my own being. Everything else I'd borrowed from other sources.

I read the talk once again to Mr. Zapiski. It seemed a shadow of its former version, the heart gone from it. Mr. Zapiski listened intently. He took deep breaths, he grew calm, he wiped his face and lips, he nodded approval. Then he lit another cigarette and ordered me to repeat by heart some matters of grammar—and promptly fell asleep.

I removed the cigarette from his fingers and stubbed it out in the ashtray on the end table. I had no stomach that night for books about war. Silently, I slipped out of the apartment and started home in the winter night and, as I hurried past the brewery, suddenly sensed alongside me a terrifying presence that set my knees shaking and prickled my skin, but, turning, I saw only the vacant street and patches of snow yellow-lit from the streetlamps.

A night of dread and sleeplessness followed. I tossed, I turned. I stared wide-eyed into the darkness and heard Mr. Zapiski saying, "*What? What? What?*" I gazed out my window at the concrete back yard and saw Mr. Zapiski in its deepest shadows. Why had he become so incensed? Had someone close to him deserted during the Great War? I'd read in one of his books that deserters, when apprehended, were executed. Perhaps *he* had deserted? Suppose—my agitated heart churned out the fearful possibilities—suppose he had bolted from his guard post in the trenches one night and my father had furtively gone after him and brought him back? Or maybe, just maybe, *it was my father who had deserted,* and Mr. Zapinski had forced *him* back—and on returning had been badly wounded by an exploding shell? Would that account for his missing leg, the marks on his face, the scars on his head, his wretched health, his grown-old look?

And then a horrifying thought occurred to me. What if my father had indeed been a deserter? And what if the American government ever discovered that he'd fought on the enemy side and determined to send him back to his old country, would he then be executed for desertion?

Fear-ridden days and nights followed. I grew irritable, couldn't eat, lost weight. My mother became concerned, kept glancing at me with worry in her eyes. I began to wonder if one day a newspaper headline might announce the presence in America of soldiers who had fought on the German side in the Great War. ENEMIES DISCOVERED IN OUR MIDST. Would the entire family be sent back? I found myself cringing at the sight of the newspapers on our kitchen table, dreaded looking at the headlines. I would not go into our kitchen or living room when I saw my father there reading his newspaper. Once I spotted a crumpled newspaper in our garbage can and thought I saw the words "Great War" in a headline and removed it with trembling hands and straightened it out on the table and saw with relief that it had nothing to do with the enemies of America but was about a statesman who was predicting another great war, one much more terrible than the Great War itself.

One evening during that awful time, I climbed the stairs to Mr. Zapiski's apartment, carrying the usual shopping bag of food, and found a note on the doorbell that read, "Benjamin, I am sick. The door is open. Please put the food in the icebox and return in two days."

Yielding to my diffident push, the door opened wide and I stepped inside.

How stifling the apartment was—a steamy inferno of radiator heat. The wooden floor of the hallway groaned; the linoleum wobbled and buckled. In the kitchen food-encrusted pots and dishes cluttered the counter and filled the sink, and old newspapers lay on the table and chairs. Roaches rushed crazily across the floor and walls and vanished into drawers and appliances. I imagined rats moving stealthily in the spaces between the walls.

I put the food in the icebox—a nearly vacant and malodorous white cavern—and had turned to leave when I heard a cry from beyond the portieres that separated the hallway from the rest of the apartment. Someone had called my name in a high-pitched voice I could not recognize.

I stood terrified.

The voice called to me again. "Benjamin, is that you?"

It was Mr. Zapiski.

"Yes."

"Come here and help me!"

I rushed through the hallway into the parlor. There, with windows sealed and shades drawn, the air was even more stifling than in the kitchen.

"Where are you?"

"I am in the bedroom."

I hurried across the parlor, bumping my knee painfully against an end table, and cautiously entered the bedroom.

It was a small room, with pale-green walls. A yellowing shade covered the single window. The stagnant air carried scents of medicine and camphor. I saw an old wooden chair, a narrow bed, a worn carpet, an old bureau with a mirror that stood tilted to the right. The room in the mirror looked oddly distended, a grotesque funhouse reflection, walls bare of pictures. Mr. Zapiski lay in the bed beneath a shabby gray blanket, his tall skullcap on his head. On the night table next to the bed were some books and bottles of medication. He lay on a crumpled white pillow, looking forlorn and gasping for breath.

"Benjamin, be so good as to go to the medicine cabinet in the bathroom and bring me the bottle with the red label."

That I did quickly. With a shaking hand, he poured the liquid into a teaspoon, swallowed it down, and lay back on the pillow. I stood staring at him and found that I couldn't take my eyes off the space in the bed where his right leg should have been but that lay flat beneath the blanket alongside the rise of the left leg.

Some minutes passed and his breathing eased. I had in the meanwhile looked about the room and noticed at the side of the bed his wooden right leg and stared in fascination at the length of wood and the misshapen dark shoe attached to it.

"Benjamin."

I took my eyes from the leg on the floor.

"Tell your father that I fell in the snow and am hurt."

I nodded.

"Benjamin."

He was propping himself up with his arms. The empty space where his right leg should have been gave him the look of half a man.

"Be so good as to give me my leg."

I hesitated.

"It's on the floor next to the bed."

I bent and picked up the leg. An assemblage of wood, straps, grooves. Strangely cold to the touch despite the overheated room. And heavy, awkward. Holding it made my skin crawl.

He took the leg. Straps dangled awfully in the air.

"Now go home, Benjamin, and return in two days knowing backwards and forwards the rules I asked you to memorize."

I started for the bedroom door.

"Benjamin."

I stopped and turned. He was still sitting up, clutching the wooden leg with both hands.

"If there are any books you want to read, you may take them with you."

My face turned hot. I hurried through the apartment without taking any of his books and left the building. The night was bitter cold. As I passed under the trestle a train roared by overhead, its lights flickering and flashing through the darkness, and I thought I heard over the rhythmic click and clatter of its wheels a high-pitched wail like that of a child crying. But there was no one else in the street.

When I told my father that Mr. Zapiski was ill, he put on his overcoat and hat and rushed out of the apartment.

And now for the conclusion. A grand success it turned out to be, my *rite de passage*. My mother, proud. My father, accepting as his due the congratulations of our clan. My siblings, jealous. My classmates, envious of my ease with text and talk. My teachers, all lavish with praise. Myself, a light-headed turmoil of emotions: pride, joy, smugness, and exultation, as if victorious in—in what? Is this what it's like to be triumphant in war, I asked myself at one point that day, this climbing soaring surging explosion of emotion? Then what is it like to lose, to be among the permanently wounded, the hopelessly defeated?

As for Mr. Zapiski, he congratulated me, and that pleased me more than the praise of all the others. My anxiety about whose side he and my father had fought on during the Great War soon faded. My mother sent me to him regularly with packages of food, and sometimes my father handed me envelopes with money to give him; but we rarely talked. On occasion he would offer me a book from his library, which I'd return unread. I had discovered other interests: sports, girls. My winter with Mr. Zapiski became an increasingly remote interlude. I had mastered a melody and a grammar that I now put to regular use, for my father insisted that I read periodically from the Scroll of the Law during services in our little synagogue. I turned into an accomplished reader. People who babbled regularly during prayer would fall silent as I chanted. I became quite adept at dramatizing events like the Creation, the Flood, the binding of Isaac, the Exodus from Egypt. I developed a distinctive panache when it came to reading aloud about the various wars fought by the Israelites during their desert wandering, and in particular the Song of the Sea, which celebrates the drowning of Pharaoh and his army as they pursued the Israelites through the Red Sea. Mr. Zapiski came over to me one day and thanked me for the way I had read the section on the war against the Amalekites. He looked pale, shaky. His eyes were moist. He seemed shabbier than ever.

And then one evening my father announced at our supper table that Mr. Zapiski was returning to Europe.

I was stunned.

Day after day, from the radio and the newspapers, all we heard from Europe was the lunacy of approaching war.

"Why?" I asked.

"He wishes to return to the history he left behind," said my father, with anger in his voice.

I stared at him in bewilderment.

My mother nodded sadly, as if she understood.

The next day I went to see Mr. Zapiski in his apartment.

About two years had passed since my last lesson. Nothing had changed inside those dim and airless rooms. The creaking linoleum, the worn furniture, the shabby rug, the shelves upon shelves of books about war. He welcomed me in his hoarse voice and brought me into the parlor and ordered me into the chair with the encompassing seat and protruding springs that I once again felt upon my rump and spine.

"Your mother did not give you anything for me?"

"My mother doesn't know I'm here."

He coughed. "Does your father know you are here?"

"No."

"What is the reason for the secrecy?"

"Is it true that you are going back to Europe?"

He shifted his right leg slightly. "And what business is that of yours?"

I said I was curious.

"Your father has already told you that I am going back. Why do you ask me if I am going back if you already know that I am going back?"

"I wanted to be sure."

"You wanted to be sure. Why is it important for you to be sure that I am returning to Europe? What do you care what happens to Isaac Zapiski?"

I mumbled a response I can no longer recall.

He was silent awhile. Then he coughed and said, "I see you in the synagogue and in your home, but we never talk. Tell me what you are doing."

"I go to school, I do sports."

"Your grades are good?"

"Pretty good."

"I'm sure they are. What sports do you like?"

"Swimming, running, basketball."

"What do you like to read?"

"Sherlock Holmes. Books about detectives and stuff."

"You no longer read my books about war."

"I don't like war and I don't like history."

He sighed. "This America of yours is not a country that values history. Where I was raised, history was the heart and marrow of a person. I am returning to the inside of myself that the war forced me to leave behind."

I've cited precisely what he said: "I am returning to the inside of myself."

Then, abruptly, he asked me to leave. He was tired, his leg hurt, he had things to do the following day.

The night before his departure he huddled with my parents in their bedroom, and I heard their voices raised in anger. My mother said repeatedly, "Isaac, Isaac," and my father seemed beside himself, but they were speaking Polish and I understood nothing.

When they emerged from the bedroom, Mr. Zapiski patted my cheek with a trembling hand, mumbled some words of farewell, coughed, and hurried out, accompanied by my father, who was in the blackest of moods. My mother choked back tears.

The next day he sailed for Europe.

Weeks went by.

A letter arrived. Mr. Zapiski was in Vienna.

I asked my father, "Why is Mr. Zapiski in Vienna?"

"He is trying to get into the university."

"Will they accept him?"

"Of course not. Austria hates Jews more than Germany does, if such a thing is conceivable."

"Did you save Mr. Zapiski's life during the war?"

"Whatever gave you that idea?"

"Did he save yours?"

"He gave me his mask during a surprise gas attack and went to find one for himself but was a minute or two late."

"How did he lose his leg?"

"When I was carrying him to the aid station a shell landed near us."

"Was he deserting?"

"What?"

"Was he planning to desert?"

"Where do you get these crazy ideas?" But why the sudden nervous glance at the door and window? And the lowered voice like a reflex, and the abrupt, "Enough curiosity, go do your homework." He was silent for a moment, looking at me through narrowed eyes. "Listen, I'll tell you what I told you already. You can't begin to understand how war binds soldiers together. Only soldiers grasp that. May you never know from it."

"But why did he go back? Won't there be another war?"

"He would rather be there in war than here in peace. He went back to catch up to himself."

I didn't understand that but felt it might be best to stop asking questions about Mr. Zapiski. A few weeks later, my father announced during supper that the new store he had recently opened was doing well and we would soon be moving to a larger apartment a few blocks away, in a house across from a park. In our language, "a few blocks away" often meant another world.

We would make good use of the added wall space in the new apartment, my father added.

"For what?" I asked.

"For the books."

"Which books?"

"Mr. Zapiski's books."

Mr. Zapiski, it turned out, had left his entire library in my father's care.

A month after we moved, Germany invaded Poland and the war broke out. We stopped receiving mail from Mr. Zapiski. As time went by and it became clear we might never hear from him again, he literally began to haunt me. Oh, yes, in the old-fashioned way, like a ghost of sorts. I would think of him, see him quite clearly in a waking vision or a dream, wonder if he was still alive, ask myself if he would have appreciated the way I had read trope that morning in the synagogue. With the entire world now at war, I began to read some of the books he had given my father. How orderly they stood on the new shelves in the hallway and eastern wall of the living room in our sunlit apartment. My mother had dusted them; indeed, had insisted on doing the task herself, turning away the help offered by me and my sister. "Go, you do your homework, and I'll do this." She labored with light shining from her eyes and memories softening the lines on her face. And so, as I read the books, there was no dust in the bindings and the mustiness was gone. I read books in English and Yiddish, books about the causes, tactics, military operations, and statistics of the Great War; books by and about generals, politicians, ordinary soldiers; books of memoirs and diaries. Why was I so captivated by those books? A youngster beguiled by the gallantry of war? A sudden necessary tethering to the trope teacher? Why? Crucial connections fail me here. There were two English books that I read with absorption, though not with full understanding, during my last year in a Jewish parochial high school: *Anti-Semitism Yesterday and Tomorrow* by Rabbi Lee J. Levinger, and *Anti-Semitism Throughout the Ages* by Count Heinrich Coudenhove-Kalergi. In all my years with my parents, my teachers, my friends, and the trope teacher, no one had ever really taught me about anti-Semitism, no one had sat me down and said: Listen, the world hates us because they say we killed their god; they say we are in league with the devil to destroy the Christian religion; they say we poisoned wells, we murdered Christian babies and used their blood to bake matzos, we loaned money to poor people at very high interest, we've been punished by God and made to wander eternally across the face of the earth.

In the book by the rabbi I read:

> The German Jews considered themselves good Germans; they wanted nothing else; they volunteered for service in the World War, were deeply grateful and proud of their recently given civil rights. Of all the discriminations of the Nazi regime the one they resent most deeply is the exemption from the military draft, which converts them into second-class citizens.

In the book by the count I read:

> For nearly twenty centuries the Jews have been disarmed and ever since they have not been the subjects

of war but its objects. They can no longer conquer through war, but suffer through it.

And I read:

For the sake of their faith the Jews have waged a world-war against the whole of Europe for twenty centuries, and they have acquired the right to consider themselves as an heroic nation of the first rank. All just men are bound to admit this, for war and fight are two very different things. Besides, wars are not the only touchstones of bravery. To most men it will appear easier to go out to war than to cling to their convictions in front of the stake.

And I saw illustrations of Jews in the fifteenth century wearing Jew badges; a medieval ghetto set on fire by a mob; Jews before the tribunal of the Inquisition; a synagogue in Palestine looted by Arabs; a middle-aged, balding Jew forced to walk the streets of a Nazi city, wearing a sign that said *Ich bin Jude;* he looked a little like Mr. Zapiski. Was that the world to which Mr. Zapiski had returned? What a confusion rose in me upon reading those two books! And immediately upon graduating from high school, I enlisted in the army. Oh, yes, I could have applied to a rabbinical school and received a draft deferment; or, failing that, waited to be drafted; it might have given me added months with my family. But I was a little berserk by then, decidedly out of control, in flaring rebellion against my parochial-school world, which I felt stifling me, and bloated with manly visions of fighting the armies of Hitler. And also, somewhere along the margin of my thoughts and feelings, was the insane notion that in Europe I might meet Mr. Zapiski! My decision to enlist in the army was met with grim and silent resignation from my father and a cry of dread from my mother. And from then on Mr. Zapiski became a sort of talisman to me—a creature of magic and enchantment. But that, Davita, is another story. Thank you for the coffee and donuts. I must now bid you good night and look in upon my wife.

BENJAMIN WALTER RETURNED HOME, CLIMBED THE stairs, and found his wife asleep. She awakened some time later, sweating and shivering, and he tended to her.

When the coughing subsided, she could speak again. "Is it very difficult for you, Benjamin?"

"I do love you, Evelyn."

"If things become very bad—"

"My darling—"

"—you should get a night nurse."

"Things need not become bad for quite a while. You'll come round this time as you did before."

"But if things do, Benjamin."

"You are going on about it a bit much, my dear."

"Am I? All right. My mind keeps jumping back and forth. Earlier, I was remembering our week in Prague."

"Isn't it strenuous for you to talk?"

"Yes. But I'll talk anyway. How remarkable."

"What?"

"I remember those Peruvian street musicians in front of our hotel on the square."

"Oh, yes, those musicians."

"Their red headbands and red-and-black ponchos and their guitars and little drums and odd wind instruments and the Indian music they played."

"They kept us awake until three in the morning."

"And remember those booths selling Russian military caps and medals? Such an inglorious end to that awful empire."

"Perhaps you shouldn't talk, my dear."

"Wasn't it in that lovely restaurant, not far from the little house where Kafka once lived, that I was terribly ill for the first time?"

"You're tiring yourself."

"Was I coughing then?"

"The coughing began in Amsterdam."

"Those Prague doctors hadn't a clue as to what was the matter, did they? The thrush on my tongue, the seborrhea in my eyebrows. Imagine, all of them leaving the hospital at one o'clock in the afternoon and going home for the day, and locking the patients in their rooms. A quite inefficient system, don't you think? One wonders what they saw in it for so many years."

"Countries get sidetracked, just as people do."

"I suppose. Do you think you might wipe my face?"

"Of course."

She said, after a brief while, "I find that I miss the children."

"Shall I ask them to come? They'll come immediately."

"Do you want them to?"

"I think not."

"You are in no mood for sentimentality. Am I right, Benjamin?"

"I don't want to share you with anyone else now."

"In some ways, you are more English than I am. Or at least you play at it well."

He was quiet.

She said, "How my mind jumps about. Do you know what I'm remembering? The song I made up and sang to you the second or third night you asked me out."

She sang weakly to a familiar tune:

> *Oh, when you Yanks came marching in,*
> *You mucked our language, drank our gin;*
> *You wooed our girls, and all the while*
> *You gave your lives for the English isle.*

He listened and was quiet. And then said, "You were the best thing that happened to me in the army. You were my very dearest friend."

She murmured, "I would so very much like to complete my book on Virginia Woolf. Do you think I might live long enough to accomplish that? Do leave me alone now, Benjamin. I am so bloody, bloody tired."

And she closed her eyes.

Now he sat gazing out his study window at I. D. Chandal, who was at a window of her kitchen, wearing a pale-blue housecoat and half-moon eyeglasses. She sat at a table, writing intently and looking preposterously bloated, the yellow light falling cruelly upon her pudgy features and gray hair. A trick of the light? Fatigue? The medication affecting my vision?

After a long moment he felt himself a voyeur and looked away.

The next morning he emerged from the house and walked to the edge of the woods, where he gazed up into the branches and leaves of the huge oak: green and blue shadows and the golden wash of early sunlight and the stunned faltering aftermath of a serious wounding. Lightning, he remembered, traveled at one-third the speed of light; its force at the point of impact quite unimaginable. The lightning bolt had struck the oak, seared the crown, spiraled downward along the contour of the trunk, and cut deeply into the bark, sending chips and huge slabs of wood flying in all directions. He shivered, having suddenly remembered a battlefield bombardment. But the smell was different here.

He turned away.

I. D. Chandal stood near her newly turned patch of soil, at a small bed of firethorns, trowel in hand, watching him. She wore her tight jeans and jersey. Small, trim, clear-eyed, cheerful.

"Quite a night in my kitchen, Benjamin."

"The coffee and donuts were splendid."

"You'll finish telling me your story?"

"Oh, yes."

"Then I'll get us some more donuts for tonight."

Her lips shaped a buoyant smile. She looked at the oak. "You'll need a tree surgeon. I know someone."

"Please ask him to clear away the debris but do nothing to the tree until I talk to him. Oh, yes, and ask him to check the woods for a ram."

She stood watching as he went to the garage and slid his lean frame into the old Saab, started the engine, and backed slowly down the driveway. Just before his rear tires reached the street he caught a glimpse of her through his front window standing on the lawn and staring up at the stricken tree, and was chilled by the look of rage he saw on her face. A fury so palpable he thought he heard her shouting. Angry at whom? At what? A very strange woman. Standing there at the edge of the woods with a trowel in her hand, and apparently screaming. Perhaps calling for the ram?

3

THAT NIGHT HIS WIFE WOKE AND HE CALMED her and brought her a fresh nightgown and changed her pillowcase and sheets. Later he sat working on his memoirs and from time to time turned to gaze at I. D. Chandal in a second-floor window of the Tudor. An odd-looking creature when she sits writing. Some kind of biological anomaly? An alteration in her body chemistry? Absurd! More likely a poorly manufactured windowpane.

In the morning he left the house and, striding past the stricken oak, entered the woods. Two or three times a week he took a walk through the woods to the cemetery. Cool bluish pools of shade that morning; a cloying moisture in the air; the crowns kindled to golden light by the sun. East of the woods lay the cemetery, stately acres of green meadow rising gracefully to a mound at the far end, on which had been built the mausoleum of a noted local family, one of whose sons, William Henry Bullock, had perished at Winfrey field in the battle of Chickamauga during the Civil War, and another, Robert William Bullock, in the Ardennes Forest during the last German offensive of the Second World War; the garrulous real estate agent had delivered the somber details in response to Benjamin Walter's probing. Near the edge of the cemetery, he stopped and stood gazing at the length of sunlit meadow. Insect life in the air and the rich scent of warming grass. Rows of stones: many old, weathered, leaning; others polished, straight, names and dates still clear. Generations of life, casualties of battles fought as far back as the Revolutionary War, and many children; but most appeared to have lived the conventional span of years. He returned after a while, walking slowly through sun-spangled shade along the leafy, unexhausted earth and the tangled roots. How calming, these woods; trees living and dying as nature intended.

Later that morning he sat in his university office reading

the manuscript of the memoirs. After a while he rang for his secretary. She stood before him, a dark-haired woman in her early forties. He handed her the manuscript, wishing to be rid of it for a time.

"It's an early draft of the first chapter. You may run into some blurry patches here and there."

"Professor Walter, have I ever had any trouble reading your handwriting?"

After she left he sat gazing out the window at the trees. There was a knock on the door.

A young man stood uneasily in the doorway, dressed in a dark suit, a white shirt, a dark tie. Handsome and muscular; long blond hair gathered in a ponytail, the lobe of one ear ornamented with a gold ring. He remained in the doorway, awkward and hesitant, then stepped into the office and closed the door.

"I just got back," he said in a low voice.

"I beg your pardon?"

"The funeral was yesterday."

Benjamin Walter suddenly remembered: Yale. Someone sick. "My sympathies."

The young man jammed his hands into the pockets of his trousers, hunched his shoulders. "I can't believe he's dead."

"I'm very sorry."

"He used to get depressed. They'd give him pills so he could stay level, but it made him sleepy and he couldn't do his work. Whenever he went off the pills he just, like, well, folded up into himself. He was a really great guy, good family, never did drugs, worried about AIDS, wouldn't screw around, just me and him, okay? And two days ago he flew back home, walked over to the bridge near his house, and stepped off. Two women saw him. He climbed up on the rail and just stepped off."

A suicide, thought Benjamin Walter, and suddenly recalled his years at Oxford, where one student jumped out of a fourth-floor window and another took cyanide crystals. He'd read Dante one spring and remembered now the passage on the Seventh Circle of Hell. The Woods of the Suicides. Their souls encased in the thorny trees; the leaves being devoured by the frightful Harpies. As the Harpies ate, blood poured out of the suicides' wounds, which enabled the souls in the trees to speak. The souls within the trees speaking only as the blood of the suicides gushed forth! Like Mr. Zapiski's shrill tale of the treatment of prisoners by the tyrant Phalaris: roasting them alive inside that huge bronze bull. The screams of the prisoners turning to music; the blood of the suicides turning to speech. Connections?

Listen to him, this sad young man, he seems unable to stop talking.

"Once I found him in his room with a loaded gun between his legs. His father's gun. I talked him into putting it away and didn't tell anyone about it. I'd go up to Yale some weekends and we'd hang out and he'd ask me to watch out for him if he ever had too much to drink. The signal that he was drunk was when he started to sing, 'Whiskey after beer, have no fear. Beer after whiskey, mighty risky.' Sometimes when he'd come out of one of his depressions, he'd think he could dodge bullets. I had to watch him real close then. I loved him, and he just walked off the bridge, like he thought he could fly."

Benjamin Walter felt pain in his fingers and saw himself tumbling head over heels toward a forest very far below. Tall trees waiting.

"You know, this is the third person I've gone to high school with who's committed suicide. Something out there is killing my friends."

"There are people here who can help you."

He shuffled his feet, blinked. "I'm ready for the exam."

"I beg your pardon?"

"You said you'd give me a makeup exam."

"Perhaps you should wait a day or two."

The young man removed his hands from his pockets and fixed his eyes upon a point behind the head of Benjamin Walter. "Allan, you sonofabitch!" he suddenly roared. "You were my best friend! Why'd you do that? You said you'd never do that!" His shouted words reverberated inside the office. He choked back a cry. "Sorry, sorry, it's making me a little crazy." He turned and strode out of the room, closing the door.

Benjamin Walter stood staring at the door. He thrust his hands under his armpits to still their trembling. Assaulted by a rush of images: Evelyn in her bed and I. D. Chandal at the window and the newly turned earth of the garden and the scarred oak and the eerie sounds of voices from afar and a uniformed man lunging at him with a bayonet. A shadow fell across the window. When he looked he saw only the cool blue sky and sunlight on the spring trees.

HE LUNCHED WITH ROBERT HELMAN IN A SMALL second-floor restaurant near the university, staring without appetite at the feta cheese in his Greek salad. Robert Helman, in a gray tweed jacket, red bow tie, and dark rumpled slacks, sat over his vegetable soup, looking fretful and displeased.

"You seem tired, Benjamin. Is it Evelyn?"

"Actually, I expect Evelyn will be on her feet again soon. Tell me, have you ever read anything by the fiction writer I. D. Chandal?"

"I don't read fiction. I have no patience with plots and narratives."

"I'm intrigued by the clever ways she connects things."

"No doubt a nineteenth-century pen working on twentieth-century horrors."

"Why are you so testy today, Robert?"

"I have a nineteenth-century story for you, Benjamin."

"Not especially interested."

"It was told to me by a boy in Theresienstadt."

"Theresienstadt?"

"I was teaching him the section in the Torah about the binding of Isaac, so he could read it in celebration of his bar mitzvah."

"Excuse me, you taught trope in Theresienstadt?"

"Why are you surprised?"

"I didn't know."

"I never told you, so you didn't know. I was sixteen at the time. In Theresienstadt there were all kinds of classes during the day, and concerts, operas, lectures, and cabarets at night. Hunger, dysentery, disease, and culture. And in the early mornings—transports to Auschwitz. That's how we lived. Anyway, I was teaching this boy, I didn't even know his name at first, he came to me one day and said he'd heard I knew trope, would I teach him—I can see him clearly, pale, thin like a stick, big dark eyes—he wanted to learn the section about the binding of Isaac so he could read it to his family on his bar mitzvah, and I said I would be happy to teach him, so we found a corner somewhere under a staircase and I was teaching him the section sentence by sentence, he had a sweet tenor voice, not loud, with a beautiful vibrato. One day he broke into tears. We were crouched under the stairs, I remember there was a children's art class nearby, and four people were sitting on the stairs discussing Mann's *The Magic Mountain,* and the boy was crying uncontrollably. I asked him why he was crying, and he said he remembered a story his Uncle Jakob had once told him about the ram."

"The what?"

"The animal sacrificed in place of Isaac. The ram."

Benjamin Walter had the distinct sensation that someone had placed heavy hands upon his shoulders and was propelling him in every direction.

"I asked him what his uncle had told him that could make him cry so, and he said, 'The ram was from the heavenly Garden of Eden, a beautiful animal, golden skin, magnificent head. Uncle Jakob said that just as there was a

Garden of Eden in this world, so is there one in heaven, where angels and animals live in peace, and that day everyone in the Garden was watching Abraham binding Isaac to the killing place on Earth, it was as if the future depended on the events of the next moment—surely all Creation would be transformed with the death of Isaac and the end of the Jewish people—and suddenly the ram pleaded to take Isaac's place. But the ram was beloved by the angels, who refused to let it go, and the ram cried out, "The future must be saved!" and in a single leap it bounded from the Garden and vaulted off a bridge of stars and hurtled through space to the mountaintop near Abraham, and called to him in a human voice not to slaughter his son. Three angels flew after the ram to bring it back, but the ram deliberately entangled its horns in a thicket and they couldn't release it and it called again to Abraham, who unbound Isaac and managed to free the horns and sacrificed the ram in his stead.'

"The boy was crying for the ram?"

"And because he thought that *he* was the ram."

"He?"

"He, we, all of us were the ram."

"Where did he get such an idea?"

"He was a very clever boy."

"If all of you were the ram, who was Isaac?"

"I asked him that."

"And he said?"

"The civilized people of the world."

"He said that?"

"I told you, he was a very clever boy."

"And who was Abraham?"

"I asked him that, too."

"And?"

"For a long time he wouldn't answer. When I asked him again, he said, 'Maybe the ones who are holding the knife.' "

After a moment, Benjamin Walter said, "What happened to the boy?"

"He read splendidly for his bar mitzvah and gave a talk describing the ram, its beauty and wisdom, its self-sacrifice to save the future of Creation. A crowded room, a clandestine gathering. Everyone cried. Four days later, he was shipped to Auschwitz, where they killed him right away. There you have it, Benjamin. The sacrifice of the ram. A nineteenth-century story. Connections, yes?"

"It explains nothing."

"Every story is some kind of explanation, which explains why I dislike stories and do not read I. D. Chandal. I became a historian so I would not have to explain anything, only recount the evidence, the facts." He looked around. "Where is our waiter? I'm going to have to leave you, Benjamin, unless you've finished eating."

"I'll take care of the check."

"No, let me."

"Why are you so angry today, Robert?"

"I have a meeting with the provost about the historian whom Fox wants to bring in."

"Oh, yes, the language-deprived woman."

"I will tell the provost that if he and Fox intend to make her an offer, I intend to make a telephone call."

"To whom?"

"To the one who funded the chair and has in mind the funding of another."

"You know him?"

"We were in the war together."

"What do you mean? I thought—"

"In the same barrack in Auschwitz. I saved his life when they herded us through the woods ahead of the Russian army."

Distinctly, someone held Benjamin Walter by the shoulders and was pushing him steadily backward into a landscape thickly befouled with death. How his arms and legs ached.

"Life connects us, Benjamin, not artifice. Ah, here's our waiter."

THE DRIVEWAY HAD BEEN CLEARED: NO TRACE OF the splinters and the fallen limb. He parked the Saab and walked on painful legs to the oak. The spiraling scar seemed inconsequential in the late-afternoon sunlight. Surely the lightning-wounded wood would soon dry, scab, heal.

How still the street was, the air calm, the woods serene. I. D. Chandal was nowhere to be seen. The length of soil she had cleared from the lawn lay planted with infant mist-flower, goldenrod, coleus, impatiens. At the end of the garden, where it approached the woods, she had rooted a bush with strikingly twisted branches. What a day's work she had put in!

Inside the kitchen the nurse was preparing a clear broth for Evelyn. His wife was so much better today, thank the Lord, the nurse said. Her color was greatly improved, her strength returning. The tree man had been there earlier, and would the professor believe what he'd told her? The oak tree had taken the lightning bolt meant for the house. Yes, that's what he'd said, those very words. The mysterious ways of the Lord. Now she would bring the broth to his wife and then give her the sleeping medication, it was good for her to sleep long and deep. Did the professor need anything? Benjamin Walter said he would take the broth to his wife and spend a bit of time with her. He went upstairs and found Evelyn awake and sitting up in bed.

"It appears you'll be able to finish your Virginia Woolf after all."

She began to cry and he comforted her and fed her the broth and waited until she was asleep and the nurse had gone.

He ate some chicken in the kitchen and went back upstairs. From the window of his study he looked out at the Tudor and saw it was dark. He had forgotten to take his medication and his arms ached painfully. Downing the pills in the bathroom, he gazed upon himself in the medicine-chest mirror and saw eyes that brimmed with memory.

Back in his study he sat at his desk, apprehensively reading the pages typed by his secretary. How very sad, the story of Mr. Zapiski, she'd commented upon returning the manuscript. She'd no idea Professor Walter came from such a background.

Cool dry night air blew through the open window. The Tudor was strangely dark. Where had she gone? The clock on the wall above the framed fragments of headline read close to eight. He stared at the headline.

M RI NS TACK B TWE   SE D AR ONNE OREST

A different time, a different war. His father's and Mr. Zapiski's war. Each generation and its own conflagration. But why, really, had he framed and hung those headlines? A connection between his war and theirs?

He would need to write the chapter about his war. But as much as the first chapter had resisted being written by him, he himself now resisted writing the second. The obstacle was not a paucity of memory but a surfeit. Memory, once begun, swelling to a detonation, a blazing eruption. Do I need to do this? Weary, weary. Fingers in pain. Drop it. An act of hubris, these memoirs. Give yourself some well-earned years of rest. Attend to Evelyn. Put the deathwork aside.

The light came on in the kitchen of the Tudor. He closed the window and in the very next instant, it seemed to him, was standing at her door, she in tight jeans and jersey. He gazed at her openly and without shame as she swung the door wide and stepped back.

"I saw your light."

"Please come in."

"I'm not interrupting?"

"No, no."

"I noticed you were busy with your garden today."

"Isn't it pretty? Especially the mulberry bush. Watch how quickly it grows. Its leaves turn a marvelous golden color in the fall."

They entered the kitchen. For some reason, he expected it to be different this time. But nothing had changed. He saw the same bleak yellow light; cherry-wood cabinets; 1950s stove, sink, and refrigerator; reddish floor tiles; wooden table and chairs; light-green paint and bare walls; and piles of newspapers on the table.

"Coffee? Donuts?"

"Thank you."

"How is your wife?"

"Much improved."

"That's wonderful news, Benjamin. And how are you?"

"Tired, achy, struggling with the memoirs."

"Too many memories or too few?"

"Far too many, tumbling over each other, difficult to sort out."

"How fortunate for you! The floodgates have been opened. Let it all pour through."

"Not so easy to do, I'm afraid. I've begun to doubt the entire effort."

"Doubt? What do you mean, doubt?"

"I'm not sure of its worth."

"What are you saying, Benjamin? You want *sure*? Go to your tax collector, get hit by lightning, that's sure."

"I didn't bargain on it being so—disquieting."

"You want memory *and* comfort?"

"Having frequent nightmares. Bits and pieces of memory skittering about like the squirrels on my roof even when I'm driving. Cannot talk to Evelyn, of course."

"Why don't you talk to *me*, Benjamin? Who can better appreciate a story?"

Her presence across the table—intoxicating. Blue eyes, oval-shaped features, high cheekbones. No makeup. Her face without a wrinkle. How does she manage that? And alluring breasts. An image of his hands cupping her breasts, fingers caressing the nipples.

She sipped coffee, studied him over the rim of her cup. "Well, Benjamin, are you going to tell me your story?"

DO YOU KNOW ABOUT THE FINAL OFFENSIVE OF THE German army against the Allies in the Ardennes forest? It began in early December 1944. At first, thousands of our men deserted, and by the time it ended, thousands were dead. In January, of the thirty-six men originally in my platoon, four were left.

We all did odd things to stay sane and alive. We talked to photographs of our fathers and mothers and sweethearts and wives and children. We kissed crucifixes and stars of David. We made vows. The second day of the Ardennes offensive Mr. Zapiski suddenly appeared beside me. Dark suit and hat and tie. Not an image in my head but actually there. I heard his raspy voice and smelled his cigarette breath. How I welcomed him! I was overjoyed. He walked with me and slept with me. He would chant the trope of passages from the Scroll of the Law, and I would quietly chant along with him. In firefights he would tell me clearly when to zig to the right and when to zag to the left, when to lie prone, when to jump up. Whenever we were being shelled, he would show me which tree to get behind and where to dig my hole. He would run alongside me, holding on to his dark hat. Strangely, his wooden leg seemed not to encumber him. He kept me alive through that terrible time. The Germans hacked us to pieces in the forests, but finally we pushed them back and straightened the line. By the end of that winter, we were moving forward again.

One morning we were reconnoitering through some woods with five or six tanks, all that remained of a battalion. A chill morning and a gray-white dawn, with ground mist covering the roots and curling up around the tree trunks. Suddenly the Germans started to pound us with artillery and tank fire. The proximity shells were exploding on contact with the treetops, and the coniferous trees and hardwoods were falling all over us, showering us with jagged splinters, and one of the guys near me caught a piece of wood in his neck, like an old-fashioned arrow. I distinctly heard Mr. Zapiski tell me to crouch behind a tree and fire into the underbrush up ahead, which I immediately proceeded to do, though I saw no enemy. Suddenly a soldier in a green uniform and helmet emerged from the underbrush, bleeding from a wound and lunging at me with his rifle and bayonet. I shot him in the face and stood near him, vomiting. Our tanks were returning fire. It went on for a few more minutes. And then it grew very quiet. I looked around and trembled. Mr. Zapiski was gone.

The infantry was ordered to advance ahead of the tanks. We moved forward through the woods, our squad in two fire teams, advancing and covering. The ground mist was absorbing the smells of the tank exhausts, which intensified the other smells: cordite and moist earth and leaking sap and newly shattered trees. My squad had just leapfrogged forward and I thought I saw something moving up ahead, but it was only the mist eddying around the shredded fragments of a tree trunk.

Then we were out of the woods and in a meadow. The mist was thinner and a breeze had risen and suddenly there was a different smell in the air, and we stopped.

The smell was like nothing I had ever experienced before—not like the charred-wood and broken-stone odors of bombed-out towns and villages, or the blood-and-gunpowder stink of a field after a firefight, or the sweaty stench of combat soldiers. It was a pungent, acrid, throat-tightening odor, and it was up ahead and moving toward us.

Then the whole forward line stopped, and we could hear the tanks behind us stopping, too.

Up front the lieutenant was in a crouching position with his binoculars to his eyes, and behind us the tank commanders were searching through the mist with their periscopes.

And then the order came down to hold our fire. I thought I saw something moving through the mist.

The lieutenant put down his binoculars and stood up.

Something moved past him. Perhaps "moved" is not quite the proper word. Something shuffled and scraped past him, a shadow of some sort. Then another shadow. A host of shadows came through the mist, some crawling on their hands and knees. They were about twenty-five yards away, and they kept coming.

The first thing we noticed was their ghastly emaciation. Then we saw their wide and dark eyes. And then we saw that they had no teeth, only rotting stumps.

Two of them were advancing directly toward my squad. I heard voices, but couldn't make out what they were saying. They kept on moving toward us and one of them stopped about three feet from me—a grotesque figure of a man; the stench that rose from him!—and he reached out and grabbed hold of my arm, and croaked at me, "Warum?"—and my blood ran cold. He said again in Yiddish, "Warum?"; and added in Yiddish, "Why did you take so long?"; and again, "Why? Why?"—and I gaped at him in horror and pulled my arm away, and he went shuffling and stumbling off toward the woods. There must have been about thirty or forty of them; they all disappeared into the woods. Later I found out that most of them had traveled laterally and died in the woods; only about half a dozen made it to the other side.

We were ordered to move on. Whoever those apparitions had been, they were not our problem. We were merely infantry, ground-pounders; as far as we were concerned, those people were only a piece of information: there was something up ahead we had to watch out for.

The ground mist soon lifted. We advanced toward a slight rise. Behind us came our tanks. There was not an enemy soldier in sight. Then we spotted smoke beyond the rise.

When we got to the rise we saw some sort of encampment about a mile away: tall fences and low buildings and guard towers with machine guns. We advanced toward it slowly and could smell it, and most of us gagged and some vomited as we went along.

From a distance we could see that the gates were open. We leapfrogged, doing reconnaissance by fire, toward the guard towers. It turned out they were deserted. Bodies lay on the perimeter fence. We charged through the gates.

Half-human ghoulish creatures stood near the buildings, staring at us as we entered. They seemed not to know what to do or say. It had rained recently; the ground was a quagmire. There were hard, narrow paths through the mud, and duckboards had been laid down, and we deployed rapidly.

The stench was horrendous: the foulest of pigsties; an open cesspool of reeking excrement. Hot, thick, pungent. A putrid, cloying, acidic smell that seemed to coat our palates and throats. The camp was about a half-mile long by a half-mile wide. We went past squalid buildings that looked to be barracks, and then a broad open space, and an inner encampment of well-kept buildings, and a brick building with a chimney that turned out to be a crematorium, and beyond that we came upon the most heart-numbing sight I have ever witnessed: a vast graveyard, trenches upon trenches of putrefying whitish bodies stacked one on top of the other like wood.

And there I found Mr. Zapiski.

He lay half covered with earth and quicklime in a trench in the mass cemetery; and facedown on the ground, reeking and begrimed, alongside a duckboard; and rotting into the mud near the fence, decaying in his urine and excrement; and among the murmuring phantoms we found in the barracks who gaped at us when we entered and began a low keening when we told them we were Americans, one of them crying out in a broken voice, "Why did you take so long to get here?"

"Warum?" I heard him say. And again, "Warum?"

The lieutenant asked them, "Where are the guards?"

They did not understand him.

I translated his question into Yiddish.

They stared at me, stunned. A soldier with a weapon, in an American uniform, speaking Yiddish!

"Most ran away," one answered. "A few are still in those houses." He pointed toward the rear of the camp.

The lieutenant sent our squad over to secure the houses.

Two of the houses were empty. We found six guards inside the third, all drunk, their holsters empty, but still wearing their helmets.

The sergeant asked them, "Where are the others?"

They stared at him, muttering in German.

"You fucking bastards," the sergeant said. "Where are the others?"

"Where are the others?" I said to them in Yiddish.

One of them, a corporal, stiffened and looked at me.

"Where are the others?" I asked again.

He said, drunk and sullen, "They took the vehicles and ran off. There wasn't enough transport for all of us."

"He says they took off and left them behind," I said to the sergeant.

"Tell him if he's lying I'll have his ass," the sergeant said.

"If you are lying we will kill you," I said.

The corporal trembled. "It is the truth."

"He says it's the truth."

One of the guards, a tall heavy-shouldered man with a jutting lower jaw and a pockmarked face, suddenly said, "What kind of German do you speak?"

"New York German."

"That's not German."

"Warum? Is that okay German?"

"You are not speaking German."

"What's going on?" the sergeant said.

"Go fuck yourself, you piece of shit," I said to the guard. "Is that good enough German for you?"

He muttered something, his fingers twitching.

"I am one of those you were killing!" I suddenly shouted.

He stiffened. His face grew red. A Jew shouting at him! He reached for his empty holster.

Absently, as if in a dream, I heard scurrying sounds and shouts.

An M1-Garand rifle is a semiautomatic weapon, with eight bullets in a clip. The rounds have a muzzle velocity of 2,800 feet per second and an impact velocity of one and one-half foot-tons per square inch. That amounts to ten to fifteen tons of pressure at the point of impact.

I did not have to raise my weapon but simply pointed it at him.

I fired twice. Both bullets hit him in the chest. The second must have struck bone; he was lifted about six inches off his feet and thrown against the wall behind him and fell dead. On the wall were blood and bone from the exit wounds.

There had been only two rounds left in my clip. It had ejected with its characteristic clink. I shoved another clip in.

"Was that good German?"

The other guards shrank back.

Faintly, through the pounding in my head, I heard the sergeant say, "Cease fire!"

I turned the weapon upon the cringing guards.

The sergeant said, "As you were, soldier!"

I pointed the weapon downward.

The sergeant said, "What the fuck was that all about?"

"He reached for his pistol."

"What pistol?"

"His holster. And he was wearing his helmet." I turned to the guards and asked in Yiddish, "Are there more camps like this?"

They glanced at each other.

"I asked them if there were more camps like this," I said to the sergeant.

"Jesus, Mary, and Joseph," the sergeant murmured.

He ordered me outside.

I walked around the camp. Everywhere I went I saw Mr. Zapiski, dead and dead and dead in the vile exhausted earth.

The sergeant, reporting the incident to the lieutenant, made a point of the German's threatening gesture and the fact that they hadn't fully surrendered because they were still wearing their helmets, and the lieutenant determined that my reaction was justified, and the matter was dropped.

Ten days later, I came down with a bad case of diarrhea. Within twenty-four hours I was burning with fever. Terrible hallucinations accompanied the fever. Lights kept flashing on inside my head illuminating frightful scenes: I was shooting the German guard over and over again; then I was killing the other guards; then I was running through the camp chanting at the top of my lungs the trope to the biblical account about the attack of the Amalekites, and the melody drifted through the meadows along which we had advanced; it penetrated the ruined woods, and there the human shadow who had grabbed my arm heard it and threw back his head as he walked shuffling and staggering and began to chant it too in his croaky voice, sounding precisely like Mr. Zapiski, and he stumbled against a shell-blasted tree and the tree opened itself to him and he vanished inside.

It turned out that I had contracted typhus.

From the field hospital I was evacuated to an American

hospital in England where I lay ill a long time. Then I was sent for convalescence to a place in the English countryside. I remember sleeping a great deal and being fed and waking once after a bad dream about Mr. Zapiski and seeing a lovely face gazing down at me with profoundly earnest concern. The face of Mr. Zapiski slowly dissolved and the face of a young English nurse took its place, creamy white skin, pink islands on her cheeks, no makeup, straight nose, full lips, and sad gray eyes. In time I discovered the reason for her sadness: she had lost her fiancé during the Ardennes offensive. She was of the English upper class, her family going back centuries. I had lost my trope teacher and fallen in love with her; she had lost her fiancé and fallen in love with me. Both of us were sick to death of the worlds from which we had come, where disgrace seemed to stare at us from nearly every human face, and so we made our own new creation. I crossed the threshold of my young life; the man deserted the boy. I did not return home, and no doubt broke my parents' hearts. I married in England, took my degrees in England. Quite trying at times, those postwar years, everything scarce and no true acceptance of me by her family—but how happy we were! I did not return to America for the funerals of my parents, who had disowned me, had actually sat in mourning over me and recited the Mourner's Kaddish, because Evelyn would not think of converting out of the Church of England. Finally, I returned to America to teach, and discovered, during a telephone conversation with my sister, that my father had given Mr. Zapiski's library to a local high school. I have no idea what the school did with the many Yiddish, German, and French books. My brother has in his possession Mr. Zapiski's Bible, the one from which he taught me the trope. He intends to use it, he says, when he teaches his two sons the trope.

There you have it, Davita. My narrative.

A SILENCE FOLLOWED. BENJAMIN WALTER NIBBLED at a donut, sipped coffee.

"No comments?"

"I'm a little breathless, Benjamin. That's a knockout story."

"May I use your bathroom? Among the many things ailing me these days is a swollen prostate."

He returned to the kitchen some minutes later to find her at the window looking out at the woods.

"Your story will keep me awake tonight, Benjamin."

"My apologies."

"No, no. Stories that keep me awake are my life's blood."

"I should go back."

"Did you really forget about your Mr. Zapiski?"

"Oh, yes. Entirely."

"And now you'll be able to sail right through to the end."

"I've already written the end. It was the beginning I couldn't write."

"The story you just told me is part of your beginning?"

"It is the myself that predates what I am now. And having recalled Mr. Zapiski for my memoirs, it is my intention to put him out of mind again as quickly as possible."

She was still looking out the window. "A pity."

"Mr. Zapiski? An antique, a disgrace. He should never have gone back to Europe."

She pointed out the window. "I meant the tree."

"The oak?"

"It will have to be taken down."

"The oak will have to be taken down?"

"It will be dead in two or three years. The tree surgeon said the lightning seared through it, crown, core, and root."

Frightful images of broken trees, shattered woods. "How very sad."

"Benjamin, did you leave the lights on in your study?"

"I don't recall."

"There's no one in your house?"

"Except my wife."

"I thought I saw someone in your study."

"Not likely."

"I look forward to meeting your wife after her recovery."

"I'll tell her. But there's no chance of full recovery."

"I'm sorry to hear that, Benjamin. Is it cancer?"

"No, it is, I regret to say, acquired immunodeficiency syndrome, from tainted blood she received some years ago during a surgical procedure. We take it a crisis at a time."

"I'm truly sorry to hear that."

"Yes, well, we rarely get to choose our own destiny, though this borders a bit on the absurd. I should go."

"Come back anytime for coffee and donuts, Benjamin. An open invitation. You needn't bring more stories."

"It occurs to me, Davita, that our ram has not appeared."

"But you say your wife is better."

"The future, as I told you, is bleak."

"A ram comes always as an astonishment. Do you know what a ram is, Benjamin? R-A-M. A random act of menschlichkeit."

"You know about rams."

She turned to look at him. "My stories are about what the world is like when there are no rams. Benjamin, as a person whose specialty is war, doesn't the ram interest you?"

EVELYN STIRRED AS HE ENTERED THE BEDROOM; she opened her eyes, raised her arms to him. He went to her bedside and held her. Frail, thin almost to emaciation, but the fever gone. She would regain much of her strength and weight; for how long, no one knew. They had been told about the hazard of a third pregnancy. The surgery and the transfusions, everyone had then thought, saved her life. Now, as it turned out—a life for a life. Roar with rage against the void. The very day of the diagnosis she'd said, "We've given each other the entire middle of our lives. I've no regrets, I've had a truly wonderful life with you, but one's end, you know, belongs with one's beginnings. We've little control over our beginnings and endings; we're in the hands of others. So I ask you to promise me that you'll send my body back to my family for burial in England."

He had given his word. They had trusted each other with their lives; she would trust him with her death.

He waited until she was asleep and went into his study. The halogen lamp on the desk was on; it sent a focused light onto the area where the manuscript lay and left the rest of the room dim. He stared at the framed headlines on the walls, barely able to make out the words, and remembered, with a lucidity that forced upon him a sharp intake of breath, Mr. Zapiski's stumbling walk and rasping voice and dusty war library. He noticed that the kitchen in the Tudor was dark, the house itself, exterior lights off, seeming to fade into the night. He leaned across his desk to open the window. A light came on in a third-floor window of the Tudor and he saw I. D. Chandal at a table, writing. He glanced at the clock on the wall over his desk—a few minutes after eleven.

He found himself at the ornate wooden front door of her house. The old-fashioned doorbell echoed dully inside.

There was no answer.

Above the doorbell was an antique knocker. He used it a number of times and stood listening.

No one came to the door.

He walked to the side of his house and looked up. There she was, visible through the closed third-floor window. How attract her attention? A shout might be overheard and bring the police.

He walked to the rear door that led to the kitchen and tried the knob. The door swung open.

Inside he stood still until his eyes grew accustomed to the darkness. He moved through the dining room and living room. At the foot of the stairway, in the entrance hall, he called, "Davita," and listened as her name rose, echoing.

How could she not have heard? Possibly the door to the third floor was closed. He could go to his own house and telephone her from there. But he didn't know her number. Certainly the operator would give it to him. But he craved to see her as she sat at her desk. A craving beyond lust. A view of the act of creation, the forging of connections.

He climbed the curving stairway. The carpeted steps creaked and groaned.

All five doors on the second floor were open. He peered into each room. Four were empty. In the fifth, an old chair and dresser, an unmade bed. Towels and toiletries in a small bathroom with a white porcelain sink and an antique claw-foot tub.

At the end of the hallway, a narrow uncarpeted wooden stairway led upward into darkness. Slowly, he climbed the stairs and came to a closed wooden door. He pushed the door open and found himself inside a vast dimly lit ballroom, with stained-glass windows, a wide-planked oak floor, a vaulted ceiling lacy with lights and shadows. Antique furniture stood about as in a storeroom: floral-patterned stuffed chairs, eagles and dragons carved from their arms and legs; long tables, their tops cut with zodiacal markings; lacquered Oriental dressers; desks of Victorian design; canopied beds. On the floor lay three piles of carpets adorned with mythic bestiaries, richly plumed birds, enchanted gardens, densely treed woods. The possessions of the previous owners. Why had it all been moved to this floor?

Against the far wall, before a window, I. D. Chandal sat at a rolltop desk, clutching a pen with three fingertips of her right hand, writing. She sat about forty feet away, bathed in yellow light from the lamp on her desk, and he made out plainly her rotund features and thick lips and double chin and uncombed gray hair and face glistening with sweat. The pale-blue housecoat she wore could not conceal the buttocks and thighs that spilled over the edge of her chair and the immense breasts pushing against the desk. She paid no attention to him as he came alongside the desk. He heard her breathing, the wheezy breathing of an asthmatic, and inhaled her sweat. She was writing on one side of a large spring binder. He wrote that way, too, leaving the other side for inserts, if needed, at a later time. The heat that rose from her! He saw her lift her eyes and look out the window directly at his house and return to her writing. She moved her lips, mouthed words in silence, cocked her head this way and that. "Warum," he heard her say, and stood cold and trembling, listening to his heart. She gazed again out the window and, following her line of vision, he saw the dark portals of his house. At the rear above the roof stood the oaks, darkly reflecting the outside lights.

A sudden bright rectangle appeared in the wall of the house. Someone had turned on the light in his study! He was able to see directly into the room: the framed head-lines on the wall; his old chair and recliner; the top of his desk with books, magazines, journals, and the manuscript of the memoirs. Was Evelyn walking about?

A shadow fell across the desk. Benjamin Walter, the skin

on his scalp rising, saw a form slide slowly into his chair. It sat still a moment, then lifted its eyes and stared at him directly through the window.

Dark clothes, white shirt, dark tie, tall black skullcap, graying beard, in the moist lips a cigarette with a long gray ash arched like a melting candle.

I. D. Chandal took a wheezing breath. "Hello, Benjamin. You have a nice home."

He was unable to respond. The pain in his arms and legs; the hammering of his heart.

"A place full of connections."

The light in the window winked out.

Benjamin Walter stood frozen with horror.

I. D. Chandal murmured, "Causes, connections, and rams. All over the place."

He stared at her and then at the house.

"Please go home and let me finish my work." Her tone was sharp.

"But—"

"Go home." Her voice had risen.

"My dear Davita—"

"I'm sorry, but now you're interfering, Benjamin."

"But I feel—"

"Benjamin, leave!" The lashing fury in her voice. What had he done to deserve that?

Inside his house another window abruptly ignited. His wife's study. Everything in it—books, papers, journals, wall pictures—arranged with an English sense of order. And on her desk, the manuscript of her book on Virginia Woolf.

A shadowy form glided into view, stood over the desk.

Benjamin Walter, roaring with rage and dread, rushed from the third-floor ballroom and down the stairway and out of the Tudor. Breathing with great difficulty, a reddish luminescence flashing before his eyes, he paused at the foot of the stairs in his living room and saw only the dim night-light. Evelyn stirred when he entered the bedroom, but did not wake.

He hurried into her study. It was dark; nothing appeared to have been disturbed. In his study, he switched on the ceiling light. The manuscript of the memoirs lay on the desk where he had left it. Glancing outside, he saw I. D. Chandal still writing at the third-floor window of the Tudor. What was that? He threw open the window and saw a shadowy figure limping along the driveway toward the woods at the back of the house. A burglar! Call the police. But then he heard the whispered word "warum" and the trope chant began from the woods. Slowly rising and curling like early-morning mist, drifting. From splintered trees and barbarous graveyards; and entering through the open window and also coming from the wall of headlines behind him and the piercingly recalled apartment of Mr. Zapiski. A long moment passed before he recognized that the word and the chant had risen from him, from his own lips. And it was then that he broke through the ramparts into the illumined entry of himself and saw as he had never seen before the exposed roots and tangles of long-buried connections, and was overcome with an infinite sorrow.

A NOTE ON THE TYPE

This book was set in Monotype Dante, a typeface designed by
Giovanni Mardersteig (1892–1977). Conceived as a private type for
the Officina Bodoni in Verona, Italy, Dante was originally cut only
for hand composition by Charles Malin, the famous Parisian
punch cutter, between 1946 and 1952. Its first use was in an edition
of Boccaccio's *Trattatello in laude di Dante* that appeared in 1954.
The Monotype Corporation's version of Dante followed in 1957.
Although modeled on the Aldine type used for Pietro Cardinal
Bembo's treatise *De Aetna* in 1495, Dante is a thoroughly modern
interpretation of the venerable face.

Composed by Creative Graphics,
Allentown, Pennsylvania
Printed and bound by R. R. Donnelley & Sons
Harrisonburg, Virginia
Designed by Virginia Tan